Edge of Heaven

~

10-18-03

To Joe
Blessings
Eva McCall

Edge of Heaven

Eva McCall

Historical Images
Asheville, North Carolina

Historical Images is an imprint of Bright Mountain Books, Inc.

Cover design by Carol Schell Bruckner

Printed in the United States of America

ISBN: 0-914875-27-2

Library of Congress Cataloging-in-Publication Data

McCall, Eva, date.
    Edge of heaven / Eva McCall.
       p.   cm.
    ISBN 0-914875-27-2
    1. North Carolina–History–1865- –Fiction.   I. Title.
PS3563.C33414E3   1997
813'.54–dc21
                                       97-40066
                                        CIP

In memory of Lucy Davenport Carpenter

Edge of Heaven

≈ *1* ≈

Lucy Davenport's pa reached for the last corn fritter and sopped up the sorghum molasses on his plate. "Better eat up, girl. Can't please no man with that stack o' bones."

Lucy's dark eyes sparked. She dropped her fork. "Don't aim on pleasing no man!" She picked up her tin plate and called to Jasper, the speckled hound that lay by the woodbox. The old dog perked up his ears, slowly wagged his tail, and rose from his warm spot by the stove.

Lucy raked the scraps from her plate. Jasper caught them in midair. She threw the plate toward the dishpan, but it missed and landed on the floor. Jasper rushed to lick it, then ambled back to his spot by the stove and promptly went to sleep.

"Pa, this here's eighteen and ninety-five," said Lucy. "In this day and time, you just don't marry girls off to men that they don't know. Besides, this man ain't from our Georgia mountains, and I don't want to leave my mountain where Ma's buried. And Pa, how about you? Who'll cook for you?"

Edmund Davenport stood. His large shoulders hunched forward. His blue-green eyes flashed. He slammed his fist against the table. "Now see here, girl! You'll do as you're told. It's way past time you had yourself a man. And you know as well as me, there ain't no men here on the mountain. Besides, your sister Clara Belle had herself a husband when she was just fifteen. Allie had her one at thirteen."

Lucy knelt down to pick up the plate. "I'm eighteen, Pa. I'm growed up now."

"What you mumbling about, girl? Speak up!"

"Nothing, Pa. Just talking to Jasper."

Lucy's father pointed his finger at her. "That's another thing, girl. You and them there critters. Ain't natural fer a young woman like yourself to be so all-fired friendly with even the wild animals. Now

3

your poor dead ma'd want me to see that you was all properly married off. That's what I'm a-fixin' to do. So you just get yourself all dooded up and a good supper made 'cause I'm a-bringin' a friend here tonight. Maybe we can fix you up with him. You know folks is already a-sayin' you're an old maid."

Lucy stood, rooted to the rough plank floor of the log cabin, waiting for her pa to finish his lecture and leave.

"Hear me, girl?"

"Yes, Pa."

"Well, see to it. I've gotta be going. Work's a-waitin'."

Lucy watched her pa as he straddled his work horse and rode away. She often wondered about this work he went to, but that was man's business. Today, her job was to fix a meal and make herself look good for her pa's friend. She finished the breakfast dishes, looked at the half-empty bag of cornmeal, then over at the full can of fat-back drippings on the stove. She nudged the sleeping hound that lay at her feet. He opened one eye and looked up at her.

"Sure can't make a decent meal from what's in this kitchen, but why should I worry about making a good meal for a man I ain't never seen—one my pa plans on marrying me off to! But this man's company, and Ma'd want me to feed him good . . . so I guess I'd better see what I can find to cook."

≈   ≈   ≈

Lucy walked along the banks of Tate Creek looking for a pool of good mountain water for fishing. "Ain't many good fishing holes up here," she said to herself, "but I'll give this one a try." She held up her bait can of squirming worms. She reached into the can and pulled one out. "Sorry, little worm, but I got to do this. Trout won't bite without bait, and without fish there won't be no supper for Pa's friend." She held the worm in the air and watched it wiggle. "I'm in kind of the same spot as you, little worm." She threaded it onto her hook. "There! You'll whet the appetite of the big brown trout over yonder." She threw her fishing line across the dark pool of water, then smoothed back her hair. How would she look to her pa's friend? Maybe he wouldn't like her. She'd try not to look too good.

4

Soon there was a tug on the line. Lucy pulled. The fish fought. She struggled. The fish swam behind a log. Trapped, if she stayed on the mountain. Trapped, if she went away. Trapped! There was no getting away from some things. The fish fought harder. "You ain't giving up so easy are you, fish? Maybe I won't give up so easy either."

Finally, the fish began to tire. Lucy eased him toward the bank. When he was close enough, she knelt down, slipped her fingers through his gills, and lifted him from the water. She put the lid on the can of worms and headed for home.

≈   ≈   ≈

Lucy bent over the cookstove frying the trout she'd caught for her pa and the man he was bringing home. Black hair, parted in the middle, hung in long plaits over her shoulders. The faded print dress she wore hung loosely on her thin frame. She looked down at bare toes peeking from beneath the hem. Her pa had told her to look good. Maybe he wouldn't notice that she hadn't tried too hard, but he would notice her bare feet.

She pushed the frying pan to the back of the stove, ran into her lean-to bedroom off the kitchen, knelt down, and pulled a pair of high-button shoes from under the bed. With the hem of her dress, she wiped the dust from them. Sitting on the bed, she squeezed a dirty foot into one, only taking time to button it halfway up. She walked around the room. It hurt, but she could bear the pain till after supper. She grabbed the other shoe and jammed it on.

Glancing at herself in a piece of broken mirror propped on her makeshift dresser, she brushed up a few loose strands of hair. Her hair—she wished she could curl it or something, but there wasn't any use. It was too coarse. And her dress—it had patches sewn all over it, but she didn't care. Her other two weren't any better. She did have a new apron Clara Belle had sent her. She'd wear that. She grabbed it from a drawer and tied it around her slim waist on her way back to the kitchen. There! That would have to do.

In a few minutes, Lucy saw her father and his friend ride up to the barn. She craned her neck to get a better look at the man, but the trees between the house and the path blocked her view. She took the

5

cornbread from the oven. Maybe if she ignored them, they'd go away. But no such luck.

Her pa called, "Loo-ou-cy, where you at?"

"In here, Pa, making supper. You get washed up; I'll set the table."

"Supper can wait, girl. We have us some talkin' to do."

Lucy bit her lower lip, fighting back tears. It hurt to think she'd probably be leaving the only home she'd ever known.

≈   ≈   ≈

The talking was done. It had been settled. Lucy would become the bride of her father's friend, Holman Carpenter. She hadn't done much of the talking. Every time she opened her mouth, her father scolded, "Now girl, I'm your pa. I know what's best fer a young girl like you. A girl needs a man to look after her."

Lucy watched Holman from lowered eyelids as he shoveled in his second helping of trout. He reached for his third helping of poke salad. Wiry blond-red hair stood up on his wrist. It looked to her like there was more hair on his arms than on his head or in his mustache. Maybe if he were handsome like Clara Belle's husband, she could go along with her pa's plan, but she could see now that she needed to find some way out of this. No way was she going to let him touch her. And eat! It would keep her busy just cooking for him.

Holman rubbed his mouth with the back of his hand. "Some cook I'm getting myself," he said.

Lucy shoved back her chair. "Where do you think you're going?" asked her pa.

"Just gonna give Jasper my leftovers." She picked up her plate.

Her pa reached for another piece of cornbread. "This here girl won't eat you outta house and home. Never seen such a picky eater. Rather feed the confounded animals than eat herself."

"She'll have to grapple for her food at my house," said Holman. "There's thirteen more mouths to feed. Pickings get mighty slim sometimes."

Lucy dropped her tin plate. It clattered onto the table. She turned to stare, wide-eyed, at the man. Catching her breath, she spoke in a low, even tone. "Thirteen what, Mr. Carpenter?"

6

"Thirteen young-uns, of course. Didn't your pa tell you that my wife died six months ago, and she left me with thirteen young-uns to raise? The oldest one is fifteen and the baby is six months. My woman died giving birth."

Lucy cupped her hand over her mouth. No wonder! Thirteen young ones in fifteen years! That poor woman had spent most of her life being "in the family way." She dropped her hand and looked back at the little man. A smile played around the corners of her mouth. He was little, but then, rabbits were little too. Well, Mr. Carpenter, this girl's not going to be in the family way by you. She was going to find a way to get out of this.

Holman turned to her pa. "This here's a good business deal for both of us, Mr. Davenport. My work and all keeping me away from home, I need someone to take care of the littl'-uns so the older ones can go back to school in the fall. I think we've hit on a good trade."

"Trade!" Lucy felt her temples throbbing as she faced her pa. "Pa, what does he mean, trade? I thought you just wanted to find me a man—a man to take care of me. Seems to me like I'm gonna be the one doing the taking care of! What's in this for you, Pa?"

Edmund Davenport stomped his foot. "Now see here, girl! What I'm doing is my business. You're my girl. I'm just seeing to it that you have a family. That's what every girl needs. Now I've got work to do in the barn. See to it that you're ready to leave with Mr. Carpenter in the mornin'."

Holman rose and turned toward Lucy. "I'll be picking you up on my way down the mountain. Seems I'm getting myself a bargain."

Lucy watched them go. Her own pa making out that he had her best interest at heart and sending her off with some strange man to some godforsaken place! What did this man Carpenter mean by their trade? Maybe money? Things hadn't been too good for her pa lately. No, her pa wouldn't sell her. She cooked his meals, scrubbed his floors, and washed his clothes. He wouldn't gain anything by taking money. She could see them currying their horses in the barnyard. They were in deep conversation. What was this skinny, big-eared man to her pa? He didn't seem like the kind he'd pick for a friend, let alone a husband for her.

Lucy's dark eyes danced with anger as she called to Jasper. The old hound pushed himself up and slowly moved toward her. "For Pa's information, I'm gonna find a way to get away from him as soon as I can. I'll play along with his little game, but first chance I get . . ." She shook her head in disbelief. "There sure ain't nothing but a few scraps left."

The dog looked up at her, his big brown eyes begging. She set the plate down for him to lick. "Pa'll let you starve for sure. And him—I wonder what he'll do for food tomorrow. Well, maybe he'll 'preciate me when he has to hunt up his own food. Serves him right!" She wiped the last plate.

In her bedroom, Lucy looked around at the sparse furniture. Wasn't much, but it was home. Her pa didn't have any right to send her away. Maybe he'd change his mind or she'd find a way out of this before morning. She reached down, pulled off her shoes, and rubbed her feet. The back door slammed and she looked up. Her pa stood in the doorway. "Pa, you sure you want me to go?" She picked up her pillow and hugged it to her chest. "Pa, did you hear me?"

"Yeah, girl. I heared you. Don't you think you'd better get your belongin's together?"

Lucy flung down the pillow. "Ain't got that much to take. That is, if I go!"

"Now see here, Lucy. It's been decided. No use talkin' no more."

"But Pa . . . !"

Her pa turned and walked away. His huge shoulders drooped. She wondered if he loved her the same way she loved him. The only other time she'd seen his shoulders sag was when her ma died. She blew out the lamp, and her own shoulders slumped as she crawled into bed and wiped a tear from her eye.

≈   ≈   ≈

Daylight peeped through the heavy morning fog that pressed against the only window in Lucy's room. She reached for the same faded dress she'd worn yesterday and slipped it over her head. In a few short hours she'd ride down her mountain with a complete stranger. He'd probably want her to bed with him and mother his thirteen children. She picked up her pillow and pulled off the pillowcase. Gathering her few belongings, she stuffed them into it. There! Her pa got what he wanted. She could take care of herself. She'd been doing it anyway since her ma died.

In the kitchen she set her sack on the table and listened to her pa's snoring coming from the loft. She'd have to hurry. That Holman man would be here soon. The back door squeaked as she let herself out into the dampness of the early morning fog. Her bare feet glided over the hard, red Georgia clay as she climbed the narrow mountain trail. Now and then, a chipmunk or a rabbit scurried in front of her, but she never stopped. She had to say goodbye to her ma.

Out of breath, Lucy pulled herself up on a huge rock at the end of the path and gazed down. The mountaintops stood clear and blue above a sea of fog. The sky began to turn crimson. She sat down, crossed her legs Indian style, and waited.

She leaned forward in anticipation. The rays streamed from behind the mountains, and as surely as a clock's hand moved from second to minute, the sun burst forth from its hiding place.

Lucy caught her breath. It was beautiful. No, it was more than beautiful. It must be the edge of heaven. Could that be the reason she felt so close to her mother here? Could her ma's spirit be part of this magnificent light?

Her ma had told her stories about heaven before she died. She'd also told her about how her Cherokee forefathers were driven from these mountains, how they'd traveled by foot, old and young alike, to a reservation in Oklahoma. She'd told her how some of them had hidden out in the mountains, and how later, a few years ago, they'd been given a reservation in Cherokee, up in North Carolina.

Lucy looked at her hands and feet. Yes, she was dark like her ma had been. She felt the coarse black hair that hung over her shoulders. She didn't need a mirror to know that she looked like an Indian.

"Loo-ou-cy. Loo-ou-cy." She sat still listening to her pa's voice as it echoed from mountain to mountain. Usually when her pa called, she'd hurry, but today, she didn't rush. Let that Holman man wait. He'd probably be doing a lot of waiting. She grasped a gold locket that hung on a frayed blue ribbon around her neck.

"Ma," she began, "Pa done gone and found me a man. He says that's what you'd want him to do since I'm eighteen. But Ma, this man, he's old—maybe forty—and he has thirteen young-uns. If I do go home with him, I'll try to mother 'em." She stopped talking and buried her head in her arms. Her thin body shook with sobs.

The fog began to drift away. Lucy felt the warm rays of the sun on her shoulders and looked up. Her sobs ceased. It was as though her ma had wrapped her loving arms around her. "I can't, Ma. I just can't sleep with a man I don't love."

A cloud blotted out the sun for an instant and then floated away. "I know you understand, Ma. I'll do as Pa says for as long as I can, but I ain't making no promises. And I don't understand this deal Pa's got with this man. I don't want to cause trouble for Pa. Maybe the first chance I get, I'll run away to Clara Belle's." She held the locket between her thumb and forefinger. For a moment she let her finger rest on the inscription, *Love*. Was her ma right? Would love ever happen to her? No, not the way things were looking. Love was nowhere in sight. She looked up. The sun filled the sky with a blaze of red, orange, and yellow.

"Ma, I won't be here tomorrow, or any other morning, but every time I touch this locket you gave me, I'll remember your love." She pressed the locket to her lips and let it drop. "Maybe when I get off this mountain, I can sell my locket and buy you a tombstone. I know you always looked at them in the mail-order books that Clara Belle brought to us. You liked the ones with the angels in the corners. I got to be going, Ma. Pa and his friend will be waiting for me."

≈　　≈　　≈

Lucy picked up a pail of water on the bench by the back door and went inside. No fire burned in the old wood-burning cookstove this morning. She shuddered. She hadn't realized how damp it felt outside. Though it was May, the fog made everything wet and the day gave her chills. She looked around the kitchen. Her pillowcase was gone from the table. There were only two eggs left in the bowl on the cook table. She was sure a fox had gotten the last hen a few nights ago. There was still some cornmeal left. Maybe her pa could make some more corn fritters for his breakfast. All the fat-back grease had been used to fry the fish last night.

From the narrow window over the cook table, she could see her pa and that Holman man talking. Old Jasper lay nearby in a patch of sun. She guessed he wouldn't be around much longer, especially with food being so scarce. Could be a good thing she was getting away, especially with her pa not wanting her and all. She let herself out the back door and moved as silently as a cat toward them.

Holman glanced up. "We were just passing the time of day while we waited for you. Your pa says you often run off by yourself in the morning." He winked at Edmund. "Now, remember, I'm gonna be your boss. I like my woman in the kitchen where she belongs."

Lucy looked at the bay mare that waited. Her pillowcase sack hung from the saddle horn. "You might like your woman in the kitchen, Mr. Carpenter, but I ain't your woman yet." She turned to face her pa. "I'd of fixed you some breakfast if you'd built a fire."

"That's all right, girl. I got me some things to care fer this morning. Mr. Carpenter here is in sort of a hurry to get going. Are you ready?"

"Yes, Pa, I reckon so."

Her pa put both of his hands on her shoulders. Her hand crept up and touched the bony knob of his wrist. "I know you'll do what's right, Lucy," he said. "I've done my best fer you. That's what I'm a-tryin' to do now. It's no life fer a girl here on this mountain."

Lucy's lips formed a tight line. She spoke in a low determined tone. "And me, Pa? What about what I want? Did you ever think a life here on the mountain, close to Ma's grave, might be all I wanted?"

"This is fer your own good, Lucy."

She withdrew her hand from his wrist and choked back the hurt inside. Mr. Carpenter straddled his horse and reached his hand down to her. She hesitated. In all her life, no one had *ever* offered to help her on a horse. Her face flushed. What kind of woman did he think she was? Didn't he know mountain women knew how to mount a horse? Before she knew it, he'd swept her up behind him. The horse lunged forward. Her arms flew around his waist. She felt a breathless stirring in her body as excitement gripped her. She looked back at her pa, but she couldn't wave. She had to hold on.

11

≈ 2 ≈

Holman Carpenter reined his horse to a stop in front of the general store and tied her to a hitching post. "Come on, Lucy," he said. "We've got us some shopping to do."

In the store Lucy hovered close to the front door. She eyed four old men seated around a checkerboard that rested on the top of a keg. They seemed not to notice her. She let her eyes travel along the walls that were lined with large barrels. They came to rest at a long counter in the back. A middle-aged man with coarse gray hair that stood on end stacked yard goods on a shelf.

"Morgan, where's Icey?" asked Holman.

"She's in the back. Can I help you?"

"No, it's Icey I want to do business with today."

"Icey," called Morgan. "Holman Carpenter's here. Says he's got some business to do with you."

The door to the back room swung open and a woman appeared, wiping her plump hands on her apron. Her graying hair, piled high on her head, accented the roundness of her face. "What can I do for you, Holman?"

Holman leaned against the counter. "See that girl over there? She's Edmund Davenport's youngest girl, Lucy. I'm gonna marry her. I've been a-needing a woman around the house since Mary died."

Icey stepped in front of the counter and peered at Lucy. "Folks around here has been a-saying she's getting too old to get a husband."

Holman laid some money on the counter. "Ain't a *real* wife I'm a-needing, Icey." He motioned for Lucy. "Come here, girl. Icey's gonna help you get into some new clothes while I make some arrangements for our wedding. I'll be back about four. See that you're ready."

At the door he looked back at the girl who was to be the next Mrs. Carpenter. *Old.* He was the old one, but age didn't matter. Mary was the only one he'd ever love. A tightness formed in his throat, and he swallowed as he closed the door behind him.

Icey reached for a bar of soap from one of the barrels. "Come on, Lucy. Let's get you scrubbed up before we try on new clothes."

Lucy followed the woman through the door into the living quarters. Icey took a large tin tub from a nail on the wall, picked up a steaming kettle of water from the stove, and began to pour it into the tub. "Get them rags off."

Lucy clutched her dress tight across her chest. "What if I don't want to get married?"

Icey took her by the arm and marched her over to the tub. "Sometimes, when we're young, we don't know what's good for us. Now, just take off those rags and crawl into this nice hot bath that I've made for you. You're gonna feel lots better once you're into some nice new things. New clothes always did make me feel good."

With her back to Icey, she removed her clothes and stepped into the warm sudsy water. Before she knew what was happening, Icey had snatched up her old dress, raised the stove lid, and dropped it into the fire. "Be back in a minute."

Icey disappeared into the store. A few minutes later, she came back with an armful of dresses and a wad of white net. She laid them over a kitchen chair, picked up a large towel, and gave it to Lucy. "Dry off with this and get behind that screen over there." She handed Lucy three dresses to try on.

Three dresses. They sure didn't look like the feed sack ones she was used to. She touched the fabric of a pale blue dress with wonder. It felt so soft.

"Which one do you want to wear to be married in?" asked Icey.

"The blue one, I reckon, if I have to wear one."

"Good choice, Lucy. My mama always said a girl married in blue would be true to her man."

"Humph! Might be if I had one to be true to, but Holman Carpenter sure ain't my man." She stepped from behind the screen.

Icey cocked her head to one side as she admired the way Lucy looked. "My, ain't you as purty as a speckled pup under a red wagon. Come on over here. Let's see what we can do about your hair. Wish we had time to roll it up in rags to make it pretty, but we ain't."

"I just always braid it."

"No, it won't look good with them Indian braids hanging down. I'll just wrap the braids around your head like a wreath. Besides, that'll give me somethin' to fasten this little veil onto. I made it for you while you was a-washing. It won't be big enough to come down over your face, but it'll make you look more like a bride."

Someone opened the store door. "That'll pro'bly be Holman. You act nice to him, you hear? I'll be right back." As Icey left, Lucy's eyes darted around the room as she looked for a way out, but the only way was through the front room.

The door slammed and Icey was back. "Holman said the arrangements was made," she said. "He wanted to see his bride, but I wouldn't let him. It's bad luck for the groom to see the bride in her wedding dress. Sent him on over to Parson Cook's house."

Icey opened the front door. She noticed Lucy's bare feet and laughed. "Can't have them bare toes showing with that new dress. Better find you some shoes before we go any further." She pulled several boxes from a shelf and rummaged through them. "Here," she said, holding up a pair of white slippers. "They can be my wedding present to you. Ain't many folks in these parts that has any use for somethin' like this."

As they walked across the street, Lucy looked down at her feet. Shoes weren't the only thing she was getting, but Holman sure wasn't new—not with thirteen children. She hated her old high-buttoned shoes, but she hated this man more. She might have to marry him, but she sure was *not* going to bed with him.

A woman walked across the muddy street. Lucy watched her as she lifted her colorful skirt to avoid the mud. The woman nodded. The blue ribbon on her hat fluttered in the wind. Her bustle swished as she stepped onto the plank sidewalk. A man with long sideburns tipped his hat as the woman passed. Lucy watched. No man had ever tipped his hat to her.

"There you are," said Holman as they entered the parson's house. "Thought you both had run out on me."

"Naw, I just forgot the bride's shoes," said Icey.

14

"I've married folks barefooted before," said Parson Cook. "Now, you two stand right here. And Icey, we'll let you stand up with the bride since you've done such a fine job fixing her up." The parson turned to his wife. "Dear, it's time to start."

His wife went to the pump organ in the corner and began to play. When the music stopped, Parson Cook read the vows. Holman moved closer to Lucy and put his arm around her waist. When it was Lucy's turn to say "I do," she opened her mouth to protest. Holman's arm tightened.

She lowered her head and mumbled, "I do." She crossed her fingers behind her back and thought, *I don't.*

After the ceremony, the parson consoled Lucy. "Now dear, don't you be embarrassed. We've all been young." He looked at his wife with a loving expression.

"That's right," said the parson's wife, "but believe me, one of these days you're gonna look back and laugh about this day." Lucy kept her head bowed.

"We're going over to the hotel to have a bit of supper," said Holman to the parson. "Would you and your woman care to join us?"

"That's mighty thoughtful of you, Mr. Carpenter, but I've got some calling to do."

Holman turned to Icey. "Of course you and Morgan will come, won't you?"

Icey pranced toward the door. "Course—it's free, ain't it? I'll get Morgan and meet you over there." Lucy watched her leave. Maybe, just maybe, Icey'd help her.

At the hotel dining room a waiter greeted Holman and showed them to a table next to the window. Lucy marveled at how green the grass looked. She was sure the bubbling stream that ran along the edge of the grass would be cold since it came from the mountains in the distance.

Another waiter appeared from behind the double doors at the back of the dining room. "Would you all care for something to drink?"

"We'll just take water now," said Holman. His gaze never left the window.

Lucy turned and looked at Holman. He sure wasn't acting like he did before the wedding. And what about this man, dressed in funny looking clothes, asking what he could do for them? At home, if she'd wanted something to drink or eat, she'd have to get it. The man bowed and left the room. Before he returned with the water, Icey and Morgan arrived and Holman ordered the meal.

Icey plopped down on a chair. "Well, here we are . . . thought I'd never get Morgan moving . . . sleeping as usual beside the stove." She scooted Lucy's pillowcase sack under the table toward her. "Thought you might be a-needing these. I put in a new nightgown and some hairpins. You'd look prettier with your hair pinned up."

Morgan sat down. "This better be worth it, Icey. Most of these here places don't feed you enough to walk across the street for."

The waiter appeared at Morgan's elbow and set down a platter of fried chicken. Holman watched Lucy eat. Had this girl ever seen this much food? He had, but most of the time it didn't do him much good with all those mouths to feed. When they had all stuffed themselves, Icey giggled and said, "Morgan, come on. Let's go. The newlyweds don't need us for what comes next!"

Morgan stood and rubbed his stomach. "Guess that's so. I've been married to you forty years, and you ain't taught me nothing yet."

"Morgan Crawford, you can just sleep in the store tonight for saying that!"

Morgan looked at Holman and winked. "Might as well, for all the good sleeping in your bed does me." Icey chased Morgan from the dining hall with her umbrella.

Holman watched them leave. "Morgan's always carrying on like that," he said, with a twinkle in his eye, "but they must have somethin' going for them. I think Icey likes his teasing. Come on. I'll show you our room." Holman took her belongings from under the table and led the way up two flights of stairs. He set her belongings on a red velvet chair by the door. Reaching into his pocket, he took a key and inserted it into the lock.

Lucy picked up her pillowcase sack and followed him into the room. Holman held up the key. "I'm going across the street to play some cards with the boys. Don't get no ideas. I'm locking the door."

16

In the hall Holman dropped the key into his pocket. Locking the new bride in her room sure wasn't how most men would celebrate their wedding night. But before Edmund Davenport had talked him into this deal, he hadn't counted on taking a bride, especially one who didn't particularly want to be taken. Anyway, Edmund was a friend, a friend who needed his help.

≈   ≈   ≈

Lucy heard him turn the key in the lock and walk away. She rushed to the door and tried the knob, then ran to the window, and yanked on it. It wouldn't budge. She grabbed a poker by the fireplace and pried. It still wouldn't budge. She saw Holman leave the hotel. She dropped the poker. He waved to her. She turned her back on him.

When she was sure he was inside the building across the street, she began to work on the window again. Finally, it gave way. She pushed it open as far as it would go, raised her skirts, and slung her long legs out the window. Her breath caught in her throat as she clutched the sill. It was two stories down to the street. "Don't look down," she told herself, "look out or up—anywhere but down." Her eyes searched for something to help her escape. No trees. No ledges to grasp or walk along. If only she had a rope. She sat still, thinking. She crawled back into the room, flung the quilts off the bed, and snatched up a sheet. After tearing it into long strips, she knotted it into a ladder. She fastened the rope around the bedpost, then dropped the other end outside. She took a deep breath and climbed back onto the windowsill. Her hands searched for the rope. She tested it, then flipped over and slid toward the ground.

Before her hands hit the first knot, a man screamed, "Look! Look up there. A woman is hanging from the window!" Desperately, she tried to lift herself up. The sheet rope gave, and she dropped again. Her feet searched for a place in the building to catch her toes.

Someone else yelled, "I think she's trying to kill herself."

Nowhere could Lucy find a place to put her feet. Against her better judgement, she looked down. In the gathering dusk, a sea of upturned faces swam before her. Her eyes met Holman's. A look of astonishment covered his face.

17

Morgan yelled from across the street, "Hey, Holman, ain't that your new bride a-hanging up there?"

Lucy watched as the look of amazement vanished and was replaced with a glint of cold, hard anger. She had to do something. To let go and drop was out of the question. She tried again to hoist herself up on the rope. Instead of going up, her hands slipped even further down until they hit another knot. She wouldn't look down again. She had to find a way out of this mess. If she pushed from the side of the building, maybe she could swing hard enough to drop beyond the crowd. At least she'd have a running chance—that was if she was able to run. She drew up her feet and swung herself toward the hotel. As her feet touched the building, her eyes caught the glimpse of an open window. She pushed away with all her strength and let the rope swing toward it. She was only inches from the window when she let go of the rope and grabbed the sill.

A cheer rose from the crowd. Lucy willed herself not to look down. She pulled up until her chin was even with the sill. She gasped. A man's bare backside glared at her. A moan rose from the pit of her stomach. Here she was, afraid of being trapped in a room with a new husband, and she was climbing into a room with a man with no clothes on. She glanced down at the ground. Holman had moved closer to the building. Fury distorted his face. She looked in the window again. Oh well, better a smiling backside than a bedding with that Holman! She pulled herself up onto the windowsill. There was no backing out now. She swung her legs through the open window. As her feet touched the floor inside, a tall, dark-headed man whirled and grabbed a towel to wrap around himself. It was all she could do to suppress a giggle. The urge didn't last long because the window slid down and caught her midriff, leaving her half-in, half-out.

With a bath towel wrapped around his waist and shaving cream covering his face, the man walked over to the window and peered out at her. Now it was his turn to laugh—and laugh he did! A slow chuckle eased its way up and out his mouth as though it were a separate part of him.

Lucy twisted and turned, trying to free herself. She could still hear the crowd below. It wouldn't take Holman long to find this room.

She'd have to get out of here. "Help me! Please, somebody help me!"

The man put his hand on top of the window, pushed it up slightly and watched her squirm. "Well, I must say. I've been thinking that I should take myself a bride, but who would have thought one would blow right through my open window?"

Lucy's hand flew to her hair. The little net veil that Icey had insisted she wear was still intact. She yanked it off and dropped it. She heard a woman on the ground yell, "I caught it! What does that mean?"

Lucy didn't care what it meant. She only knew what it meant if Holman caught her in here. She pushed on the window. "Please help me! I'll explain. Please!"

With one hand, the man lifted the window higher. She scrambled inside and made a dash for the door. As she reached for the knob, the man caught her by the shoulders and whirled her around. "Young lady, I do believe you owe me a thank you."

"Uh! I guess I do. Thanks. Now I have to be going." She tried to turn back to the door.

The man's fingers dug into her shoulders. "Not so fast. It's not every day a bride climbs in my window. Let me get a good look at you." He held her at arm's length and eyed her up and down.

Lucy pulled loose and grabbed the doorknob again. "I promise you, it's not what it looks like." Before he could grab her again, she was out the door and down the hall. She ran, not knowing where she was going. Stairs! They must lead to the second floor. If she could only get back to her room, maybe Holman wouldn't think to look there. With the speed of the wind that blew across her mountain, she ran up the stairs. At the top, she paused. Which way now? She looked to her left. No, that didn't look like the way. It had to be to her right. There—it was the room with the red velvet chair outside the door.

Lucy reached for the doorknob, then remembered Holman had locked it. She dropped into the chair and buried her face in her hands. A floorboard squeaked. Holman would be here any minute! She looked up. The door to their room opened from the inside and there he stood. She waited, expecting him to whale the tar out of her.

19

Holman didn't say a word, just yanked her inside and slammed the door. He walked to the window, closed it, picked up the poker, and jammed it between the window and the casing. He turned toward her and dangled the key inches from her nose. His eyes narrowed to cold blue lines in a flushed face. "Don't try that again!"

Lucy stepped backward. Fear gripped at her gut. Had she pushed him too far? Holman whirled and stepped into the hall. He slammed the door so hard the floor shook.

As Lucy heard the click of the lock, defeat settled over her like the May fog moving over the mountains. She lay on the bed for a long time wondering what to do. Suddenly, she sat up. An extra key! Why hadn't she thought of that before? Maybe there was one hidden somewhere. She searched every drawer and even looked under the edge of the rug. No key! Defeated, she sat down on the bed. Now what was she going to do? She studied the door. An idea began to take shape. She went to the door and picked up the brass chain hanging from the doorjamb.

"Locks work both ways, don't they?" she reasoned aloud. "Why not?" She slipped the night bolt into place.

≈   ≈   ≈

The next morning Lucy sat up in bed. For a few seconds, she couldn't remember what had happened. She looked down at the blue dress. Like a flash flood, the realization of the day before washed over her. She heard steps coming down the hall. She waited for the door handle to turn. The steps continued down the hall. Her stomach reminded her it was time to eat. Maybe if she screamed loud enough someone would hear her. She slipped out of bed and tried the door. It was locked, and the night bolt was still in place. She wondered where Holman had slept last night. A soft knock interrupted her thoughts. The knock became louder. Lucy held her breath.

"Lucy, you in there? It's me, Icey! Let me in."

Lucy unlatched the door. The handle turned. Icey stood there with a wide grin on her face. "Where'd you get that door key, Icey?"

"From Holman, who else? Gotta give you credit, girl. Never thought you'd be smart enough to put a man in his place on the first night."

"What're you talking about? Where's Holman?"

"Over at the store with Morgan."

"What's he doing over there?"

"Sleeping off a hangover. Anyway, where'd you expect him to go last night after what you did? He took such a ribbing from the men that he got dead drunk. Morgan carried him over to the store and they both slept there."

Lucy giggled. "Well, Morgan had company in the store. Tell me, Icey, would you have made him sleep there anyhow?"

"Course I would." Icey plopped herself down on the bed. "You got to learn, Lucy, to use what you have when it comes to a man. Most of 'em talk big, but at heart they're gentle as lambs."

Lucy walked to the window and looked out. "Icey, what's the name of this town?"

"Clayton, Georgia. Why do you ask?"

"I got a sister in Atlanta. How far is that from here?"

"It's about a hundred miles south of here. If you got a hankering to go there, Lucy, I'd forget it if I was you."

Lucy turned to look at Icey. "Why do you say that?"

"No place for a young girl like you. Believe me, Lucy, you'd be better off going with Holman."

"Where's that, Icey?"

"To Franklin, North Carolina. About a half-day's ride from here."

"Is that close to Cherokee?"

"I reckon so. Why do you ask, Lucy?"

"Ma's people live there on a reservation. She told me all about how the government rounded them up and sent them to live over there."

"That's right. I'm sure you'd be happier there than you'd be in Atlanta, but if you decide to stay with Holman, you can handle him. You proved that last night. I'm gonna fix Morgan some breakfast. Come over and have some. I always think better on a full stomach. Anyway, you have to pick up your new clothes."

"I reckon I do need to eat. Come on, Icey. Let's go get that breakfast." As she closed the bedroom door, she thought that Icey's advice wasn't half bad. She'd go with Holman to Franklin, and she'd stay till she could find a way to get to her ma's people.

≈ 3 ≈

Holman jumped from his horse and helped Lucy down. "This here's your new ma, young-uns."

"Don't want no new ma—want *my* ma." A little girl in front of the group turned and buried her face in the skirt of her older sister. Lucy felt the girl's pain. She wanted to cuddle her and smooth the soft, blond curls from her face. Instead, she waited, rigid. For what, she wasn't sure.

A taller boy stepped forward. "My name's John, I'm fifteen. I'm the oldest."

Lucy smiled and extended her hand. "Proud to meet you. Looks like them there pants of yours could take a couple of patches on the knees." John looked down and blushed. His freckles popped out like a case of the measles as he pulled on his left ear.

Lucy gave him a pat on the shoulder. "Don't you worry none. I'm good at sewing on patches. My ma taught me before she died."

The girl with her face buried in the skirt peeked up. Her big blue eyes still glistened with tears. "You don't have a ma, either?"

"That's right, honey. My ma's been dead for five years."

"Did your pa get you a new ma?"

"No, but I was bigger and didn't need one so much."

One of the other boys moved up beside John. "This here's Arthur," said John. "He's fourteen. Me and him do most of the chores. He's big as me, but he ain't no smarter."

Arthur flexed his muscles and grinned at Lucy. His chest bulged with pride. "If you need protecting, I'm your man."

Lucy gripped his hand in a firm shake as she noticed how his brown hair shone in the late afternoon sun. "I'll remember that, son. Who're those two redheads over there?"

John moved over by the twins. "These here's the twins, Harley and Carl. They're eleven. About all they do is fish."

Lucy held out a hand to each boy. "I like fishing, too."

"Bet you can't bait your own hook," said Carl.

Lucy smiled at the boys. "I can even dig my own worms."

Holman took Lucy's belongings and handed them to her. "That's all the boys. The rest of them is girls. The one with the baby is Dovey. She's thirteen. The baby is Martha. Martha's the one my woman died birthing."

The baby grinned and reached out her chubby little arms to Lucy. Dovey's grip tightened around the baby, pressing its soggy diaper closer to her bony hip. Lucy felt an urge to pull the long stringy hair back from Dovey's face.

"The next one's Annie May. She's ten. She's small for her age."

Lucy looked straight into the eyes of the little girl. She held a small ragged quilt under one arm. She couldn't look any whiter if she was a ghost. Those dark circles under her eyes—could she be sick or something?

"The one there in front of Annie May is Mary. She's five. Them two blond heads over there are the other twins. Their names are Nannie and Fannie. They're seven. The sassy one hiding behind Dovey's skirt is Hattie. She's nine." Hattie raised her head and stuck out her tongue at Lucy. Lucy pretended she didn't see.

"The littl'-un here in front is Lou Ellen. She's three. Where's Emily?"

Dovey shifted the baby to the other hip. "Asleep, Pa. She didn't sleep good last night. You know she's two. I think she's cutting her jaw teeth."

"Poor little Emily. Did you give her some paregoric? You know, that's what your ma'd a done."

"Ma taught me how to take care of the young-uns, Pa. I don't need no help." Dovey cut her eyes toward Lucy. Lucy felt her throat tighten. She could tell Holman loved his children, and he must have loved their mother. Well, *she* wasn't their mother, and as far as Dovey was concerned, she'd have to let her know right off that she didn't plan on filling her ma's shoes in any way.

"Dovey, why don't you show Lucy the bed your ma and me slept in. She'll be sleeping in it from now on." Holman led the horse to

23

the barn. Lucy slung her belongings over her shoulder. *Only if she was sleeping in it alone!*

Dovey turned to her. "I see Pa's done and got him a squaw for a wife. Too bad we don't have a tepee for you to sleep in. But since we don't, come on." She started for the house and called over her shoulder, "I ain't got all day."

By the time Lucy caught up with her, Dovey had stepped inside the house. "This here's the front room. That ladder goes to the loft where the boys sleep."

Lucy glanced up at tattered quilts that hung over the edge. It sure looked to her like some new quilts were needed here. Her gaze came back to the front room. There was just enough cane bottom chairs for them all—guess she'd have to sit on the hearth. That big old fireplace sure could keep a whole parcel of toes warm in cold weather.

"The kitchen's over there." Dovey pointed to a door beside a pump organ on the other side of the room. At the back of the front room, she pushed open a door to a large bedroom. "All us girls sleep in here. Ma's bed is the one over in the far corner. I've been a-sleeping there. It's yours now. It's a feather bed. Nice and soft. The other three beds is straw ticks. Only thing is, you'll have to sleep with the two littl'-uns, Lou Ellen and Emily. They're worrisome some-times—'specially Emily. She's teething."

Lucy looked at the sleeping young-un on the bed. "I don't mind that a bit. At home I slept on a corn-shuck tick so I ain't used to a soft bed. If you have an old quilt, I'll make me a pallet over here by this other door. I can even use my belongin's for a pillow. That way, I'll be out of the way."

"Pa wouldn't like that." Dovey placed Martha in a wooden cradle between the two beds nearest the door where Lucy stood. "That door leads to the kitchen, too. It's a big old room built across the whole back of the house."

Lucy studied Dovey's face. The girl's jaw was set. Lucy knew Dovey was only doing what her pa had said. Instead of arguing with her, Lucy sat down on the feather bed, leaned back on her arms, and felt the feathers puffing up softly around her fingers. She could feel Dovey's defiant eyes boring holes through her and could see right

24

now that she was going to have to take a stand with this young-un.

"Where's your pa sleep?"

"Him and Ma used to sleep in this bed out in the front room. But when Ma died, Pa said he couldn't stand to sleep in her bed. We moved it in here, and I've been sleeping in it with the littl'-uns. Pa sleeps out in the hayloft when he's home. Ain't here much of the time. Guess we'll be moving the bed back to the front room now that you're married to Pa. Then we'll have to find a place for the two little girls to sleep."

Lucy never let her eyes leave Dovey's face. "The way your pa and me choose to sleep is *our* business."

"And the way these young-uns is raised is *my* business. Ma left me in charge of them, and I plan on staying in charge. Now I've got to get some supper started."

Dovey was gone before Lucy could answer. She could hear her slamming pots in the kitchen. Should she go in and offer to help? No, Dovey had made herself clear. She didn't want her help in any way. It was going to be awfully crowded in here, but that was all right. Better than being alone with Holman. She reached for the doorknob, then hesitated. Maybe she should take her belongings and leave. No, it was getting late and she didn't want to get lost in these mountains. Besides, Dovey had said Holman wasn't home much. She'd take Icey's advice and give this a chance. In the meantime, she'd go outside and look around.

≈   ≈   ≈

In the barn a calf bellowed a lonesome cry. Lucy patted it on the head. "You want to see your mama, littl'-un?" Lucy's mind wandered back to the first few weeks after her ma had died. She had felt so lost. "Ma, I've found myself here amongst thirteen motherless young-uns. Their pa ain't around much. So far I've been able to keep away from him. I guess I'll stay till I can find me a way to Cherokee and your people. Dovey don't want my help. She don't like me, Ma. And Hattie, she's so sassy. I don't much care. It ain't my job to make them like me."

A hen began to cackle in the hayloft. Lucy took a few steps toward

25

the ladder and looked up. She wondered if there was a nest of eggs up there.

"Where do you think you're going?" Lucy turned in time to see Holman step around the corner of the barn. Her pulse quickened at the sound of his voice. Why hadn't she remembered Dovey saying he slept in the hayloft when he was home? She shouldn't have come out here.

Holman stepped in front of her, placed one foot on the ladder, and leaned his arm against the side wall. Her foot searched for a rung on the ladder. As her toes curled around it, she pushed herself up.

She backed up a couple of rungs. Now they were looking eye to eye. "I was just gonna look for eggs. I heard a hen cackling up in the loft."

Holman watched her like she was a mouse and he was a tomcat getting ready to pounce. "I think you'd better leave the egg hunting to the young-uns. They've been doing it long enough to know where to look. Wouldn't want you wandering around and getting lost."

Lucy never took her eyes off Holman. She bet he wouldn't want her to get lost. Then who'd look after this herd of young ones? "You don't have to worry, Mr. Carpenter. I ain't planning on getting lost."

"Talking about plans," said Holman, "I think you and me had better clear up some things. For one, I have no plans of making you my *real* wife. This arrangement is strictly business, but you know as well as me I had to marry you. Wouldn't look right for me to bring home a young woman without the benefit of a parson."

Lucy wanted to back up the ladder farther, but his eyes held hers. She studied his face. She wasn't afraid of him because she could take care of herself. Hadn't she outsmarted him on their wedding night? He didn't look as old as he had at her pa's, or as little either. And his lips—how would they feel on hers? His arms rippled with lean hard muscles. A slow blush eased its way up from her neck and turned to a hot burn as she let her gaze drop.

Holman removed his foot from the ladder and stepped back. "Look at me, Lucy. As for as what happened at the hotel, maybe we can just forget that and start over. I'm sorry I got mad. Guess if I was in your place, I might try the same thing. You know, this ain't easy on me

26

either. I've got to go in the house and try to explain you to the children." He turned to leave, then hesitated and turned back. "Lucy, I made a fair trade with your pa. The way I see it, you're honor-bound to hold up your pa's part of the bargain. I'll do my part." He turned and strode toward the house.

Seething inside, she watched him go. Her pa had traded her off like an old plow mule or a sack of corn. Well, she'd show them. First chance she got, she'd get away from this place. Slowly, she let out her breath. She'd stay here out of the way till Holman had finished his meeting with the children.

≈   ≈   ≈

Everyone crowded around the table, all talking at once. Holman slammed down his fist. "Quiet! It sounds like a beehive in here."

The voices hushed as all eyes turned toward him. He knew he was going to have to do some explaining. He mopped his brow. Why hadn't he thought of the way the children would feel when he'd made his deal with Edmund? But he *had* thought of them—especially Dovey. She was the one who wanted to go to school so bad, but without someone here to watch the little ones she'd have to stay home. He'd have to make them understand that he wasn't trying to replace their ma.

Holman cleared his throat and twisted his mustache. "I know you-uns wasn't a-counting on me bringing home a wife so soon after your ma's death." He coughed again and looked around the table at his children. Not a single one moved or uttered a sound. Holman felt his sweaty palms against the table. "There's school, you know, and lots of work around here, and I'm gone a lot of the time." Still, not a sound from any of them. Only the eyes watching—watching for him to say or do something to explain what he'd done. "Well, don't any of you have anything to say?"

John made a muffled sound like a pig grunting.

"If you have somethin' to say, John, speak up."

John pulled on his left ear. He looked at his brothers and sisters. His face turned red as his eyes met his pa's. "It ain't that we don't want you to be happy, Pa, but you know how much we loved Ma.

27

It's just gonna be hard with another wom . . ." John's voice failed and a steady stream of tears rolled down his cheeks.

Holman felt the pain of his loss twist like a knife in the gut. He knew the young ones were hurting, but so was he. Another woman here—*here*, in Mary's kitchen—here, mothering her children—but he wouldn't have her *here* in Mary's bed. No, that wasn't in his plans. How could he make them understand? Slowly, he felt his hurt turn to anger. He watched the bunch of stony-faced children. Why should he have to explain Lucy's presence? He was the father and these young ones were his responsibility. He was doing what he had to do to make sure they were seen to. Working at a job he didn't like was enough to deal with right now.

Holman slammed his fist against the table again, but this time there was no request. His anger penetrated the air. "She's your new ma. That's the way it is, and you'd better mind her!"

Annie May tugged on Holman's pants leg. "Pa, what's her name?"

For a moment Holman studied the upturned face—a face that reminded him so much of his loss. "Her name's Lucy and she's from Georgia. She ain't got much of a family, and she's a real good cook."

Hattie flounced around the table. "I ain't calling her nothing! And as for cooking, I'd rather eat Dovey's."

Before Holman could say anything, someone said, "Not me." A whole chorus of "not me's" filled the room.

"I ain't let you all starve yet, have I?" asked Dovey.

John patted Dovey on the back. "You ain't bad, Sis, but I can't say it won't be good to have a change." His arm tightened around her shoulder.

Dovey pulled away from him. "Well, John, if you thought a change was needed, why didn't you offer to cook? Who says cooking is only woman's work?"

Holman went to the bedroom and brought Emily into the kitchen. "Here, feed this young-un some supper and keep her awake for awhile. Maybe she'll sleep tonight. I got to be going now. I've got me some business to take care of a ways off. I'll be gone about two weeks. You know I don't like to be gone like I am, but a man's got to make a living. See that you keep a eye on Lucy. She's new to these parts. It would be easy for her to wander off and get lost. If I come home and she's gone, I'll tan your hides—all of you!"

"Yes, Pa," they replied in unison as Holman left the room.

≈   ≈   ≈

Lucy heard the door slam. In a little while, the clop-clop of hooves faded away into the distance. Holman was gone. She started for the house. Might as well face the children. There wasn't much hope of getting away right now with all those eyes watching her.

The door squeaked as she slipped into the kitchen. Whispering suddenly stopped and all eyes turned to her with stony looks. Lucy's first impulse was to just take her belongings and leave, but then she remembered her earlier talk with Dovey. Now was the time, if she planned to stay, to let them know she wasn't taking any backtalk from any of them. She straightened her shoulders and moved around the kitchen, opening drawers, peering at shelves, and poking around in a bucket of potatoes on the floor.

Finally, John eased around to where she was inspecting a slab of bacon. "Is there somethin' special you're looking for, Lucy?"

She shook her head, then came over to the table. "What I'm looking for ain't in jars or pans. It ain't even on a shelf. What I'm looking for is down inside you young-uns."

Dovey stepped closer. With palms against the table, she leaned toward Lucy. "I know you're gonna try to make us feel sorry for you, but I want you to know right now it ain't gonna work. We've been a-making it on our own since Ma died, and we can keep on a-doing it. We don't need no outsider telling us how." She turned to face the others. "Do we?" Every head bobbed in agreement.

Lucy knew they would stick together. She hadn't wanted to be bossy, but it seemed there was no other way. "All right, if that's the way you want it! I was a-hoping we could all be friends, but it's a-looking like I'm just gonna have to take charge!"

Dovey's cheeks grew red. "What do you *mean* take charge? Didn't I tell you this afternoon *I* was in charge?"

Lucy leaned toward Dovey. They were only inches apart now. "You told me your ma left you in charge of the young-uns. You can stay in charge of them, but I'm running this kitchen from now on. Starting in the morning, I'll do the cooking."

Dovey wheeled around. "You-uns get to bed! Ma'd want me to take care of you." She glared at Lucy. "Ain't no heathen gonna keep me from it!"

Lucy knew the talking was done. She might as well go to bed. Tomorrow, she'd show them she could cook.

~ 4 ~

The next morning, Saturday, brought rain—not a mist but a downpour. Lucy woke to Martha's cries. It seemed to her that the baby had cried all night. She threw back the covers and crawled out of bed. Sure sounded like a sick baby to her. Well, that wasn't any of her business. Cooking was her business, and she'd better get out in the kitchen and get started.

Lucy found the cookstove already hot. John stood at the window watching the rain beat against the panes. He turned as she came in. "I know you said last night that you'd take care of the cooking, but are you sure you know what you're getting into?" John grabbed the milk buckets and reached for his coat.

Lucy took a large knife from the cook table and jabbed it into the slab of bacon she'd examined last night. "Breakfast'll be ready by the time you get back," she said firmly. She'd show them she could cook. There wasn't anything to it—especially when there was something to cook. Half the work was finding it. She began looking around for flour to make biscuits. She'd seen some large barrels on the back porch last night.

On the porch, she brushed the dust from the lid of one of the barrels. The letters on the top looked like the same ones she'd seen on the flour sack back home. She sure wished there had been a school on her mountain. It would be nice to know how to read. She pulled off the cover and found the barrel did contain flour. She filled a large wooden bowl and returned to the kitchen. Once the biscuits were in the oven, she began to carve the bacon. Soon, the whole slab was sliced and the smell of frying bacon filled the room.

John came in with a pail of milk and a basket full of eggs. He set them on the cook table and looked at the full platters of biscuits and bacon. "Lucy, how much bacon did you fry?"

"The whole slab. Do you think there'll be enough?"

"Enough! Of course there'll be enough. Everybody will love you for cooking so much, but what'll we eat till Pa gets home?"

Lucy's eyebrows drew together in puzzlement. "Why do you say that, John?"

"That was store-bought bacon. It was s'posed to do till Pa comes home with some more. This time of year, we're out of our own, so Pa buys it."

Lucy looked at the basket of eggs. "We can have eggs. There seems to be plenty of them."

"I don't think so, Lucy. Dovey's awful fussy about how the eggs are used. I guess it's 'cause the chickens run loose, and we don't always find them."

Lucy cracked an egg into a bowl. "Ain't none of Dovey's business how the eggs are used. I'm in charge of the cooking now." John shrugged his shoulders and began to pour the fresh milk through a cheesecloth strainer. Lucy finished the eggs and took the bucket from him. "This is woman's work. I need some more water to heat for the dishes later."

While John was gone, Lucy studied the pile of bacon. It did seem like a lot, but she had all the grease from it, so she'd be able to make a whole bunch of gravy. She'd as soon have the gravy as the bacon. Of course, she'd been raised on gravy; maybe these young ones wouldn't like it. Well, she'd just have to hunt up all the hens' nests she could find and feed them plenty of eggs. If Dovey had something to say, she'd do like she had last night and let her know it wasn't any of her business.

"So you think you can cook better than me? And where'd you get them eggs?" demanded Dovey as she stood in the doorway clutching a fretful Martha to her thin chest.

Lucy dropped her dishrag and faced Dovey. "The way I see it, Dovey, ain't a question of who can cook better, but who's gonna do it. In case you've forgot, I'm the one in charge of the cooking, so it ain't none of your business where I got the eggs or how I use them."

"Well," Dovey said, rocking the baby in her arms, "I try to save them to put under the setting hens. Won't be no new chicks if you cook up all the eggs."

Lucy raked the scrambled eggs onto a platter. "You can fetch the young-uns now. All I have to do is bake another pan of biscuits."

Dovey looked at the cook table, and her eyes widened. "Just how much bacon did you fry?"

Lucy took more biscuits from the oven. "All there was. I already know that I cooked too much. John told me."

"You mean you fried the whole slab? You're only s'posed to fry one slice for each person. I guess we'll have to eat gravy till Pa gets home."

"Gravy ain't bad if it's made right. I grew up eating it. Can't say I'm no worse off for it."

Dovey looked at the jar full of bacon grease. "Well, I hope you're as good a cook as you think you are—there ain't none of us crazy over gravy."

Martha squirmed and let out a sharp cry. Dovey patted her on the back and snuggled the baby against her shoulder. Lucy shot Dovey a questioning glance. "What seems to be wrong with the baby? I heard her fussing in the night. Is she running a fever?"

Dovey clutched the baby tighter. "Ain't none of your business what's wrong with her. If you ain't no better at caring for young-uns than you are at cooking, you'd kill her." She wheeled and left the room.

Lucy jerked the last pan of biscuits from the oven. She burned her finger and the pan dropped to the floor. Biscuits rolled everywhere. The children began to stumble in still half-asleep. As she picked up the biscuits, she made a vow to find where the hens were laying their eggs. She'd try to make sure the family didn't have only gravy to eat because of her being so stupid.

≈　≈　≈

The ritual of Saturday night baths had begun. Mary sat in the large washtub, rubbing a bar of soft lye soap into her blond curls. John pulled at his left ear thoughtfully. "Sounds to me like Martha might not be feeling too well. Does she have a fever?" He reached over and touched Martha's head. "I think she feels a mite warm."

Dovey pressed the baby's head to her cheek. "She sure does. Oh,

Martha, what're we gonna do? Pa's gone. Please don't get sick!"

Lucy heard the panic in Dovey's voice. Maybe she'd take some advice from her if she were scared enough. "Ma always gave us snakeroot tea when we had a fever."

Dovey held the baby closer and glared at Lucy. "You ain't gonna use your Indian poison on my baby sister. John'll go for the doctor."

John pulled harder at his ear. "Seems Ma used to give us *some* kinda tea."

"But what kind?" asked Dovey.

"I don't remember. I think sometimes she gave us catnip. Let's give her some. If she ain't no better in the morning, I'll ride for the doctor," said John.

Lucy filled the kettle and set it on the stove. "Catnip won't bring her fever down, but it'll make her sleep good. I saw some out by the front steps, John. Go get it, and I'll make catnip tea for her. If she's still got a fever tomorrow, I'll go looking for some snakeroot."

Dovey hugged the baby tighter. "No, you won't! John'll go looking for the doc." Dovey sponged the baby's face with a wet cloth.

Mary sloshed water onto the floor as she stepped from the tin washtub. "I sure hope it's not raining too hard for church tomorrow. I like to get dressed up in my good clothes and go."

Lucy looked out the window at the rain. Sure wasn't nobody going anywhere in this rain, not even church. Too bad, she would kind of like to go. Of course, Dovey wouldn't want her to.

≈   ≈   ≈

On Sunday morning little rivers of water ran down the hills, split, and ran around both sides of the house. John already had a fire in the stove and was watching the rain come down. He turned when Lucy came into the room with Martha. "The baby ain't no better this morning?"

Lucy tried to lay Martha down but she began to whine so handed her to John. "No. She fussed all night. Don't guess Dovey'll like it 'cause I got up with her, but she's wore out. I know she didn't get a lick of sleep. It feels like the baby's still got a little bit of fever."

John felt Martha's head. "What do you think we ought to do? You

34

know this time of year we have to watch out for typhoid fever."

Lucy shook her head. "It ain't been hot enough for the fever yet. Besides, that's usually after a flood when all the water gets poisoned."

John looked out the window. "If it keeps this up, we'll have a flood, and you know Dovey's gonna want me to fetch the doc."

"We better dig some snakeroot. I think I saw some in the woods out near the barn."

John pushed the baby toward Lucy. "You can't go out in this rain. Besides, what's snakeroot?"

"It's a weed with bunches of white flowers on the top and roots to make a tea out of. The tea is good to bring down a fever. Ma used it all the time."

John hesitated. "You know Dovey ain't gonna let you doctor the baby. She don't want you messing with the young-uns."

"She might not have a choice if the rain keeps up."

John set the baby on the floor. "Well, I'll go get the snakeroot just in case we have to use it."

Lucy could see the doubt in his eyes. "Do you know what you're looking for? If you take care of Martha, I'll go." Lucy reached for a coat and put it over her head.

John picked up the baby. "Don't you go wandering off too far. It would be easy to get lost in this rain."

"Don't worry, John," said Lucy. "I won't lose sight of the barn. And I'll hurry. I'm sure Martha's fever is just from cutting teeth. My sister's babies always had that problem. See how she's drooling? She'll be a lot happier when her fever is down."

Lucy stepped into the gushing rain. She could barely make out the barn as she groped her way through the downpour. Beyond the first clump of trees, she found several bunches of snakeroot. She knelt down in the mud and yanked at it. As the plant weakened, Lucy fell back with the long snake-like roots in her hand. She got up and made a dash for the house. Halfway there, the ground melted from beneath her feet. Cold water rushed around the lower part of her body. The current pulled at her. Fear clutched at her heart. She'd heard talk about underground streams and this must be one of them. The rain must have softened the ground enough to cause it to give in. She

35

couldn't lose the snakeroot, so she threw it as far as she could. Her coat slipped from her shoulders. She dug her fingers into the wet earth. She had to find something to hang onto. She didn't want to drown out here. Her fingertips touched a mass of tangles and then a tree root. She gratefully clung to it.

Slowly, she edged her fingers up until she had a good hold. The root loosened, and the current tugged at her body. She couldn't lift herself up by the root. She looked around for something else to use to hoist herself out of the water. Nothing. She shivered. The heat of the kitchen sure would feel good right now, even if Dovey were there.

Lucy felt her dress and apron being sucked around her legs by the rushing water. If she could get her apron off, maybe she could use it as a rope and lasso a tree limb. With her left hand, she struggled with the knot, but it only tightened. The root gave again and she slipped. Water engulfed her up to her armpits. "Help!" she called. "Please! Somebody, help me!" Her pleas for help were lost in the teeming rain. Frantically, she kicked her feet, hoping to find something to dig her toes into to keep from drifting underground.

"Moo-oo-o," came a muffled sound from her left. A cow! Wildly, she twisted around. All she could see was the swish of a tail. If only she could reach it! Her toes touched a rock. She braced herself on it and shoved toward the rim of the hole, digging her elbow into the soggy earth. The tail swished only inches from her face. She let go of the root and grabbed at the tail, but missed. She shoved her elbow deeper into the ground and reached again. She caught it! With lightning speed, she grabbed on with her other hand.

The cow bellowed as Lucy yanked on its tail. "Get up, cow! Get up." She felt her hands slip. "Move, cow, move! If you don't want both of us to drown, you'd better move, 'cause I ain't gonna let go."

The cow moved, but not the way Lucy had hoped. She backed up and Lucy felt herself being lowered into the water. Desperately, she hung on. The hair on the tail brushed her nose. "I'll bet you'll move if I bite your tail." Her teeth clamped down.

The cow lunged forward. Lucy's body was hauled from the water, but her troubles weren't over. The cow didn't stop. She ran like the devil toward the barn. Lucy's fingers instinctively tightened. No, this couldn't be happening. Drowning would be better than being dragged to death. All she had to do was let go, but her fingers seemed frozen to the hairy rope. The cow made a quick turn. Lucy's body swiped a tree. She closed her eyes and waited for death.

≈　≈　≈

John watched for Lucy as he rocked the baby back and forth in his arms and talked to Dovey. "Oh, Dovey, I wonder what's happened to Lucy. She should have been here long ago."

Dovey went to the stove and yanked at the door of the firebox. "It would serve her right if she got lost and had to spend the day out there. Don't know why you're so worried about her." She put an old quilt down behind the stove. "Looks like Martha is finally sleeping. Lay her down over here."

John laid the baby down. "Did you ever think, Dovey, she might not want to come back? She don't owe us nothing. And how do you think you'll get to go to that school you love so much if it weren't for Lucy being here? I sure hope nothing's happened to her."

The baby whimpered. Dovey patted her on the back as she ignored John's concern for Lucy. "You think the baby's worse, John? You tend to the fire. I'll just set here by her for awhile."

John picked up a handful of wood from the box by the stove. "You know Pa'll have all our hides if we let anything happen to Lucy. And, Dovey, you'd better hope the snakeroot tea breaks the baby's fever. I'd never make it to town in this rain—'specially on our old plow mule. You know how she hates storms. Pro'bly couldn't even get her out of the barn."

A look of terror flashed across Dovey's face. "Oh, John! You just have to go. We can't let anything happen to Martha. Pa'd sure enough have our hides."

John turned toward the window. "Dovey, it don't take much for the valley to flood. What would you do if I went for the doc and somethin' happened to me? Then you'd sure be in a fix. Even if Lucy does come back, I don't think you and her could make it here alone."

Hattie came into the kitchen and squeezed in front of John. "Let me see what you're looking at." She wiped the windowpane with her sleeve. "Ain't nothing out there but water. Sure glad it rained. I didn't want to have to go to church, anyhow. I'd as soon be a heathen like Lucy."

John patted Hattie on the head. "I doubt she's a heathen, Hattie. Maybe we're all being too hard on her. Could be we need to give her a chance."

Dovey wheeled around angrily. "Chance! Seems we gave her that yesterday morning—and you see what happened. If you didn't, you'll know when you have gravy for breakfast this morning."

"I ain't gonna stand around here fighting with you about how we should treat Lucy." He reached for his coat. "Pa told us not to let her get lost, and I'm gonna go out there and find her."

Dovey grabbed her coat. "Hattie, you stay in here with Martha. She's asleep. Be quiet and don't wake her; she didn't sleep good again last night."

"Dovey, I don't think you should go out in this rain. We can't afford to have you sick, too."

"I'm gonna go, John. I don't trust that Lucy woman. I want to see what she's up too. Bet you a dime to a dollar we don't find her."

"Somehow, I think we will. Don't know why, but I have this gut feeling she's in trouble."

Dovey stepped out into the rain. "It would serve her right if she was—pay her back for barging in and taking over!"

John followed Dovey out the door. "I'm gonna look over this way. Could be she lost her way in the rain. You look toward the back of the barn."

Dovey walked toward the barn. Had John been right? Maybe she should have stayed in the house out of the rain. Lucy sure wasn't worth being sick over. What she saw next made her laugh. Yes, it was worth being sick over—she sure wouldn't miss this! "John, come here. Quick! Look over yonder at the cow. She's running like the devil's after her—and ain't that Lucy hanging onto her tail?"

John ran up beside Dovey. "It sure is. I hope she ain't hurt. If she is, we'll *really* need the doc."

Dovey turned on him with fury in her eyes. "You'd go fetch the doc for some half-breed and not for your own sister!"

"I've got to stop that cow, or we're gonna need a pine box instead of the doc. I'll run around behind the cow and herd her into the barn. Don't you let her run out this side."

Dovey bent over and clutched her stomach as tears of laughter ran down her face. "You're crazy if you think I'm gonna help you catch that cow. Seems to me she'd just let go of the tail. You can chase the cow down if you want to. I don't care what happens to Lucy, but I do want to see what she's up to."

John caught the cow as she made another swipe around the tree. Lucy's eyes were shut tight, her knuckles white from hanging on. Dovey ran up to where she lay. "And you know so much about taking care of young-uns! Just look at you. Who's gonna take care of you while you mend? Ain't gonna be me—I got enough to do."

John knelt down. "Can you hear me, Lucy? Are you all right?"

Slowly her eyelids opened, and she tried to move. "John, I . . . I fell . . . in a . . ."

"Never mind, Lucy. Try to stand up, but first let go of the cow's tail."

Dovey was laughing again. "You expect her to know how to let go? If she did, she wouldn't still be hanging on. Guess we'll just call her 'Cow's Tail Lucy' from now on."

John reached down and helped Lucy stand. "You sure you're all right, Lucy?"

Lucy tried not to look at them. She'd messed up breakfast and now the snakeroot. What had happened to it? She started toward the woods. "I've got to find the snakeroot."

John took her arm. "Don't worry, Lucy. I'll go back for it when you're in out of this rain. Come on. Let's go." He and Dovey herded the cow toward the barn. Behind stumbled a mud-soused Lucy.

≈   ≈   ≈

Dovey held the baby tighter as she watched Lucy work. "You're crazy if you think I'm gonna give that stuff to this baby!"

Lucy set the pan off the stove and strained the water through a cheesecloth. "It's ready now. We'll let it cool for a few minutes, then if Dovey won't give it to her, I will."

39

Dovey screamed at Lucy. "I told you she's not taking that stuff!"

John put an arm around Dovey. "Now Dovey, we don't have no choice." He peered down at the brownish water in the pan. "Shouldn't we just try to get her to drink some of it?"

Lucy stirred a spoonful of sugar into the tea. "She's too little to drink. We'll have to do it this way. Now, you take her and just lay her back. It won't be bad."

Dovey clutched the baby even tighter and backed toward the door leading to the front room. "You'll have to give it to her over my dead body! She's my sister and she's in my care. That's what Ma wanted." Her eyes flashed as John moved toward her. "I'm warning you, John! Ain't no Indian gonna come in here and poison my baby sister."

The baby began to scream. John reached for her. "I know Ma left you in charge of the young-uns, but with Pa gone, I'm the man of the house. I'm gonna do what I think best. Now, you just go on in the other room and let me and Lucy do what we have to."

Dovey yanked the baby back from John. "No, John! You ain't gonna do it."

Lucy put down the cup of tea. "All right, Dovey, calm yourself. We won't give the baby my medicine. We'll do what you want to. John, go get the doc."

John tugged on his ear. "But Lucy, you know I won't get there in this storm."

The baby screamed louder. "Go, John, and watch for that underground stream I just fell in. I almost drowned. Would have, if it hadn't a been for the root I was able to hang onto till I could grab the cow's tail. Hurry. The baby sounds like she's hurting bad. Let's just hope it's not too late."

Dovey touched the baby's forehead. A puzzled look crossed her face. "Her fever ain't no worse. John, what do you think is wrong with her?"

John grinned. "I'd say she's just scared of all the screaming that's going on."

Dovey relaxed her hold on Martha and glared at Lucy. "Think you're gonna scare me into giving in, do you? Well, it won't work!"

Lucy sat down at the table and wiped her face on her apron.

"Dovey, I'm sure the baby's just cutting teeth. It would be a shame to, send John out in this weather if that's all it is." She picked up the cup of tea. "Tell you what. I'll drink the tea in this cup. If nothing happens to me in a little while, will you let us give the baby the medicine?"

Dovey watched Lucy. "Well, I guess if you don't die at least I'll know you're not trying to kill her. I still don't think it'll help her. I'll let John do what he thinks is best." She turned to John. "You just wait till Pa hears about you letting her give Martha heaven knows what."

John tried to comfort Dovey, but she pushed him away. "See how that rain's coming down, Dovey? Ain't seen it rain this hard in a long time. The creek is out of its banks by now. You'd better hope Lucy's medicine helps the baby. And as for Pa, I don't think we'll have to worry about him coming home for awhile."

Lucy finished drinking the tea and reached for the baby. "Let me take the baby for a little while, Dovey. You look wore out."

Dovey turned away. "Ain't none of your business how I look. And I'll keep Martha with me—no telling what you'd do to her if I turn my back." She stomped out of the kitchen.

Lucy handed John some more tea. "When Dovey calms down, take this in and spoon some down the baby. I'm gonna start breakfast." She needed to stay busy. The steady squeak of Dovey's rocking chair from the front room sounded like the ticking of a clock, a clock that could mean the difference between winning or losing for her.

≈ 5 ≈

A week later the flood waters were down. Lucy waited on the front porch of the Carpenter house for the sun to creep over the mountains. Her pillowcase sack of belongings sat beside her. She was going to leave this place, even if it meant going against her pa's wishes. She couldn't help it.

Now that Martha was better, and Dovey had found out she hadn't tried to poison the baby, it seemed like she'd be grateful for her help. But no, she'd only gotten harder to live with. She was tired of trying to live with folks who didn't want her. Let them get along on their own. And who cared if Dovey ever got to go to school? The way she'd been acting she didn't need to go. Her pa had no business making a deal with Holman. After all, it was her life. At least she deserved to know what the deal was all about.

"You gonna go somewhere, Lucy?" Annie May looked up at Lucy with her ragged quilt tucked under one arm.

Lucy knelt down and motioned for her to come close. "Yes, Annie May, I've got to go. My ma's got family around here, and I want to go see them."

The little girl shook her head. "I know why you're really gonna go. It's 'cause we ain't been nice to you." Lucy lowered her head. "Ain't I right? That's why you're gonna go, ain't it?"

Lucy felt the touch of Annie May's hand on hers. She knew these same little fingers were also finding their way to her heart. She'd have to be careful and not let them get too hard a grip. One thing she didn't need now was attachments. An ache filled her heart as she thought about all she'd left on her mountain. No, she wouldn't let herself get too close.

"I'm sorry Dovey's been so mean to you. It's her that's making the others not like you. Would you stay if I told you that I like you?" Annie May's pleading eyes looked steadily into Lucy's.

Lucy took Annie May's hand in hers. "I like you, too, but it's hard to stay where you're not wanted."

The little girl's arms slid around Lucy's neck. "I like you. Please say you'll stay. You can come with me to see the deer feeding."

Lucy looked at the sky as she tried to ignore the arms that clung to her. Dark clouds rolled over the mountains. There'd probably be no sun today, and from the way it looked, there'd be rain again. It couldn't hurt to stay another day or two. She unclasped the arms from around her neck. "I'll stay a little longer, Annie May, but I ain't making no promises."

"Would you come with me to see the deer feeding?"

Lucy looked up at the clouds again. "We'll have to hurry. It looks like it's gonna rain." She moved her sack to lean against the porch post. "Come on. We'll have to hurry."

Annie May dropped her quilt. "It won't take long." She grabbed Lucy's hand and pulled her toward the steps. "Let's go."

"Go where?" asked Dovey from the door.

"I'm gonna show Lucy the deer."

Dovey glanced at the quilt and Lucy's belongings on the floor. "What about breakfast?" she asked and brought her steel blue eyes back to rest on Lucy.

Lucy met her cold stare. "Who cooked it before I came? We'll be back in time to eat." She bent and picked up the quilt, handing it to Annie May.

Lucy felt Dovey's eyes on her and Annie May as they disappeared up the trail. She guessed she'd have a fight on her hands when she got back. Oh well, if the rain held off, she just might head on out today.

The trees began to thin as they climbed. Annie May motioned toward a small clearing where a doe and two little fawns nibbled at tender blades of grass. The doe lifted her head, sniffed the air, then licked one of the fawns. Lucy squeezed Annie May's hand as they watched together.

A shot rang through the morning air. The doe's head came up and she spotted Lucy and Annie May. In an instant, she vanished into the trees with the fawns at her heels.

"Who do you think's a-shooting so early in the morning?" Annie May asked Lucy.

Lucy patted Annie May's head. "Pro'bly just somebody a-hunting." She scanned the trees. An uneasy feeling settled over her. Holman had been gone longer than he should have been. Could he be out there somewhere? "Come on, honey. I think we'd better get back to the house." Another shot split the air. It sounded closer. "Annie May, you run on back to the house. Tell John I'll be there soon."

Annie May called back as she started down the trail, "Better not be gone too long, or you won't get no breakfast."

Lucy peered through the trees. There was no sign of a trail leading further up the mountain, so she began picking her way through the undergrowth of the forest. Pine needles and leaves cushioned the ground as she worked her way up the mountain. Sometimes the going got steep and she'd rest, but only for a few minutes. The trees thinned. Bushes and vines took their place. She knelt and crawled toward the top. Voices—there *was* someone up here! She edged closer and could hear men's voices.

Lucy's heart fluttered when she recognized one of the voices. She parted the vines and peeked out. Holman stood in a small clearing with his hand on the shoulder of another man. Holman's gun was tucked under the other arm. A third man stood about three paces in front of them with his gun aimed at the other two. His face looked grim, determined. "I ain't gonna do it. I don't care what you say. It's mine, and I ain't gonna give it up."

The man standing next to Holman took a step forward. "Now Luther, let's be reasonable about this. Your men could have killed me and Holman awhile ago if they'd had a mind to. Folks know you ain't a bad man—just a man trying to make a living."

The man crossed his arms and spread his legs apart as if to dare the others to come any nearer. "You know all that shooting that was going on? I meant it to scare you away."

Holman sighed. "We know you wouldn't hurt us, Luther. You have to know we're doing what we have to. We're sure you're not messed up with the men we're after, but we think it would be safer if you shut down for a little while."

The man's face relaxed. He turned toward a large boulder. "Guess you're right. Come on, let's get it over with."

Lucy crouched in her hiding place. She couldn't move if she had wanted to. She watched as the men disappeared behind the rock. She waited and her breathing filled the space around her with a vibrancy of its own. She'd have to be careful and quiet because she certainly didn't want Holman to find her here. Spying on him wasn't part of the job he had made his deal for with her pa.

Angry, high-pitched voices filled the air. She moved a few inches to gain a better vantage point. What had she gotten herself into? But she couldn't leave now; she had to know what Holman was up to.

The voices quieted, but from all the thrashing sounds she heard there must be some kind of fight going on. "Watch out, Holman! His gun!" she heard, followed by more thrashing and then a shot. Lucy let out a soft moan, then clapped her hand over her mouth. She sure hoped they hadn't heard her. She shrunk back into her covering and waited. There was more thrashing and moving around as well as mumbling that she couldn't understand.

"What're we gonna do now?" someone asked. Lucy peered out again. The men were in the clearing again.

"I'll help you get him on your horse. You can take him home. We'll meet back in town later."

Lucy stuffed back an urge to scream. There was a man on the ground, and the way it looked, he was *dead*. She watched as the men dragged the body over to a horse and tied it on. The other man mounted and rode right by the place where she was hiding. Blood dripped from the dead man's fingertips. She kept her hand tightly over her mouth to keep from being sick. Holman walked toward her. It seemed like he looked straight at her. She moved back. Holman stopped and scanned the clearing. Had he heard her? She waited. He searched the clearing, then mounted his horse.

Lucy sneezed.

Holman stopped, then turned his horse and rode around the clearing, looking into the bushes.

She scooted backward. She heard a hissing sound. Then she smelled it and there was no mistake. She'd been sprayed by a skunk!

Clutching her nose, she crawled forward. She saw the toes of boots. At this point, it was either Holman or the skunk. Before she had time to make a decision, she was being lifted from the vines by her collar.

"So you've decided to run away. I should have known I couldn't trust you to do what's right." said Holman.

"Right!" Lucy shouted. "You got the nerve to talk about what's right. A man's just been shot dead, and you can stand there and tell me I'm doing wrong. If you'd been through what I have the last few weeks, you'd already been gone. I want you to get it through your head right now. I ain't carrying out no deals made between you and my pa—'specially ones I don't know nothing about." She caught her breath and stomped her foot. "And another thing, I ain't a-running away. I was just trying to show some love to one of your young-un's."

Holman stepped back and held up his hand. "Whoa! You've got this all wrong. I ain't killed nobody. And if you're not running away, what are you doing way up here all by yourself?" The corners of his mouth turned up in a half smile. "If I do say so, you sure are mighty purty when you're mad, but what is that godawful smell?"

"I'm up here 'cause I came with Annie May to see the deer. We heard the shooting. I sent her back to the house, and I came to see what was going on. You can't say nobody was shot 'cause I saw that other man ride away with a dead man on his horse."

Holman grabbed her by the wrist and jerked her to him. His eyes narrowed, and she could feel his hot breath. "You ain't seen nothing! You hear me! You ain't been on this mountain, and you ain't seen nothing." His fingers dug into her arm. "Look me in the eye and tell me you ain't never been here."

Lucy tried to work her arm free. Holman caught her around the waist and pressed her close. The fight left her. She was tired. Tired of it all. Why fight? She wasn't gaining anything. She let out a sigh and felt her body sag against Holman's. For a moment she closed her eyes. How good it would be if someone cared about her. Annie May's arms were the first she'd felt around her since she'd left her mountain. Suddenly, she realized Holman wasn't gripping her waist, but instead his arm was around her shoulder. She raised her face to meet his gaze. "All I seen up here was a skunk."

"That's right, Lucy. All you seen was a skunk. Now you get on home and get some of Dovey's hard lye soap and take yourself a good bath. I'll be on in a little while."

Holman mounted his horse and rode away. The feel of his arm around her shoulders lingered. Yes, all she'd seen on the mountain was a two-legged skunk. But was it Holman? Somehow she hoped it wasn't. The hoofbeats faded into the distance, and she was left alone on the mountain with only the smell of blood and skunk for company.

≈   ≈   ≈

Lucy dreaded going back to the house. Could she act like her old self? She hoped so. She wished she'd brought her belongings so she could just head on out to look for her family. When she came out of the woods at the foot of the mountain, she saw a little white church near the edge of the road. Maybe this was the church the Carpenter children came to. Could it be the God her ma used to talk about lived at this church? She needed all the help she could get right now.

She pushed opened the door, but nobody invited her in. She looked down at her dress. It was just as well—she wasn't fixed up enough for God. She sat down in a pew. What was she going to do? She hoped somehow she could get away from here soon. How was she going to face all those young ones now? And their father with a dead man whom he had probably shot, or at least it looked like he could have. Well, sitting here worrying about it wasn't going to help. She'd better get on back. If she knew John, he'd be out looking for her soon.

Lucy heard the door open and she ducked behind the pew. Maybe Holman had come looking for her. Maybe . . .

The door squeaked louder. "Lucy, you in here?"

She sat up. "It's you, John! I was just a-fixing to come on home."

"Annie May came home without you. Said you'd went off looking for somebody shooting a gun. I was afeared you got yourself lost or in some kind of trouble. Pa'd be awful mad at us if we let somethin' happen to you."

"I'm all right, John. I just needed to be alone for a little while. Church seemed to be as good a place as any." No matter what, she couldn't let anyone know what she'd seen or heard.

≈   ≈   ≈

Later that day the sun beat down on Lucy as she scrubbed the boys' overalls. She straightened and rubbed her back. When the boys came in from the field, she'd have them fetch more wood. She punched down the white clothes with a broomstick. There was still another pot of clothes to boil, but the dark clouds that had threatened rain this morning were gone. There'd be more shade from the old walnut tree later this afternoon, so she'd finish the wash then. Suddenly a bell tolled. It sounded like it was coming from the church.

The children came running from all directions and gathered in a cluster. Lucy shaded her eyes with her hand and looked toward the church. "What's going on?"

Hattie wormed her way to the front of the group. "Guess somebody's dead. The bell rung like that when Ma died."

Lucy cringed. *Dead.* There sure was somebody dead, and she'd seen him this morning. She swallowed and wondered if she could hide her feelings.

"Wonder who died?" John asked.

"It's already tolled ten times," said Arthur.

"Listen!" demanded Dovey. "How can we count with you all gabbing?"

"Why are you counting?" asked Lucy.

"Anyone, even a dumb Indian that rides on a cow's tail, ought to know when a bell tolls, it's for the dead," said Dovey. "If you count the tolls, it'll tell you how old the person was. Be quiet and listen."

"Twenty," said Arthur.

The children counted. "Twenty-one, twenty-two, twenty-three." On and on the bell tolled. Each toll sent chills up Lucy's spine.

"There's a rider coming up the road." Arthur announced.

Hattie danced around in circles. "Maybe it's Pa."

John started back toward the barn. "Whoever it is will pro'bly know who's dead."

Harley counted aloud. "Thirty-six, thirty-seven, thirty-eight."

The tolling stopped. The children looked at each other. "Who is it?" asked Lucy.

Dovey shrugged her shoulders. "Could be about anybody."

"The rider is Pa! It's Pa!" Hattie shouted.

Lucy shivered. Only this morning she'd seen Holman standing over a dead man. And he'd made her say she hadn't seen anything. The last thing she wanted was to have to deal with these children and a funeral, let alone what she knew about Holman.

Hattie ran to give her pa a hug. "Where you been so long, Pa?" asked Dovey, as she took his bedroll. "You said you'd be home in a week or two. It's been almost three weeks."

"Business took longer than I thought, Dovey."

John ran up to the horse and grabbed the reins. "This horse has been rode awful hard. You're always yelling at me and Arthur if we ride a horse too hard."

Holman patted the horse on the flank. "It was necessary, but don't let me find you doing it unless you have to. Walk her till she cools off."

Dovey pushed her long hair off her face. "The bell was tolling, Pa. Do you know who died?"

The stern expression on Holman's face changed to sadness. "Yes, Dovey, it's Luther Jones. He was shot this morning."

"Shot!" Shock registered on every face.

Dovey dropped the bedroll. "Why? He was an elder in our church. No one would want to hurt him."

Holman picked up the bedroll and slung it over his shoulder. "I guess you could say it was an accident."

"How did the accident happen, Pa?"

"I'm not free to say, Dovey. Just that there was some shooting, and Luther got shot."

"I can't believe Mr. Jones is dead. You've got to be wrong, Pa."

"Wish I was, Dovey. They're neighbors, and we've all been good friends. They'll be expecting some of us by."

"I ain't gonna go. I just can't face 'em." Dovey turned and ran toward the house.

49

"I'd go, but I've got to go back to town. Some things I got to finish up," said Holman.

"What're you gonna ride?" asked Arthur.

"I'll take the mule and the wagon. I got to get supplies." Lucy was glad Holman hadn't forgotten the supplies. Even she was getting tired of gravy.

Holman turned to Lucy. "Well, I see you ain't run off on me. Don't s'pose I can count on you to go by the Joneses' and help out tonight for the vigil? They can always use an extra woman in the kitchen. Be right nice if my new missus was one of them women." He headed toward the barn before she could answer.

Lucy stared after him. How could he just ride in here and act as though she'd always been his missus? It seemed to her he expected an awful lot from a woman he'd made a deal for—a woman he'd not bedded. He'd even given her orders on the mountain. Maybe she should go on up to the Joneses' and make sure that Luther was the same man she'd seen Holman with this morning. That was what she'd do. As soon as the horse cooled off and her supper chores were done, she'd have John take her up there. It would be a good way to avoid Holman tonight.

≈   ≈   ≈

John reined the horse to a halt in front of the Joneses' old farmhouse, dismounted, and helped Lucy down. "You sure you want to do this, Lucy?"

She slid off the horse. "Yes, John. Your pa expects some of us to come and Dovey's too upset. Besides, it'll give me a chance to get to know some of the neighbors."

John tied the horse to the rail fence. "I'll go in with you. People in these parts don't cotton to strangers. 'Specially if they're . . ." He looked away.

Lucy blushed. "You needn't feel bad, John. I know how folks feel about Indians. I don't want to cause your family no shame."

John took her by the arm and guided her toward the porch. "It's not that, Lucy. People just don't like outsiders." He nodded to several men who stood on the porch talking. "See that bunch of men? Just ignore them when you walk by. They'll for sure look you over good."

A chill crept up Lucy's back. She turned and looked down the road, trying to avoid the men that had already begun to stare at her. She pointed to the road. "What's making all that dust?"

"That's just people coming up to pay their respects to the family. It'll be like this till he's buried."

"When'll they bury him?"

"Pro'bly tomorrow. Can't keep him too long. The neighbors will sit up tonight." John opened the door. Lucy hesitated and drew in a deep breath, then stepped inside. Had she done the right thing coming up here? Maybe she'd just get a look at the body and go back home. She sure didn't owe Holman anything. And the Joneses—she'd never met them so she didn't owe them anything either.

For a moment she could swear she smelled the scent of fresh blood. Her stomach churned, and she closed her eyes. She opened them and took a step toward the coffin. Sure enough, it was the man she'd seen Holman with on the mountain. She shook her head as if to clear away the image of the face, but it stayed. She felt John's hand on her shoulder.

"You all right, Lucy? Ain't you never seen the dead before?"

"Yes, but not one that's been shot."

"Come on. Let's go in the kitchen. I want you to meet Bessie."

Lucy moved away from the coffin. She wasn't sure she wanted to meet Bessie or anybody else. Inside the kitchen the oil lamps on the big oak table gave a ghostly effect to the room. Lucy raised her hand and watched the shadows of her fingers race across the floor and crawl up the wall.

"Bessie, this here's my new ma, Lucy," said John. "She wanted to come help out. Pa said to tell you he'd be by later."

Bessie removed bread from the oven. She raised her eyebrows as she looked Lucy over. Finally, she extended her hand. "My name's Bessie. I'm Luther's oldest sister. I live here with his family and help out with the young-uns. The missus ain't too well. Can you cook?"

John smiled. "She can if you tell her how much."

"That won't be no problem. See that bucket of taters over there? They need to be peeled."

"I've got to get going," said John. "I'll come for you in the morning, Lucy. Bessie, let us know if there's any more we can do."

Lucy began to peel potatoes. Looked to her like Holman had already done his part helping out. What would John say if he'd seen what she'd seen? Would he be so eager to offer their help then? She heard Bessie give a weary sigh.

"Thanks, John, but don't guess there's much to do now 'cept bury my poor dead brother." Lucy watched John leave. How would she ever get through the night with this strange woman? She guessed it would be better staying here than going home to face Holman though.

Bessie put more bread in the oven. "When you're finished, you can tell people there's a fresh pot of coffee ready."

After finishing the potatoes, Lucy wiped her hands on her apron and pushed open the heavy wooden door. A circle of people sat in ladder-back chairs. From here the corpse seemed to be only sleeping. How she wished that was so. How she wished she'd never gone on the mountain. How she wished she'd not taken Icey's advice. "Coffee's ready," Lucy announced.

Before she closed the door, something brushed against her leg. She looked down in time to see a dark shadow dart past her into the room. "Get 'em! Don't let that cat get to the body!" someone yelled. A group gathered protectively around the coffin and swatted at the cat. All Lucy could see was the cat's green eyes as it darted around the room and finally made a beeline back toward the kitchen. Before Lucy could move, the cat shot between her feet and she lost her balance. A man caught her. As he stood her up, she caught a mean look in his beady eyes beneath a mess of stringy hair. He sure looked like a real mean mountain man to her.

"Seems you'd better stay outta the way, girl."

Lucy straightened her skirt. "I didn't come up here to be in the way. I came to help Bessie, and she says to tell you the coffee's ready."

"Well, see to it that's all you do. We've got us enough trouble a-brewing."

She went to the stove and got the coffee pot. He'd think there was trouble if he knew what she knew. Maybe she'd go to the sheriff. But how? She didn't even know where to find the town. Also, it could be the sheriff was already here. She'd ask Bessie later.

One by one the mourners finished their coffee and returned to watch over the body. Bessie took the last of the bread from the oven. "Ain't much to do till it's time for the midnight supper. Want to set in with the others for awhile?"

Lucy wasn't eager to sit in a room with a corpse, especially *this* corpse, but she'd do what was expected of her. The hushed mourners hardly noticed her slip into a chair near the coffin and glance around at them. Some slumped in their chairs, tired from a hard day's work. Others sat with closed eyes. She looked up at the coffin. Why would Holman have any dealing with the kind of people that killed?

Sobs broke out from someone at the back of the room. Lucy turned to see a small childlike woman standing in the doorway. Lucy watched her stumble toward the coffin and throw her body over the corpse. Bessie went to the woman and put her arms around her. "Come, Effie. You need your rest for tomorrow."

Lucy followed them into the kitchen. Bessie said, "Can you go put the coffee on? It'll soon be time to warm up the vittles for the midnight supper."

Lucy watched as Bessie guided the woman toward a door of the kitchen. Her heart ached for the widow. She shuddered and turned to the stove.

The midnight supper didn't take long. Few people wanted to eat. Bessie cleared the table. "Better keep the coffee going the rest of the night. They'll need a lot to keep them awake. You want to set in here or with the others?"

Lucy poured the dishwater into the slop bucket. "Could we just set out here at the table?"

Bessie slung the dishrag over the side of the dishpan. "Fine with me."

"Bessie, could I ask you somethin'?"

"You can ask; can't say I know the answer."

"The sheriff, is he here?"

Bessie's head jerked up. "Why do you want to know?"

53

Lucy shrugged. "Just wondered. Guess I thought since it was a shooting, he'd be around."

"Well, not as I know, but if I was you, I wouldn't get too nosey."

The clock struck two. A commotion rose in the other room, and Lucy pushed the door open. Something moved across the room. A dark shadow loomed against the window. The people in the room were as quiet as the corpse. The same stringy-haired man moved toward the window with caution and pushed back the curtain. The black cat leaped toward the coffin and landed on the edge. Before it regained its balance, the man scooped him up. A dog howled outside.

Another man walked to the window and stared into the dark. "Will this night ever end?" he asked.

Finally, the rays of the morning sun peeked over the mountains, chasing all traces of ghostly shadows from the valley. Heavy sighs could be heard from some of the mourners as they filed onto the front porch. Lucy turned and walked back into the empty room. Someone had removed the chairs. The casket stood closed, waiting to be moved to the church. She went back to the kitchen.

Inside, Bessie prepared breakfast. "Need some coffee, Lucy?"

"That sounds good, Bessie, but I can get it." She took a cup from the cupboard and poured it full of the steaming black brew. She sat at the table and looked around the room. The cat that had looked so large last night lay sunning himself in the kitchen window. The shadows that had played across the room now gave way to real shapes. Bessie looked rested, not as weary as last night. "Bessie, why did your brother get shot?"

Bessie's blue eyes looked intently into Lucy's. She reached out and cupped her large calloused hand over Lucy's. "Remember what I said last night, dearie. Some things are better not talked about."

Lucy got up and walked to the back door. She turned and looked at the scene before her. She suspected this room held a lot of well-kept secrets.

≈　　≈　　≈

54

As Lucy started home from the Joneses', the sun didn't have to struggle to shine through the fog. The air felt clear and crisp. Dew bathed the grass along the wagon trail. The rays of the sunlight caused the dew to sparkle like stars. She took a deep breath and slowly let it out. "Ma, what am I gonna do? I've been here nearly a month. Annie May and John are the only ones that like me. John said he'd come for me this morning, but I wanted to walk so I'd have some time to talk to you. Your family in Cherokee is my only hope. Maybe I can find a way there soon. And this shooting, Ma. I saw Holman and another man on the mountain with Luther Jones, the dead man. Guess that don't mean Holman shot him but it could've been. I like Bessie, Ma. If I were to be around here, I think I could count on her to be my friend."

By now Lucy was at the foot of the mountain. A rider came toward her. "Ma, somebody's a-coming. I hope it's John and not Holman."

John reined the horse to a halt in front of her. "Thought I told you I'd come and fetch you this morning. What are you doing way down here?"

"There was nothing else I could do there. Figured I'd better get on home and help with the young-uns, seeing the funeral's today."

"Pa's home. Said he'd be here till Luther's buried and the Joneses was seen to. He was mighty surprised that you'd gone up there last night, but he acted pleased."

"Is that right? When did he come home from town?"

"Late last night. He brought plenty of supplies. You'll be happy to know we didn't have gravy for breakfast this morning."

"Bet the young-uns were happy about that. I s'pose Dovey told your pa all about how I went and cooked all the bacon at one time."

"No. Dovey's been real quiet. Ain't said a word to Pa about nothing."

"You mean she ain't told him about the snakeroot tea I gave Martha?"

"If she has, I don't know nothing about it. Come on. Get up here and let's get on back to the house. Maybe she was just waiting for me to get gone so she could talk to Pa alone."

"Don't matter. I don't care what she tells your pa."

John helped Lucy onto the horse, and they rode home in silence. As they entered the kitchen, Holman pushed back his chair from the table and stood up. His eyes traveled over Lucy. One thing this little woman had was spirit. Something his Mary never had. No, Lucy wasn't as pretty, but there was one thing for sure, she had spunk. And he liked that in a woman. Yes, that was what he had in his new wife. "Well, I can see you're acting the way a wife should act."

Lucy flipped her braids over her shoulder. "I'll have you know I ain't acting. I'm just being me."

"Pa, I found Lucy walking home from the Joneses'. You don't have to worry about her getting lost no more. She has a good sense of direction."

Holman grinned his crooked grin. Lord, how she'd smelt yesterday morning. The lye soap must have worked. Maybe she was telling the truth about why she was on the mountain. He'd have to remember to ask Annie May about it. "I'm glad to hear you're doing good, Lucy. And it was nice of you to help out at the Joneses last night. My missus would . . ." Holman stopped and looked in the other direction.

"You don't have to be grateful, Mr. Carpenter. I only done what your wife would've done if she'd been alive. Ain't that part of my job?"

"Job!" said Holman. "So you look at this here . . ." He gestured toward the table. ". . . as a job. And just what sort of pay do you expect to get?"

John slipped from the room. Lucy was too intent on answering Holman to see him leave. "Ain't looking for no pay, Mr. Carpenter. Just trying to pay for my keep. Ain't nobody can say a Davenport took any handouts."

"Girl, get it through that thick Indian skull of yours that you ain't taking any handouts. I've taken on your care, and a Carpenter takes care of his own."

"Only part of my skull is Indian. The other part is hard Irish like yours, Mr. Carpenter. Anyhow, I'm not yours yet."

Holman's mouth relaxed. The lines around his eyes crinkled from the smile that played around his mouth. "Oh, . . ." He hesitated for a moment, then continued softly, ". . . I see what you mean. Well, girl, relax. I got me enough young-uns. Anyway, ain't been that long since I lost my Mary. Can't nobody take her place." Holman sank into his chair. Tears misted his eyes. He brushed at them with the back of his hand.

Lucy placed a comforting hand on his shoulder. "I'm sorry, Mr. Carpenter. I lost my ma five years ago, and nobody can ever take her place."

Holman looked up at Lucy. "Losses is losses. Ain't nothing we can do about them. Life's for the living. You just tend to the young-uns like you're s'posed to. Don't go getting no fool notions and everything'll be all right. We don't need no more trouble around here." He pushed back his chair and stood. "Hear me, girl?"

Lucy stood straight, never batting an eyelid.

Holman wheeled to leave. "I'm gonna be gone again after the funeral. Be sure you remember the talk we had on the mountain yesterday."

Her black eyes snapped. "I don't have to get no fool notions, Holman Carpenter. When I find a way, I'm gonna leave this place. Then you can take care of your own children."

~ 6 ~

"He's a-coming! He's really a-coming." Harley pointed down the road. "I just seen his wagon turn up our lane."

Lucy poured a bucket of water over the ashes in the hopper, straightened and shaded her eyes against the bright sun. "Who's a-coming?"

"The peddler!" Harley stirred the dark-colored liquid lye for the soap-making as it dripped from the ash hopper. "Glad he's here. I need me some new fishing line. What you gonna buy, Lucy?"

"What do you mean, buy?"

"From the peddler. What're you gonna get?"

Lucy mopped her face with her apron. This peddler must sell things from his wagon. She sure didn't need fishing line, and anyway, she didn't have money for buying. She watched the covered wagon as it rattled up the lane, and her mind raced. What she needed was a ride. When he left, she'd go with him if he'd take her, and if he wouldn't, maybe she'd just hide on his wagon and go anyway.

Harley dumped another bucket of water over the ashes. "You know he has all kinds of trinkets." He looked at Lucy's patched apron. "Bet you could get some new cloth to make you a new apron with. Them patches are awful big. I'm sure Pa'd want you to buy somethin'."

"She can't get nothing." Lucy turned at the sound of Dovey's voice. "Pa said only six of us can buy this time, and the two littl'-uns need some cloth for new dresses." Dovey pushed a few strands of hair back from her face.

Lucy wished Dovey would get some side combs to hold back her hair, but she knew if she told her to, she wouldn't. "I ain't planning on getting nothing. Besides, your pa bought me some new things when we was married."

Dovey glared at Lucy. "He bought for you? He never did buy much for Ma."

58

Harley stirred the ashes. "Now Dovey, you know as well as me that he wanted to buy for Ma, but she'd rather buy for us."

The peddler was so near now that Lucy could hear the creaks and moans of the old wagon. While this man they called the peddler was getting here, she'd go on in the house and pack her belongings. She didn't want to keep him waiting when he was ready to leave.

≈   ≈   ≈

Lucy set her belongings behind the washtub and walked toward the wagon to join the children crowding around the peddler. She caught her breath. Oh my Lord, it just couldn't be! Not the man in the hotel! She hadn't remembered the black wavy hair or the muscles that rippled under his shirt, but this *had* to be the same man. She would never forget that grin or his bare backside. Even Clara Belle's fancy husband from Atlanta wasn't this handsome. He smiled directly at her. Her heart skipped a beat. Would he remember her? She swallowed hard and hoped no one had noticed the surprised look on her face.

The peddler took down a satchel from the wagon seat. "Now, whose turn is it this time?"

Lucy felt a slight tug on her dress. She glanced down. Annie May looked up at her with a blank stare. Under her arm she held the ragged quilt. She knelt and put an arm around her. "Do you need somethin', Annie May?"

"It's my turn to get somethin'," said Annie May. "Will you help me?"

"I'd be glad to, honey," Lucy said as her eyes darted toward the peddler. He was too busy poking through his satchel to notice her. She'd keep her back to him as much as she could, but the safest place for her right now was in the wagon. Before she knew what was happening, the peddler reached down and scooped Annie May up into his strong arms. Annie May giggled. It was the first time since Lucy had been here that she'd seen her laugh.

"Let's see. I remember. You're the one who has a hard time deciding what to buy. Any idea what you want this time?"

"My new ma's gonna help me pick."

The peddler turned to Lucy and winked. Lucy could feel her face flush. The peddler's eyes seemed to slowly undress her. She looked down at the ground and dared not look up. Would he remember her? And if he did, would he say anything? She dug her toes in the dirt and waited.

"Well," said the peddler, "and where did this pretty young filly come from?"

John stepped up to Lucy and put a hand on her shoulder. "This here's Pa's new wife, Lucy. She's been here about a month. Takes real good care of us."

"Bet she does—and your pa, too! Name's Jake Crocket, madam. Pleased to make your acquaintance." He took her hand in his and kissed it. Lucy saw a devilish gleam in his eyes. It would be just like his kind to tease her. She nodded. It was best not to talk to the likes of him. Even if he didn't recognize her face, he might remember her voice. "And what are you going to get from my wagon today, Lucy?"

She didn't have time to answer before Dovey spoke up. "She don't get to have a turn. Pa bought her some new things when he married her."

"Oh, I see," said Jake, still sizing Lucy up.

Harley nudged the peddler. "Do you have that new fishing line you promised me?"

The peddler ruffled the boy's red hair. "Sure do, son. Saved some especially for you." He set Annie May on the wagon seat and went to the back of his wagon. He pulled out a box marked *fishing line*. "Saved these just for you, Harley. Find what you want. Dovey, looks like you could use some combs to hold that hair out of your eyes. Here, I have some new ones. They have pearls on them." The peddler held out a set of pink side combs. They were decorated with a tiny line of pearls across the top.

Dovey's hands shook as she took the combs. She held them as though they were eggs. "How much are they?"

"Fifteen cents for the set."

"I'd sure like to have 'em, but the little girls need dresses worse." Jake helped Dovey up into the wagon.

"I want my turn," said Annie May from the front seat. The peddler lifted her off the seat and into the wagon. "Can Lucy come, too?"

"Course she can. You and Lucy can rummage around and see if you can find something that you take a fancy to." The peddler turned to Lucy and offered his hand.

Lucy hesitated. She didn't need his help. She had climbed into many a wagon without a man's help. The peddler's eyebrow shot up in a knowing arch. He winked at her. She ignored him and pulled herself up into the wagon. Dovey climbed down. "Where's Fannie?"

"Don't know. She said she'd be right back."

"Here I am," said Fannie. They all turned to see Fannie holding Hattie's hand. There was a smirk across Hattie's face. "I promised Hattie she could have my turn."

"But Pa said she'd have to wait till next time," said John.

"I know," said Fannie, "but I want her to take my turn. Pa'll never know if we don't say nothing, will he?" Hattie broke loose from Fannie and ran toward the wagon. As she passed John, she stuck out her tongue. Lucy wondered how that one little girl always managed to get her way. If things were different, she'd stay around and find out.

"Give me a teething ring for Martha and this cloth for dresses," Dovey said to the peddler. "When you're done with the others, you can get washed up for dinner. We'll be eating soon. Pa said you could bed down in the barn loft like you always do."

"Thank you, Dovey. That's mighty hospitable of your pa. Going to be getting dark before too long. That hayloft is better sleeping than my wagon."

Dovey started toward the house. Lucy glanced toward the washtub. She'd leave her belongings and talk to the peddler about taking her to Cherokee after he had dinner. She hoped he hadn't recognized her. Maybe if he ate good, he'd forget all about her. A good meal would probably satisfy that devilish look in his eyes.

≈ ≈ ≈

Jake Crocket ate like he hadn't had a meal in weeks. Everyone but Lucy was too busy asking him questions to notice. He told them jokes, all the time keeping an eye on Lucy.

Carl scooped the rest of the potatoes onto his plate. "Will you tell us a ghost story tonight?"

Hattie gave him a know-it-all look. "You mean a haint story," she corrected.

"Same thing—haint or ghost."

Hattie stuck out her tongue at Carl. "Ghosts ain't as scary as haints." A discussion began around the table as to who was right, Carl or Hattie.

The peddler leaned back in his chair and tugged on his belt as if to stretch it. Lucy looked him in the eye, determined not to let him fluster her. "Mr. Peddler, do you know where Cherokee is?"

"Make rounds there all the time. It's over in Swain County. Them Indians is a strange lot."

"What do you mean, strange?" asked Lucy.

"Superstitious, and they sure don't cotton to outsiders."

Lucy lowered her eyebrows. "But they like *you?*"

"That's because they like all the trinkets I have. Their chief is old and suspicious of everyone."

Lucy looked down at her hands. She felt his eyes on her and heard the hiss of the match as he lit his pipe. Her heart raced. What if she went with him and the chief wouldn't give her a home? What then? She'd be at his mercy. What should she do? She was becoming fond of the children. Some of them were beginning to like her. At least she had a home here, and she'd be pleasing her pa if she stayed.

"You gonna have some new trinkets your next trip?" asked Dovey.

The peddler got up from the table. "Depends on how the Indians buy. I've got some work to do before our ghost telling. Anyway, ghost stories ain't any fun till dark."

The young-uns scrambled to do their chores. Through the kitchen window, Lucy watched until she saw the peddler sitting propped against a wagon wheel. She slipped out of the kitchen and crept quietly toward him. "Mr. Peddler?"

He looked up. "Well, if it ain't our new little filly."

Lucy blushed. "I was just wondering if you could help me with somethin'."

"That depends," drawled the peddler as he let his eyes travel slowly over her. Without glancing away, he reached into his pocket and pulled out a mouth organ. He ran his lips over the length of the keys, then wiped it on his leg.

"The Cherokees. They're my family."

He looked closer at her. "Thought there was something different about you. Been studying you. Could have sworn I'd seen you somewhere before." He rubbed his chin. "What are you doing in these parts?"

"My mother was half Indian. Before my people was put on a reservation, they roamed through all these mountains."

"Why ain't you with them?"

"My grandmother married a white man."

Jake stood. "I see. One of them kind. How did that come about?"

"My grandfather was Irish. Made moonshine and sold it to the Indians. When my grandmother married my grandpa, the tribe disowned her."

"What do you expect me to do about that?"

"I was just wondering if you'd give me a ride on over there."

The peddler dug the toe of his boot into the red clay. "What about Holman and the young ones?"

"Holman ain't nothing to me. Just took me to be a ma to the young-uns. They ain't crazy about me. Far as I can see, they don't need me."

"Hmm, I see," he grunted. "Maybe, just maybe, we could work something out." He touched the locket around her neck. "That's a pretty trinket. Indians would like that. Guess I could give you a ride for it."

Lucy clutched the locket. There was no way was she going to part with the only thing her ma had given her. She'd find something else to pay him with.

The peddler winked at her. "I still got a feeling I've seen you somewhere before. Hmm, wait a minute. I think I've got something that would look real good on you." His long legs disappeared into the wagon.

"No, wait! You have it wrong. I ain't got no money to buy anything. I just need help getting away from here."

"Don't want you to buy anything," he called. "Just want you to try this on to see how you look." He stepped down from the wagon with a handful of white net veiling.

Lucy turned her back to him. He reached out, yanked her around, and placed the net on top of her head. "Uh-huhh, thought so. You're the young lady that came calling through my bedroom window." His eyes twinkled. "Next time you decide to call, will you please rap on the window so I'll have time to put on my pants?"

Lucy twisted free. Her face flamed. "You've got it all wrong, Mr. Crocket. That was the only place I had to go. You see, Holman and a bunch of people were down below. I couldn't get away. I had to come through your window 'cause I couldn't climb back up my rope."

The peddler threw the net into the wagon. "I see you're determined to get away from Holman. Go get your things. I'll be a-leaving about daybreak. Like I said back at the house, Indians don't cotton to outsiders too much. The chief is old and cantankerous. Where are you going if they won't accept you? I can't be saddled down with a woman."

"I already thought about that. Would you bring me back?"

He shook his head. "Can't do that, little lady. I've got a lot of territory to cover. And, as I just said, can't let a woman slow me down." He blew through his mouth organ a couple of times, as though giving her time to think. "Better take your chance while you can get it." His eyes traveled from her narrow waist to her high-button shoes.

"Well, . . . when will you be back?"

"Always try to get back before it gets too cold."

Lucy gripped the locket. Maybe she'd just wait. Fall wasn't that far off, and that would give her time to figure another way to pay him. She just couldn't let him have her locket.

Jake touched her on the cheek. "You're a mighty handsome looking woman, Lucy. Be a shame to waste all that beauty on a old man like Holman. Wish I could just keep you with me, but right now . . .'" His voice trailed off.

Lucy brushed his hand away. "Think I'll just wait. Maybe you could talk to the chief and see how he feels about me coming. When you come back again, if it's all right with him, I'll go with you."

"Guess I could do that. I'll just make myself a note so I don't forget." Jake reached for a pencil.

Lucy turned to leave, then faced him again. "You ain't gonna tell Holman about the hotel, are you?"

He winked at her. "Now why would I want to do something like that? I'm sure Holman wouldn't be too pleased to know that you had seen my bare butt."

Lucy's face flamed again. She wheeled toward the house. She gave a glance over her shoulder and caught a quick glimpse of the peddler's white teeth. He was laughing at her. She bet this man had more up his sleeve than selling trinkets.

≈   ≈   ≈

The chores were done and the family began to gather on the front porch. Lucy finished in the kitchen, pushed open the front door, walked over to the porch swing, and started to sit down.

Hattie stretched her legs out. "You can't sit here."

"And why not?"

"This is the peddler's seat."

Lucy sat down on the top step, leaning against the porch post. She was beginning to see why they liked the peddler so much. He not only brought them goodies, he brought them fun and laughter. And the first Mrs. Carpenter, stuck here with all these children—it must have been lonely for her. She probably liked the peddler's visits, also.

Hattie took her legs off the swing. "Here he comes."

The soft beams from the moon filtered through the tall pine trees that surrounded the old house. The fast-approaching night had already begun to throw ghostly shadows across the yard. Lucy watched as Annie May ran out to greet the peddler. He squatted down, and she climbed on his back. Her black curly hair bounced in the moonlight. The peddler seemed to be extra fond of Annie May and she of him. Holman never paid much attention to Annie May. Hattie was his pet. Could it be Annie May reminded him too much of his first wife?

Hattie stood and waved to the peddler. "I've saved you a seat." Harley moved toward the swing. The look in Hattie's eyes defied him to sit down.

Jake slid Annie May onto the swing beside him. "Thank you, Hattie."

Harley perched himself on the railing. "You got any new haint stories this time?"

Hattie sat down at the peddler's feet. "Don't care if they're new ones. Haints are haints."

The peddler stretched out his long legs in front of him, reached in his shirt pocket and took out his mouth organ. He blew up and down the keys a couple of times and began to play a melancholy tune.

The lonesome notes echoed through the valley. Lucy's heart went back to her mountain with her pa. Why hadn't he come to see about her? Probably had himself a woman by now. Maybe that was just as well. Wasn't much she could do. This was what he'd wanted.

Finally, Jake spoke. "Yeah, I do, Harley. It's kind of a strange one. Something that happened to me over in Swain County."

Dovey leaned closer. "You mean you really seen a haint this time?"

"I saw something out of the ordinary. Can't say it was a haint. Maybe my imagination was just working overtime."

"If you seen it, you seen it," said John.

"Remember my telling you about that big white rock over in Swain County that hangs over the road?"

"The rock Pa talks about? The one folks call the Crying Rock because just before somethin' bad happens it can be seen crying?" asked Harley.

"That's the one. If you remember, it's called that because two young lovers leaped from it to their deaths," said the peddler.

"I remember," said Dovey. "It was because a poor girl loved a rich boy. His parents wouldn't let them get married, so they jumped off the rock holding hands."

"That's right, Dovey," said the peddler. "You know just one of the stories. Always seems that nobody can remember who the boy and girl were or just when it happened. Just a haint story. I never really believed it. Been by the rock lots of times myself. Never saw any-thing—just a white rock hanging over the road."

"Did you see the rock crying this time?" asked John.

Jake ran his fingers through his dark wavy hair. "More than that, John. You know, I wouldn't have been surprised to have seen red water running out of that rock. With all this red clay, it would be easy enough to explain."

"I s'pose so," said John. "Pro'bly most of the haint stories told in these parts can be explained."

"I can't explain what happened to me. Maybe some of you can. Anyway, I usually don't take the road by Crying Rock."

"Why?" asked Hattie. "You scared?"

"No. Truth is, there's some pretty bad curves in the road, and it's dangerous after dark. But the other road was washed out by the flood, so I had no choice. It was getting on toward midnight. I hadn't found a decent place to bed down. Thought I'd get by Crying Rock and camp in the hollow on the other side. I was just coming up to the rock when all of a sudden my team of horses just bowed up and stopped. Wouldn't budge an inch. Sniffing and snorting, like some-thing had spooked them. The air began to smell funny."

Lucy watched Hattie's eyes grow larger. "What do you mean, funny?"

"Kind of a warm, sweaty, bloody smell."

"Ugh!" exclaimed Hattie.

"The scent grew stronger. The horses were going wild. I climbed down from the wagon to try to calm them. Just as I walked around in front of the team, a shadow came up over the bank of the road."

Hattie scooted closer to Dovey, who sat braced against the porch railing, biting her nails. "What kind of shadow?"

"In fact, there were two of them. One looked like a boy and the other one like a girl, and they were holding hands."

John looked out into the night. "Pro'bly just a big bird flying over and casting a shadow."

"Maybe so, John, but this shadow grew longer and longer. And when it reached the Crying Rock, the rock just swallowed it up."

Hattie gulped and snuggled closer to Dovey, who had begun to look a little pale herself. Arthur edged closer to the peddler from his place on the steps. "Then what happened?"

"Just as the rock swallowed up the shadow, it let out this lonesome moan, and tears of blood began to roll out of it."

"Who-o-O, Who-o-O," came from the dark, startling the younger children.

Hattie ran to John and held out her arms. John picked her up and hugged her tight. "John, he's brought that haint with him."

"Thought you weren't afeared of nothing, Hattie," said Arthur.

"I ain't afeared of nothing, but I am afeared of haints. You'd better not laugh at me or I'll tell Pa."

"I'm not laughing, and that's not a haint. It's just an old hoot owl. He always roosts in our pine trees," said Arthur.

Hattie let go of John's neck. "I knowed that. I was just trying to scare you."

"I've seen a haint," said Lucy. Everyone turned to look at her.

Hattie slid down from John's arms and ran over to where Lucy sat on the steps. "Tell us about it, Lucy. Please!" She planted herself at Lucy's feet.

Lucy looked around to find that all eyes had turned to stare at her. The peddler leaned forward in the swing. Annie May scooted closer to him. The peddler made a choking noise. "Yeah, Lucy, tell us."

Lucy watched his face. Was he holding back a laugh? Or worse yet, was he thinking about their first meeting? She was sure of one thing. He wouldn't let her forget what had happened. She cleared her throat and said, "Don't rightly know how I feel about haints. Some folks say they serve as a warning. Could be. I seen one just before my ma died."

"What did it look like, Lucy?" asked John.

"It was a pretty little girl. She had long yellow curls and was dressed in fancy clothes. Didn't talk at all—just followed me around all night."

"Where were you?" asked John.

"I went with my sister Allie and her young-uns to a Christmas potluck down in the valley. All evening there was this little young-un following me around."

"Didn't you ask her what she wanted?" asked Dovey.

"No, she wasn't bothering anybody. When we got ready to leave, she followed us. About halfway home, we passed this house where some well-to-do folks lived. When we passed the front gate, the little girl laid down in the snow and spread out her arms and legs like she was making a snow angel. And right there before my eyes, she disappeared."

Hattie swallowed. Annie May moved uneasily in the swing. The peddler picked her up and put her on his lap. "What happened then?" asked John.

"Well, I asked my sister where the little girl went. She told me she hadn't seen any little girl. One of her young-uns asked me what I'd been drinking. And I told them there sure was a little girl following us. She just laid down and disappeared."

"Did they ever believe you?" asked John.

"Naw, they just laughed at me. I told my ma about it. She believed me. She said God had guardian angels that watched out for us and that when she died, she'd like to have some angels on her tombstone. Anyway, wasn't long after that till Ma took sick and died." She brushed at her eyes and choked back the lump that rose in her throat. Someday, she'd make sure her ma had a tombstone with angels on it.

"You think it was some sort of sign?" asked Dovey.

"Who knows?" said the peddler. "I've heard of some crazy happenings in these parts."

A cloud passed over the moon. A dog howled in the distance. Something rustled in the nearby grass. Lucy shivered. The cloud passed. A strange shadow darted across the yard. Jake stared into the darkness, then spoke in a eerie whisper. "Maybe there's more out there than the natural eye can see!"

69

≈ 7 ≈

Lucy mopped the sweat from her face with the hem of her apron and paused at the Joneses' front porch. She looked around. The black cat that had caused so much trouble the night of the wake stretched full-length on the nearby rail fence, watching some unsuspecting prey in the grass below. A flock of half-feathered chickens clucked and pecked at the green apples littering the yard. Lucy hoped Bessie's tongue would be as willing to cluck to her as these hens were to each other. A hoarse voice cut through the sultry, late afternoon air.

"What you want?" Lucy turned to face a tall, lanky boy. He carried a pail of water in each hand. His bare feet were caked with mud.

"Bessie. Is she home?"

"Yeah, she's out in the back yard. Go on around."

"Thank you." She tiptoed her way through the chicken droppings to the back yard. Bessie was stoking a fire under a tin tub filled with jars of green beans. "Howdy, Bessie."

Bessie straightened and turned to look at her with a frown. Lucy reached out her hand. "I'm Lucy Carpenter, Holman's new missus. Remember? I helped you in the kitchen the night of Luther's wake."

A smile replaced the frown on Bessie's face and she reached out her hand. "Course, dearie. I remember. Come on in the kitchen and set for a spell."

Lucy followed Bessie toward the back door. "Your son said I'd find you out here."

"That's Richard, Luther's oldest. Me and Mr. Farmer didn't have any young-uns." They stepped into the kitchen. "Have a seat over at the table. I'll get us a cup of coffee."

"Where's Mr. Farmer, Bessie?"

"Dead. Been gone nigh on ten years now."

"I'm sorry."

Bessie set a cup of coffee and a chunk of chocolate cake in front

70

of Lucy. "You don't need to be sorry, dearie. Me and Mr. Farmer had a good life—married for fifteen years."

Lucy took a sip of her coffee. "You don't look that old."

Bessie sat down at the other end of the table. "I was a child bride. Most women were in my time."

Lucy took a bite of cake. "How old was Mr. Farmer?"

"He was twenty years older than me. Didn't make no difference. He took real good care of me."

Lucy shooed flies away from her cake. Bessie picked up a leafy branch and rattled it. "Shoo! Shoo! Them pesky old flies. They're really bad in August—guess it's because it's so hot. Hope it don't rain. Hot rainy weather and flies breeds the fever."

The swarm of flies settled on the ceiling. Lucy took another bite of the cake. "Have you always lived in these parts?"

"Just down the road apiece. After Mr. Farmer died it was kinda lonely, and Luther's missus was expecting so I just moved on up here to help out. Lived here ever since. The missus, poor thing, ain't doing no good at all since Luther's death."

Lucy shifted in her chair. The night of the wake seemed so long ago, but how well she remembered Luther's death. What she'd seen on the mountain burned in her thoughts as fresh as the smell of the coffee in her cup. "Bessie, did the sheriff ever come out here after Luther was shot?"

Bessie shook her head. "Just brought him home that morning. Said someone found him shot up on Chimney Knob."

Lucy glanced around the kitchen. It didn't look like he'd been found dead from what she'd seen. Who was the man with Holman? Could he have been the sheriff? Holman told the man he was with to take Luther home. Had he or had he taken him to the sheriff to take home? "Bessie, what kinda looking man is your sheriff?"

Bessie peered at Lucy over her coffee cup. "Just a regular looking man, I guess. A little taller than Holman. Stocky built but not fat. Why do you ask?"

Lucy tried to piece together a picture of the man she'd seen. He was bigger than Holman, but that didn't mean much. Most every man she'd seen, even her pa, was bigger than Holman. From her

71

hiding place, she'd been looking into the sun and hadn't got a good look at his face. "No reason. Remember, I asked you the night I helped you in the kitchen if the sheriff was there."

Bessie rubbed her chin. "Seems like I do remember you saying somethin'. That's strange. Wonder why he didn't come. Him and Luther was good friends." She waved the fly brush again. "Could be he was too busy. I'll have to remember to ask him when I see him again."

Lucy drained the last drop of coffee from her cup. "I'd guess most sheriffs are busy." She watched Bessie for a few minutes. "Tell me about Holman and Luther. How long had they been friends?"

Bessie refilled Lucy's coffee cup. "They were young-uns together. Walked to that little school on the other side of the mountain. Course I was older than him. Him and Luther was the same age."

Lucy remembered the bell had tolled thirty-eight times. And if Luther and Holman were the same age that meant Holman was also thirty-eight. For some reason that made her feel good. She'd hated the idea of being married to an old man, but thirty-eight didn't sound *that* old. "Did you know Holman's missus, too?"

"Knew the family. She didn't go to the same school so I didn't know her from there."

"How did Holman meet her?"

"Luther and him went to a barn dance over in her community. Luther said Holman was crazy about her the first time he laid eyes on her. She sure was a pretty little thing. Long curly black hair and skin as white as yours is dark."

Lucy looked down at her hands. Well, Annie May sure did have black hair. "Does Annie May look like her ma?"

Bessie was thoughtful for a few minutes. "Guess she does, except for . . ." She paused for a moment and then continued. "She sure don't look like Holman with all that black hair. Course some folks in these parts say . . ." Bessie stopped and looked at Lucy. "I'm sorry, Lucy. I ain't got no right to say that. Just gossip, and I don't want to spread rumors."

Lucy knew from the look on Bessie's face there was no use asking any more questions about Annie May. "Holman's gone a lot. Says he has business to care for. I often wonder what he works at."

"Well, Holman's a pretty good handyman. Makes extra money sometimes fixing things for folks around here, but he's always worked on a public job somewhere."

"Does he have any brothers or sisters?"

"There was a big crowd of them young-uns. Can't rightly remember just how many but as soon as they got big enough, they headed on out west to find their fortunes. Never came back. Holman's got one brother here. He's a lawman over in Swain County."

"I see." Lucy bunched up the last crumbs of cake from her plate with her fingers and stirred her coffee with the spoon. Could it be that Holman had something to do with the law?

≈   ≈   ≈

The sun sank into the west as Lucy started home from the Joneses'. She hadn't learned as much from Bessie as she'd hoped, but it was the first woman-talk she'd had since the night of Luther's wake. "Ma, I think I've found a friend in Bessie. She seems like the mothering kind. Ain't much on gossip though. I learned that Holman's brother is a lawman. I wonder what she was gonna say about Annie May. And this public job Holman works, I wonder what kinda job that is. Guess it ain't none of my business; it's man's business. Anyway, Ma, I guess I'm stuck here till the peddler comes back. Holman ain't bothered me none 'cept telling me what my job is. Like I don't know. He must have loved Mary somethin' awful. Bessie said he loved her from the first time he met her."

The stomping and snorting of horses caught her attention. She looked over at an old shed. Two men were shoving jugs into a wagon-bed full of hay. Her heart raced. Someone was going some-where. Maybe, just maybe, they'd take her along. She hurried toward the men. From where she was, one of the men kind of looked like the peddler. The other man was shorter. He had a gray beard and long stringy hair. He sure looked like the man at Luther's wake. The sound of their voices stopped her dead in her tracks.

"Make sure you deal directly with Injun Fast Foot." The short man said to the man who looked like the peddler. He spoke way down low in his throat. It sounded like dull shears cutting through sheep's wool. There was something scary about that man's voice. There was something scary about that man! Maybe she'd better just head on home. Then she heard the ugly deep voice again. "Don't let it get into the hands of none of them other dumb Injuns. We'd have the law on us quicker'n a duck on a June bug. Ole Fast Foot's the only one you can trust."

Her breath caught in her throat, and she coughed. Before she could take another step, the man that looked like the peddler jumped onto the wagon seat. With a flip of the reins, the old wagon lunged forward and was gone.

Lucy's arms dropped to her side. Hope died like the sap in the dying trees. Wearily, she turned toward the path. Suddenly a man grabbed her by the shoulder and spun her around. "Where do you think you're going, girl? What're you doing eavesdropping on us?"

Lucy pulled free from him. "Eavesdropping! What do you mean, eavesdropping?"

The man reached for her again. "I caught you nosing around here. What did you hear, anyway?"

She took a step backward. "I ain't heard nothing. I don't know what you're talking about. All I want is to get away from this place. I was a-hoping that I could catch a ride on that man's wagon."

The man looked in the direction the wagon had gone. "Well, won't be no rides on that wagon. He's already got a load and he's gone." He glanced back at Lucy. "And just who are you, anyway?" He peered at her closer and his beady little eyes narrowed. "Ain't I seen you before?"

Lucy looked wistfully down the road and then back at the man. "I'm Lucy Dav—I mean Lucy Carpenter. And yes, I do think we met the night of Luther Jones's wake."

"So you're Holman's new missus I've been hearing about. For Holman's sake, I hope you're not like the other one." A mocking grin played around the corners of his lips. "I'd say you'd better get on home where you belong. Almost anything could happen to a young girl out here in the woods." He laughed a low chuckle, snuff dripping from the corners of his mouth.

Lucy fled down the road. The chuckle followed her. Maybe she should have stayed and found out who he was, but that laugh gave her the feeling she'd as soon not know.

≈   ≈   ≈

Holman dumped his gear in the barn and headed for the house. His step was light. He hummed a merry tune as he approached the house. Home—it sure was good to be back. Lucy—would she still be here? She'd threatened to leave the last time he'd been home. Maybe that would be just as well with what she'd seen the morning Luther was shot. He didn't need her getting too nosey. And he sure couldn't hold her against her will. Dovey would just have to find some other way to get her learning. He stepped into the kitchen.

Dovey slung her dishrag down on the table. "It's about time you got home. Can't believe you'd go off and leave us this long with that Cow's Tail Lucy woman in charge!"

Holman took a step backward. Something must be dreadfully wrong here. None of his children dared talk to him like this. He'd better try to find out before he gave her a whipping. "Dovey, you know I do the best I can for you young-uns. And as for Lucy, I didn't bring her here to take your ma's place. I just thought the littl'-uns needed a ma."

"I'm the only ma they need," answered Dovey, her voice rising hysterically.

"Dovey, you'll want to go to school next week. Ma wouldn't want you to miss. With Lucy here to help with the babies, you can go back."

"Pa, I can't leave her here with the littl'-uns all day."

"What are you talking about, Dovey? Lucy is good with the children. I've been watching her. Annie May's really fond of her."

There was a long silence. When Dovey spoke her voice sounded calmer, but Holman could see she was going to pull one of her stubborn spells. "Pa, I'm afeared she'll hurt them."

"What on earth are you talking about?"

"Well, Pa, I was a-hoping I wouldn't have to tell you about her giving Martha some strange medicine."

75

"What are you talking about, Dovey? When did she do that?"

"When we had the flood."

"Why? She must have had a reason. Was Martha sick?"

"She had a fever. We gave her some catnip the night it started."

"There ain't nothing wrong with that. Catnip makes 'em sleep." Holman got up from the table and went to the girl. He tried to put his arm around her, but she shrugged it away.

"That's not all, Pa. The next morning her fever was still up. It was raining too hard for John to fetch the doc. When I got up, I found John holding Martha. Lucy had gone to find some snakeroot to give the baby."

Holman rubbed his hand over his thinning hair. "Dovey, you know John wouldn't let her give the baby anything that would hurt her."

"She has John fooled just like she has you fooled."

Holman ran his hand over the top of his head again and turned back to the table. "Dovey, I don't know what to say to you. I'm sure if Lucy had her way she'd just as soon not be here."

Dovey wheeled to face her pa. "What do you mean, Pa?"

"Lucy's pa thought it would be best for her to get off their mountain and be with people, and I needed somebody to help with the young-uns."

"You don't love her like you did Ma?"

"There'll never be anyone like your ma, Dovey."

"I miss her so much, Pa."

"I know you do, child. But you've got to remember, the babies won't remember her like we do. They've got to have someone."

"But Pa, she can't cook as good as Ma. The first time you was gone she cooked all the bacon at one time. That's why we was eating gravy when you got home."

"She'll learn, Dovey. Give her time."

Holman looked up and saw Lucy in the doorway. "Here's Lucy," he whispered. "We'll talk later." He turned to Lucy. "Well, I see you're still here. Thought from what you said last time I was home, you'd be gone."

Lucy's eyes narrowed. "When I come and go is my business, but if you want to know, I just been up the mountain to pay the Joneses a visit. Had myself a nice visit with Bessie. She says Luther's widow ain't doing so well. It's been hard on Richard and Alice and the other young-uns, too"

Holman's voice softened. "Sorry to hear that, Lucy. I'm glad you made a call on them. I'll check by tomorrow and see if there's somethin' I can do."

Lucy picked up a bowl half full of gravy. "Dovey, I'll do the dishes."

Holman turned to leave the room. "Why don't she sleep out in the barn with you?" Dovey called after him.

Holman spun around to face Dovey. His eyebrows formed a thin straight line. In the same moment, Lucy dropped the gravy. The bowl broke in half and lumpy gravy splashed onto her bare feet. She looked at Dovey with her mouth hanging open.

"Now look what you've done," said Dovey. "Pa, I told you she was out to hurt me. That bowl, it was Ma's favorite, and she's broke it."

Holman bent to pick up the bowl. "Lucy, why don't you run on outside and wash that mess from your feet. Wait for me in the hayloft. Dovey and me still have us some talking to do."

Holman watched Lucy leave. He supposed she'd be gone when he got to the barn. He couldn't much blame her. Life around here sure wasn't any picnic. And with the way things were going on his job, he didn't want to worry about her snooping around.

≈   ≈   ≈

Darkness closed in. The hayloft felt stuffy and the scent of the stables below filled the air. Lucy paced back and forth. She should have just gone with the peddler, but now she had no choice. There wasn't any way out of here with no money. Even if she had money, she wouldn't know which way to go. She'd heard of trains, but she wouldn't know one if she saw it. She knew she'd have to answer lots of questions when Holman came.

"You up there, Lucy?"

The whole ugly scene with Dovey flashed before her eyes. Had Holman calmed her down? She could hear him coming up the ladder. She moved toward the large double doors that opened to the outside where the hay was put into the loft. She didn't want to get trapped up here with him. "I'm over here, Mr. Carpenter." The flame from Holman's lantern cast soft rays of light on the hay. Lucy couldn't see his face. "Did you and Dovey have your talk?"

"Sure did. Don't know if I got through to her or not. She stubbed up and wouldn't talk much."

"I'm sorry, Mr. Carpenter. I didn't mean to cause no trouble."

"Do you have to call me Mr. Carpenter? Holman will do. As for Dovey, she'll be all right. It'll be good for her to get back to school. She's taking the job of mothering the younger children too much to heart. Now you tell me what kind of medicine you gave Martha."

Lucy sat down in the hay near the double doors. Holman hung the lantern on a nail in the overhead rafter. He kicked over a wooden crate and sat down on it facing Lucy. She could see his face now. There seemed to be no trace of anger. "Snakeroot tea," Lucy said in a low voice.

"Instead of giving her snakeroot, why didn't you just send for the doctor?"

"It was raining real hard. Had rained all night. I was worried John couldn't get across the creek. Besides, Martha was drooling and biting on anything she could get her mouth on. Nobody's ever died from cutting teeth."

"How about the fever?"

"Ma always said babies run fevers cutting teeth. She always used snakeroot tea for fevers."

"And you took it upon yourself to doctor Martha with your ma's home remedy?"

Lucy bowed her head. "Yes, sir. Figured it was better than no doctoring at all."

Holman broke into a loud laugh. "When my Mary was alive and one of the young-uns got sick, she never knew what to do. She couldn't make up her mind about nothing, 'cept maybe going to bed with me." Lucy blushed and looked away. "I like a woman that knows her mind and ain't afeared to do what she thinks. Now, I think we had better get some sleep."

Lucy got up and moved toward the opening in the floor. "I think seeing how Dovey's upset that it would be better if you slept out here tonight. You needn't be afeared of me. I ain't gonna bother you. Your job's to look after the young-uns. Seems you're doing a good job." Holman pitched her a blanket and took the lantern from its nail. "You can bed down anywhere you like. This is my corner over here." He moved to the far side of the hayloft. He found another nail for the lantern and spread out his blanket, then blew out the light.

Soft rays from the moon filtered through the cracks in the barn. Lucy stood with her blanket clutched to her chest. Holman slid his suspenders off his shoulders. "It's too hot to sleep in your clothes. You'll be a lot more comfortable if you get out of that skirt." Holman began to unbutton his pants. Lucy turned her back on him and clung to her skirt as if someone were trying to rip it from her.

"You up there, Pa?" came a small girl's voice from the bottom of the ladder. Lucy turned just in time to see Holman yank up his pants.

"Yeah, Hattie. I'm up here. What's the matter?"

By now the head of blond curls had popped through the opening. "Ain't nothing the matter, Pa, 'cept Dovey is being awful mean to me."

"Does she know you're out here?"

"Sure does. She called me your pet and told me to just run on out here and sleep with you. Can I, Pa? Please? Please?"

"I s'pose so, as long as Dovey knows where you're at. Come on over here. You can share my blanket." Hattie smiled and cuddled down by her pa.

Lucy spread out her blanket near the opening and laid down. She was glad Dovey had sent Hattie out here. Now she didn't have to be alone with Holman. She stole a quick glance at him. He'd laid down with his clothes on. Soon he was snoring. Lucy let out a long sigh. Dovey was going to be harder than ever to live with. And then there was Hattie. How could she worm her way around all twelve of her brothers and sisters and wrap her pa around her little finger?

She wondered what Holman meant when he told her she was his kind of woman? And that old snuff-dipping man up the road. Why did he give her such a creepy feeling? Well, she had time before the peddler came back. Maybe she'd get some answers.

79

~ 8 ~

Wagons rattled into the Carpenter's yard with loads of sorghum cane. Men unloaded the wagons and stacked each family's cane in separate piles. The scent of fresh horse manure filled the air. Two men sawed and piled wood for the large furnace that held the boiler for the sorghum. The rasping of the crosscut saw filled the crisp October air with its own song.

A horse was hitched to the end of a long pole that pulled the huge iron rollers around and around. Lucy neared the man who fed the cane into the mill. Good Lord, it was the snuff dipper from the mountain! She wheeled to go in the other direction, hoping he hadn't seen her.

"You ain't gonna say howdy, girl?"

He didn't sound as rough as he did the other time. Now he sounded more like the man who had captured the cat the night of the wake. Maybe he wasn't all bad. She turned back toward him. "Is there somethin' I can get for you?"

The man stepped from behind the rollers, wiped his hands on his overalls, and extended his hand. "My name's Herby Ledford, girl. Sorry I gave you such a fright on the mountain a while back. You done and run off before I could properly introduce myself."

Lucy shook his hand. She didn't like his grip. It felt more like a warning than a handshake. Well, she'd been through too much to let some man scare her. "Tell me, Mr. Ledford, was that the peddler I seen you with?"

He didn't let go of her hand but squeezed harder. "Peddler? I'm afeared I don't know who you're talking about, Miz Carpenter." Lucy tried to pull her hand away.

Mr. Ledford caught her by the wrist and pulled her closer. His lips turned up in an ugly sneer. "If I was you I'd ferget I ever heared anything. Ain't healthy to know too much. Ain't healthy to talk too

80

much either. You ain't said nothing to Holman about our little run-in, have you?"

"No, but if you don't let me go, I'm gonna scream. Then you can tell him yourself."

Holman looked up from stirring the syrup. Did that Herby Ledford have Lucy by the arm? Why the nerve of him! He'd show him he couldn't touch *his* woman. He started toward the mill. The sound of Hattie's voice calling him stopped him. He'd have to let it go for now, but he'd have a talk with Ledford later.

The Joneses' wagon pulled into the yard. Bessie and Richard climbed down from the wagon seat. Lucy hurried over to greet them, smoothing her apron as she went. "You can take the wagon over yonder and unload it, Richard. The men will show you where to put your cane."

Richard picked up the reins. "If somebody hadn't a-killed my pa, this here job wouldn't be so bad. If I ever find the polecat that shot him, I'm gonna shoot him dead."

Lucy felt tears sting her eyes as she watched Richard drive away with the half load of straggly cane. Did Holman have anything to do with Richard's not having a pa?

"Dearie, how've you been? I've been thinking about you ever since your visit."

"Just fine, Bessie. It's been quiet—school starting up and all. Kinda nice to have most of the brood gone for the day."

"How many are in school this year?"

"All but the three littlest. Ain't too bad with just them three. But that Hattie! She's a case. Don't like school. Has a reason every day not to go. Don't know how she does it, but she gets the others to take her side."

"You won't have to worry about school this week with the young-uns being off to help with the syrup making."

Lucy wiped at a loose strand of hair. "Hattie'll be up to some mischief, I'll bet you, before the week is out."

"A young-un like her sure takes some watching. Never can tell what they're up to. Most times, give them enough rope and they'll hang themselves." Bessie glanced around. "What do you want me to do?"

"Well, there's enough help in the kitchen. Hattie's supposed to keep track of the syrup buckets and take them to Holman, but you can't count on her to do nothing."

Bessie looked around. "Where's she at?"

"I left her at the mill. See what I mean? She'd do anything to get out of doing her job."

"You see to your doings." Bessie started toward the mill. "Don't you worry a bit about her. I'll have her back here in no time."

Lucy watched the big woman walk toward the group at the mill. Young-uns! It seemed all they did was cause trouble. Well, she wasn't going to bed down with that Holman. They sure didn't need any more children around here.

Holman waited until he saw Bessie go toward the mill, then he called, "We need some buckets down here." Lucy grabbed six tin buckets and headed for the boiler. The first batch of syrup was ready to pour.

The light brownish liquid dribbled onto Holman's fingers as he poured it into the buckets. He glanced up at Lucy. "Seen you talking to Herby at the mill. Did he want somethin'?"

Lucy's heart pounded. How was she going to explain this to Holman? She remembered Herby's warning. Best to keep quiet. The peddler would be here any day now, and she'd get away from all this. "Ain't none of your business. Remember ours is just a business deal. I'll talk to who I please."

Holman looked down as he poured the syrup into the buckets. Lucy was right. Theirs was just a deal. He had no right to think of her as his woman. But he did have some rights and responsibilities as her legal husband. One of those responsibilities was to warn her about men like Herby Ledford. "I ain't trying to be bossy or act like a *real* husband, Lucy, but you'd better watch the likes of men like Herby Ledford. He ain't no good. You could get yourself in real trouble."

Lucy watched his face intently. "If you're trying to tell me somethin', out with it, or else let me take care of myself."

Holman poured another bucket of the syrup. Well, he'd done his part; he'd warned her. Now she could take care of herself. It wasn't

82

much use talking to the likes of Herby Ledford. That would only make matters worse.

Holman concentrated on the syrup again. "Just once, I wish I could get every batch to turn out good. George, come over here and put the lids on these buckets."

George hammered down the lids. "You know, Holman, everyone will have a fit if the last batch ain't thick enough. Can't have a candy pulling with runny syrup."

Holman handed Lucy a bucket. "What are you thinking about?"

Lucy shook her head. "Nothing much, 'cept how my pa would like a good mess of that syrup."

Holman kept his head bowed. Maybe he should tell Lucy about her pa's illness. No, that would only upset her, and there wasn't anything she could do about it.

Lucy batted at the bees buzzing around her head. "A candy pulling sounds like fun. How do you do that?"

Holman wiped his hands on his overalls and began to stir a new batch of syrup. "You'll get to find out Saturday night. You can help me pull."

Lucy placed her hands on her hips. "Just who do you think you are? First, you tell me who to talk to, and now you're telling me who I can pull candy with. I'll have you know I'm a growed-up woman now. I ain't one of your children you can just order around. I'll do as I please, Mr. Carpenter!" She turned and stomped away toward the mill.

Holman stopped his stirring and watched her go. What had he done now? All he was trying to do was to make her feel like she belonged. Well, Saturday night wasn't here yet. Maybe she'd come around.

"Lucy, you're right about Hattie," said Bessie. "She's up to somethin'. I think it has to do with the twins. They was wading in the branch and I found Hattie watching them."

Lucy raised an eyebrow. "That's strange. I've found her watching the other young-uns lots of times. Seems she watches more than she plays with them. Could be 'cause she's a troublemaker. I'm gonna get on in the house and see how dinner is doing. If she gives you any sass, you can just let Holman know." As she came around the barn, she found Dovey and a dark-headed boy sitting on a mossy spot of ground, kissing.

The boy jumped to his feet. "We was just talking, Miz Carpenter."

Lucy smiled at him. "What's your name, son?"

He brushed a black curl from his forehead, stepped toward Lucy, and held out his hand. "Name's Will. Pleased to meet you, ma'am. That's my pa over yonder feeding the cane in the mill."

Lucy wondered where he'd got his good manners and decided he must look like his ma. "You can visit with Dovey later, Will. It's getting on towards noon. We need all the help we can get in the kitchen. Come on, Dovey."

Lucy and Dovey started toward the house. Lucy glanced back in time to see Hattie's curly blond head dart around the corner of the barn. She'd have to see that Miss Hattie got enough rope to do a good job of hanging herself.

"I guess you're gonna tell Pa I was kissing Will."

"Does it matter to you, Dovey?"

Dovey flung her hair back with a shake of her head. "Tell what you like. We'll see who's side Pa takes."

"Dovey, I want to be your friend if you'll let me."

"I don't need you for a friend," Dovey flung over her shoulder as she ran toward the house. Lucy sighed. No matter how hard she tried with that girl it wasn't any use. Well, it didn't matter much. The peddler would soon be here and she'd be on her way.

≈   ≈   ≈

It was Saturday, candy-pulling night. The horse had been unhitched from the mill and taken back to the barn. The fire had died under the huge boiler. In place of the cane there was a large mountain of pulp left. Several children climbed to the top of it and slid down to the bottom.

Some men had gathered on the front porch of the house and were tuning up their fiddles. Everyone would dance to their music after the candy pulling, and young and old alike were pairing off for the pulling.

84

Lucy was excited. Parties back on her mountain were rare. She went to see if the girls needed some help buttering the bowls. As she rounded the corner of the house, she heard two girls arguing. "You'd better do as I say, or you'll be sorry."

"But I want to have Will for my partner," came Dovey's voice.

"If you don't ask Will to be *my* partner, I'll tell Pa I seen you and Will kissing out behind the barn."

"We was just . . ."

"I know what you was doing, and I'll bet Pa'd like to know."

"All right, Hattie. I'll ask Will if he'll be your partner first, but you can't have him for the whole night."

That little sneak! Lucy wanted to tell her she'd seen her behind the barn watching Dovey and Will. She wanted to tell her that she knew she was spying, but instead she decided to give her a little more rope.

"Lucy, where are you?"

She backed up until she was around the corner of the house before she answered Holman. "I'm here, Holman. What do you need?"

"I need someone to help me pull my syrup."

As Lucy neared the long bench by the syrup boiler, she saw Holman rolling a large brown ball of syrup around in his bowl. "I've got it ready to pull, but the pulling will take two. Would you please help me pull?"

Lucy looked at the huge ball of syrup. "What do I do?"

"Just dig your fingers into the side of this ball and pull."

Lucy dug her long slender fingers into the ball of syrup. To her surprise, it gave very little. Holman stuck his fingers into the other side. "Now just pull away from me."

Lucy backed up and the syrup pulled into a long rope between her and Holman. "What now?"

Holman moved toward her. "Roll it back till we meet."

Lucy wound the syrup until she reached him. Back and forth, back and forth, they pulled until the syrup was too firm to pull anymore. Lucy looked at the long strings of syrup. "Now what do we do?"

"Just lay it here on the bench. Time the dance is over it'll be hard enough to break and eat."

Lucy laid her end down on the bench and turned to leave. Holman laid his down and called after her. "Where do you think you're going?"

"We're through, ain't we?"

"We're through with the pulling, but it's a rule that you dance the first dance with your candy-pulling partner."

"Why didn't you tell me when you asked me to pull?" Lucy bowed her head and said in a low voice, "I can't dance."

Holman slipped his arm around her waist and began to twirl her around the yard. "I'll teach you. Just follow me."

Lucy willed herself to follow Holman's steps. The music eased the tension in her body. She felt the heat of Holman's body against hers. To her surprise she had to look up to see his face. Why had she thought him so short? Maybe because her pa was such a big man.

Holman smiled into her eyes and began to sing. "*Ha! Ha! Ha! You and me, little brown jug, how I love thee.*" Lucy smiled to herself. Holman's singing wasn't very good, but the words of the song were Holman all right. He sure loved his little brown jug.

"What're you smiling about? My singing that funny?"

Lucy giggled. "Ain't your singing. It's the words to the song."

Holman chuckled. "I got to admit that I love a nip from the jug once in awhile."

The music stopped as suddenly as it had started. Lucy stepped back. Holman drew her a little closer. "Thanks for the pulling and the dance."

Lucy's felt her face grow warm and she turned her head. John and a red-headed girl were sitting on the bench at the wash place. John's arm was draped around her shoulders. She wasn't sure, but she thought she'd seen the girl come with the Joneses' wagon. She smiled to herself. It was nice that John was interested in someone whose family was friends with the Carpenters. Hattie! She was peeking from behind a tree. She'd had enough rope. It was time to stop her.

"There'll be more dancing. If you'd like, we can dance some more," said Holman.

"Maybe later. But right now, I've got to get on in the house and see how the food is coming."

"I'll remember," he called.

Lucy came up behind Hattie and slid a hand around her mouth. Hattie squirmed and tried to pull away. Lucy caught her around the waist with the other arm and lifted her off the ground. The little girl kicked and moaned. Lucy continued toward the house. Near the back door, she set her down. Hattie turned on her with fire in her eyes. "You just wait till I tell Pa what you did. He'll run you off."

Lucy took her by the shoulders and gently shook her. "You just go on and tell, Hattie. What do you think your pa is gonna do with you when he finds out what you've been doing?"

Hattie swallowed hard. "What do you mean?"

"How did you get Dovey to let you pull candy with Will tonight?"

Hattie looked up at her with her big blue eyes. "Will just wanted to pull with me instead of Dovey. Can't you see why? I'm a lot prettier than she is."

Lucy wanted to slap her face, but instead she said, "No, Hattie. I think it was because you were spying on him and Dovey the other day and you threatened to tell your pa."

Hattie's eyes grew larger. "You're just making that up."

Lucy let go of her. "I am, am I? What would you say if I told you I saw you hiding behind the barn watching them? And just tonight I was coming around the house, and I heard you threaten Dovey. You said you'd tell your pa if she didn't get Will to be your partner."

Hattie took a step back. "You've been spying on me!"

Lucy looked her straight in the eye. "Somebody had to stop you. Bessie seen you with the twins the other day. That night the girls got sick, they told me you had caught them drinking your pa's cane juice. They said you planned on telling if they didn't do your chores this week. But that don't matter now. What were you gonna threaten John with?"

Hattie gave her a hateful look. "Ain't none of your business. If Pa knew the girls was drinking his cane juice, they'd be in big trouble."

Lucy reached for her hand. "Come on. I just left your pa in the yard. I'm sure he can settle this once and for all."

Hattie jerked her hand free. "No, Lucy! Please don't tell Pa!"

Lucy stopped. "And if I don't, what're you gonna do? Keep on spying on the others?"

She looked up at Lucy with a whipped puppy look in her big blue eyes. "I won't . . . Please, Lucy! I won't do it no more."

Lucy hesitated. "All right, Hattie. We won't go see your pa now. I'm not making you any promises, though. We'll see how you act. If I catch you threatening the young-uns any more or spying on them, you won't get a second chance. Understand?" Hattie nodded as tears filled her eyes.

"Don't pull your crying act on me, Hattie. It won't work this time." Hattie turned to leave. "Somethin' else." Hattie stopped and looked back. "Come Monday morning, you'll go to school and no backtalk." Hattie nodded and ran off into the dark.

Lucy felt a twinge of pity for the little girl stir deep inside, but she pushed it away. She was in control, and she planned on staying there—at least until the peddler came.

≈ 9 ≈

The autumn leaves blanketed the ground. Buckets of sorghum lined the canning shelves along with an assortment of canned goods. All the crops were gathered in. The smokehouse held the recently killed hogs. Lucy had never seen so much food at one time, but she'd been here long enough to know it wouldn't last long.

Holman was gone again. At the breakfast table Lucy said, "In a few days it will be Thanksgiving. How would you like to have a turkey?"

All thirteen pairs of eyes lit up. Dovey pushed back her hair. "I remember one time Ma fixed turkey. She raised some from babies. She had Pa kill and clean a big tom turkey. When she cooked it, she couldn't eat a bite of it."

Hattie grabbed a biscuit. "Why not?"

"Said every time she looked at it she could see him gobbling out in the barnyard."

Hattie smeared butter on her biscuit. "That's silly. Turkey is turkey."

Annie May frowned and reached for the gravy. "It's not silly. I know just how Ma must have felt."

Harley rubbed his mouth with his sleeve. "Course you would, seeing how you're so crazy about animals and birds."

John laid down his fork. "Where we gonna get this turkey, Lucy? The Ledfords have some for sale, but Pa's gone and we don't have no money." Lucy looked down at her plate. She sure wasn't going to buy one from that Ledford man. Even if he was giving them away, she wouldn't take it.

"Did you hear me, Lucy?"

"Yeah, John, I just had my mind on somethin' else." She looked up. "Any of you ever been turkey hunting?"

"Pa promised to take us boys sometime, but he's never home long enough to keep his promises."

"What if I take you, Arthur?"

"You! You know how to turkey hunt?"

"Been calling turkeys as long as I can remember. Pa taught me how. Killed 'em too."

Hattie moved closer. "How do you call a turkey?"

"I sometimes use a leaf. Deer tongue makes a good one to call with. You just hold it between your thumbs and blow through it, but this time of year the leaves are dead."

Arthur leaned closer to Lucy. "What're you gonna use?"

"That's easy. I'll be right back." She left the room and soon returned.

By now Hattie's eyes were shining. "What's that?"

Lucy wiped the object with her apron as her heart filled with memories from her childhood. Well, her childhood was gone. No use crying over spilled milk. She had a Thanksgiving dinner to fix. She cleared her throat before she spoke. "It's a small bone from a turkey wing. Pa took it from the first turkey I ever killed."

Hattie's eyes grew larger. "What are you gonna do with it?"

"Watch." Lucy put the bone to her lips and sucked air through it. Turkey-like yelps filled the room.

Arthur jumped to his feet. "I want to go with you."

"All right, Arthur. In the morning before daylight you and me will go on up on the ridge. I saw a flock of wild turkeys there a while back when Annie May and me went for a walk."

"Don't kill the turkeys, Lucy," begged Annie May.

"Honey, it's all right to kill for food. Anyway, if the turkeys ain't kept thinned out, they'll starve this winter. You wouldn't want that, would you?"

"I guess not."

"Then it's settled. In the morning Arthur and me will get us a Thanksgiving turkey."

≈   ≈   ≈

The next morning before dawn, Lucy and Arthur set off to hunt. Before they reached the top of the ridge they heard a turkey gobble.

"Arthur, you set right here in this thicket. I'm gonna circle around to the top of the ridge and call. When the turkey hears me, he'll run right by you to get to me."

"You mean you want me to shoot him?"

"Who else? Can you do the calling?"

"No, I don't think I can." Arthur settled himself in the thicket. Lucy helped him find an opening to aim his shotgun through. She went around toward the top of the ridge. Near the top, she felt something crunch under her feet. She looked down. The ground was covered with broken glass. Off to her right, the bushes were bent down. She worked her way through the brush. She smelled smoke. By now she had a pretty good idea someone was making whiskey.

Sure enough, a man was pouring moonshine into jugs. On a nearby bench sat a line of jars. She wished the man would turn around. It would be nice to know if he was one of the neighbors. You never knew when you might need a little moonshine for medicine. With Holman gone so much, she couldn't depend on him to get it for her. Maybe Arthur would know who owned the still, or maybe she should walk right up there and ask him his name.

Then she remembered Herby Ledford. If it was him, he more than likely wouldn't be too happy to see her. Why had he been so mean to her? All she'd wanted to do was hitch a ride on the wagon. Could it be that Mr. Ledford was doing something against the law? Making moonshine wasn't against the law. Maybe she should say something to Holman. No, she'd take care of herself like she always had. There was no way she wanted to be beholden to Holman. When she left here, she didn't want to owe him anything. She turned and slipped through the undergrowth. At the top of the ridge, she sat down on a stump. She took the bone from her apron pocket and began to blow. "Chob-alob-alob! Chob-alob-alob!"

From the turkey roost came the reply, "Chob-alob-alob! Chob-alob-alob!" Lucy answered. The gobbling grew closer. She knew the turkey was looking for a mate. She called again. A shot rang out; then there was silence. She waited quietly and heard something rustling in the dry leaves.

"Did you get him, Arthur?" No answer. The rustling grew closer. "Arthur, you all right?" Lucy tried to see where the noise was coming from. Through the morning light, she saw someone coming toward her. "Arthur, is that you?"

Her eyes widened as Herby Ledford stepped into view. She glanced around for a stick or part of a stump, anything to defend herself with. Nothing. Her only hope was to yell for Arthur and in the meantime climb a tree. She screamed. "Arthur! Come here. Quick!" She whirled and shinnied up a half-grown pine. She felt her dress tighten around her chest. Her grip on the tree trunk loosened, and Herby Ledford held her in the air, face down. She shivered as he laughed, low and deep in his throat. She screamed louder. "Arthur, hurry please! Run!"

"You little witch! You ain't nothing but trouble. I think it would be best for your health if you forgot what you've heared or seen." He set her down, turned, and vanished into the woods.

"Lucy, are you all right? I came a-running as soon as I heard you scream. What's wrong?"

She pointed in the direction Ledford had gone. "A man. He just picked me up and shook the daylights out of me."

Arthur looked around. "What did he look like, Lucy?"

Her heart skipped a beat. She couldn't tell Arthur that it was their neighbor and friend, Mr. Ledford, that was after her. He'd tell his pa and then there would really be trouble. She'd already seen one killing, and she sure didn't want to be the cause of another. "Just a big, mean-looking man, Arthur. He had an awful mean laugh. I was sure I was a goner. If you hadn't a-showed up—you just saved my life, son."

Arthur's expression of pride quickly changed to disappointment. "But I missed your turkey."

"That's all right. Who cares about an old turkey? I've got to set for a spell." She lay back against the damp leaves and wiped her face with her apron. "A scare like that takes the starch out of the bones."

Arthur wiped his face with the tail of his shirt. "You set right there and rest, Lucy. I'm gonna go out in the woods and look around."

Lucy reached up and caught him by his shirttail. "No, Arthur, let him go. I'm safe now. Ain't no use stirring up trouble."

Arthur sat down beside her. "I wonder if we're hunting on somebody else's land, but Pa said we could hunt anywhere we wanted to."

He looked down the mountain. "And I've disappointed you. I missed the turkey."

There was one thing Lucy was sure of, Ledford wasn't after her because of hunting. Then what was it? He'd said to forget what she'd heard and seen. What had she heard? All she could remember was that wagon and it being a ride off the mountain for her. And the man at the still just now—why would he care if she'd seen his still? Everybody made moonshine.

She looked back at Arthur. She had to reassure him somehow. "You scared away the man that was after me. That's the most important thing. Arthur, you could never disappoint me. Remember when I came here you said if I ever needed protecting you would do it. Well, you just did."

The boy's face brightened. "I remember that promise. You know when I said that, I was just trying to act as big as John."

"I know. Now you've proved yourself. The turkey doesn't matter. Let's get out of here."

"What about that man?"

"We'll send John back to look around."

As they started down the ridge, neither spoke. Suddenly Arthur pointed. "Look out yonder, Lucy!" A big gobbler stood in the clearing, cocking his head from side to side.

"Quick! Get in that thicket." Lucy pushed Arthur in the direction of a clump of laurel bushes. When they were hidden, she handed him the gun and blew on her bone. She took the gun back and found an opening to point the barrel through. "Now, be real still. He'll come right to this spot."

They waited motionless, speaking in whispers. "You sure he's coming, Lucy?"

"Listen, hear that? It's a strutting sound."

"Vuh-duh-yuh-you."

"Sounds like footsteps," said Arthur. "How's he making that noise?"

"He's dragging his wings on the ground."

The noise stopped. Lucy aimed and tightened her finger on the trigger. The shot vibrated down the mountain and echoed back.

"We'll have turkey for dinner after all, Arthur."

"Can I see?" He pushed away the branches. The turkey flopped through the dead leaves, his head held on by a slender string of flesh. Blood gushed onto the ground. "Can I get him, Lucy?"

Lucy caught Arthur by the pants leg. "Wait till he stops jumping around. He still could hurt you with his spurs. They're sharp as a razor and could cut you bad."

Finally the turkey lay still. Arthur tied its legs together and threw it over his shoulder. They headed toward home. Lucy knew that not only would they have turkey for dinner tomorrow, but by the way Arthur was acting, they'd also have another grown man at the table.

≈　　≈　　≈

Dovey set a wooden box on the table, opened the lid, and picked up a silver spoon. She gently wiped it off with a soft rag. Her ma had always used this silver for the holidays. She was going to use it too, and if her and Hattie's plan worked, it would serve more than one purpose. Lucy came and looked over Dovey's shoulder. "Ma always used the silver in this box when she had company coming for supper."

"It's beautiful, Dovey. Are you sure we should use it?"

"Ma'd want it used."

"Where'd she get it?"

"It was her ma's. The silver and the pump organ was the only two things her ma left her. She said when she was gone she wanted me to have them. She wanted me to use them for special family days. I figure Thanksgiving is a special day. If it's all right, I'll polish it and put it on the table."

"You do that, Dovey, and I'll finish in the kitchen."

Dovey worked and planned as she lay the silver on the table. She knew how her pa had felt about her ma. She was sure he'd send that Cow's Tail Lucy packing if she messed with her ma's stuff. She'd already taken over the kitchen. And now with this turkey killing, she'd be more of a hero to the children. She could see every day how they were looking more and more to Lucy as a ma. She wasn't going to let that happen. Her ma had left her in charge, and this Lucy

94

woman was just going to have go. If her pa couldn't see what was happening, then somebody had to make him see.

≈　≈　≈

Back in the kitchen, Lucy went about her work feeling that Dovey might be warming a little toward her. Hattie burst through the back door. "They're here! The Joneses are here. They're in their Sunday best. Do we have to dress up, Lucy?"

"No, Hattie, not your Sunday best. I do think it would be nice if you found some soap and water and washed that face of yours. It wouldn't hurt if you changed your dress, either."

"Don't want to. I'll ask Dovey—she won't make me."

"If you don't wash up, Hattie, there'll be no dinner for you."

Dovey came into the kitchen and set the wooden box on the table. "There's some spoons in here you can use for the food."

Hattie stuck her tongue out at Lucy. "Dovey, Lucy said I had to get cleaned up. Don't I look good enough the way I am? Ain't nobody coming but the Joneses." Hattie opened the box and peeked in, then reached and slipped a couple of spoons behind her back.

Dovey turned to Lucy. "Ain't you got it through your head yet that I'm the one in charge of the young-uns? You just tend to your cooking. I'll take care of Hattie." She took Hattie by the hand. "Come on, let's see if we can't find you a better looking dress."

Lucy lifted the lid on the box and took a handful of spoons. She guessed she was wrong about Dovey liking her better. Didn't make much difference. The peddler should be here any day now. She touched her locket. She could feel the letters that were etched into it. She wasn't finding much love around here, except maybe from Annie May. Could be her Indian people would accept her and love her, but even getting there had a price. These sure were nice silver spoons. She bet the peddler would like them, but they weren't hers. She wiped a spoon and put it into a steaming bowl of squash.

≈　≈　≈

Holman stepped up on the porch. The scent of turkey filled his nostrils. *Thanksgiving*—he'd completely forgotten. Where had his family gotten a turkey? He'd been promising the boys to take them hunting. He was just going to have to make more time for them. He opened the front door and entered with a big grin. "Happy Thanksgiving, everybody!"

"Pa! We didn't think you'd make it."

"I didn't either, John, but here I am."

"Pa! Pa! You're home." Hattie ran to him with outstretched arms. He gathered her into his arms and gave her a hug.

John rose from his pa's chair. "Here, Pa. You can be the one to carve the turkey."

Holman walked over to the table. He set Hattie back on the floor and gave her an affectionate pat on the head. He sat down and pulled his chair up to the table, then looked around. "Howdy, neighbors. I'm glad you could join us for this Thanksgiving dinner." He turned to Lucy. "Where's Dovey?"

"She's out in the kitchen seeing to the littl'-uns."

"Come out here a minute, Dovey," Holman called.

Dovey stuck her head around the kitchen door. "Pa! You're home! What do you want, Pa?"

"You want to come in here and say the blessing?"

Dovey bowed her head and began to pray. Lucy watched her from half-closed eyes. This girl that was still a child in so many ways had taken on so much, mothering this bunch of young ones. She hadn't missed a Sunday since the flood, taking them to church. Maybe she should go along and see if she could learn something about God. Especially if she was going to leave with the peddler. She had a feeling she'd need all the help she could get. Her ma had told her about Jesus's love, but she'd been so young she didn't really understand. If only she could read. But then, it wouldn't have done any good without a Bible.

When Dovey finished, bowls of steaming vegetables, mashed potatoes, and gravy were passed. "Now let's see what we can do to this bird. Where'd you get such a big turkey, John?"

"I didn't, Pa. Lucy and Arthur went turkey hunting and got 'em."

Holman looked surprised. "Lucy, I didn't know you knew how to turkey hunt. You're a woman with lots of talents."

"Arthur gets most of the credit," said Lucy. "Without him there wouldn't be a turkey."

"A man scared Lucy, Pa. Me and Arthur went back to look for him, but he was gone. We couldn't find any sign of him," said John.

All eyes turned on Lucy. She shuffled uneasily in her seat. "I was calling the turkey for Arthur to shoot. A man came instead of a turkey. I tried to get up a tree, but I couldn't climb fast enough. I yelled for Arthur and he came a-running and scared him off."

By now Holman's blue eyes were wide with worry. "Lucy, why do you think he was after you?"

Lucy's hands clutched the edge of the table. "I don't know." What would he say if he knew it was Herby Ledford? Could be he'd go after him and maybe kill him. Hadn't Luther been a neighbor and a friend, and Holman had been there when Luther was killed?

Holman turned to the boys. "Tomorrow we'd better see what we can find on that mountain. Richard, would you like to come with me and the boys?"

"Sure would. Can I take my gun? I want to learn to shoot better. If I ever find out who shot Pa, I'm gonna kill him."

"Richard, I told you I didn't want to hear no more about you killing nobody. Now if you're gonna talk like that, you can just stay home," said Bessie.

Richard dropped his head. "I'm sorry, Aunt Bessie. I forgot."

"All right, you can go, and you can take your gun, but you mind Holman. You hear?"

Holman gave him a pat on the shoulder. "Be down here early in the morning, son." He took another bite of dressing. "This is mighty good dressing. Just the right amount of sage."

Lucy reached for the platter of turkey. "I'm glad. I used all the sage we had. Hope maybe that peddler man will have some more."

"Don't guess you'll be getting nothing from the peddler—not till spring at least." Everyone stopped eating and looked at Holman. Lucy felt as though her heart would stop beating. No peddler—that meant she'd be stuck here all winter.

"Why not?" asked Harley. "He always comes before the weather gets bad."

"He's in no shape to come."

"Did he have an accident?" asked John.

"You could say that. They found him over by Crying Rock in pretty bad shape."

"That's where he said he saw the haint, ain't it?" asked John.

"You don't believe all that hogwash about haints, do you?" scoffed Bessie. "Ain't never seen or heard of nothing any uglier or bigger than me, yet."

Everyone at the table roared with laughter. John reached out and touched her hand. "Bessie, you ain't ugly."

"You've heard that old saying, son, that beauty is in the eyes of the beholder. I ain't found nobody with big enough eyes to hold me since my man died."

"Pa, what you think happened to the peddler?"

"Don't know, Arthur. He looked like he'd got beat up. Most of the stuff in his wagon was gone."

"Sounds like he was robbed," said Bessie.

Holman nodded. "Some folks say the Indians did it. There was some moccasin tracks."

"What do you think?"

"I think whoever done it would like us to think the Indians done it, Bessie."

Lucy saw Annie May peering around the door. Lucy motioned for her to come over to her chair. "Will the peddler be all right, Lucy?"

Lucy hugged the little girl to her breast. "I hope so, honey."

Holman looked over at Annie May. "He'll be just fine. Said he'd try to be around in the spring." He watched Lucy's face for some sign of disappointment. He'd found a note in the peddler's belongings about Lucy being family to the Indians. Had she planned on going with the peddler when he returned? Was that what the note was about, or was she just trying to find out about her family? Well, if she had plans to leave, her face sure didn't tell it. He guessed he'd have to believe she was going to carry out her pa's deal. Lord knew he was doing all he could to make life good for her here, but she could never take Mary's place.

After supper, the chatter of the girls' voices coming from the kitchen gave a homey feeling to the old house. Lucy invited Bessie and Effie to sit with her around the fireplace. She'd have to spend a lot of long cold evenings here. She wondered if Holman would be around much.

"I knew it. I knew the minute she saw them she wanted them." Every eye in the room turned toward Dovey who stood in the kitchen door.

Holman took a step toward her. "What're you talking about, Dovey?"

"My silverware. You know, what ma left me. I shouldn't have showed it to her. She really liked it. She made me use it for Thanksgiving supper tonight. Now I know she wanted to take some."

"Dovey, do you know what you're saying that Lucy did? Are you sure there's some missing?" asked Holman.

"I think Dovey knows what she's saying. And I'm also sure she'd like to believe I took some of the silver. I believe there's another person in this room who knows I didn't take it." Lucy never let Hattie out of her sight. "Dovey, could you tell us what's missing?"

"The large gravy spoon and some of the other spoons. Like you don't know!" Hattie edged her way toward the bedroom door.

"Dovey, why don't you go back to the kitchen and look again. I'm sure you'll find them. If you don't, we'll talk about this after our company is gone," said Holman.

"It won't do no good, for she has 'em." Dovey disappeared into the kitchen.

Lucy turned to Holman. "Could I have a word with you later? There's somethin' I've been a-needing to talk to you about."

From the corner of her eye, Lucy saw Hattie's head lift and tilt in their direction. Lucy raised her voice. "There's some more problems with one of the young-uns I've been aiming to talk to you about."

"We'll talk in the morning, Lucy. I'm gonna go help the boys with the chores," said Holman, as he walked the Joneses to the door.

Lucy caught a glimpse of Hattie as she slid through the bedroom door. "Dovey, I think either you or Hattie knows where the spoons are. You two are bound and determined to make my life miserable! Go ahead and tell your pa all the lies you want to. The peddler ain't coming, and I may have to spend the winter here, but I want you to know right now, I ain't taking no nonsense from you or Hattie."

≈ ≈ ≈

Holman stood in the kitchen doorway and watched Lucy roll out biscuits. He wondered if it was her devotion to her pa and his deal that was keeping this spit-fire of a woman here. He was sure it wasn't for love of him or the children. The peddler had been here and that would have been a good way to leave. She must not have been in too big a hurry to go. If she planned to go with him this time, she must be disappointed. There was also something going on with the children. He was sure of that, and he was also sure Lucy knew what it was. He needed to let her handle it. "Morning, Lucy. Breakfast sure smells good."

Lucy looked up. "You're up and about early."

Holman pulled out a chair and sat down. "Thought you and me should have our little talk before the rest get up."

Lucy cut the biscuits and put them in the pan. Holman studied the nimble fingers that placed the biscuits so precisely. There was something different about this woman—something his Mary didn't have. He sure would like to be home more and find out, but till he was done with this job, there'd be no way he could, and probably by the time he could be here, she'd be gone. He cleared his throat and spoke. "Lucy, I thought you'd like to know Dovey came out to the barn last night and told me she found her spoons."

Lucy put the biscuits in the oven. "Would you like some coffee?"

"Sure would. You gonna have some?"

Lucy didn't answer, but poured two cups of coffee and set them on the table. She pulled out a chair and sat down.

"You don't act surprised, Lucy."

Lucy traced the rim of her cup with her finger. "I figured she'd find them. Did she say where they was?"

"She said after all the dishes was done, she counted again. They was all there. I told her she needed to tell you that she was sorry. I think she still believes you took 'em and put 'em back later."

"What do *you* believe, Holman?"

100

Holman watched Lucy as she twisted the worn ribbon around her neck. It looked to him that if she washed that ribbon there'd be nothing left. "I don't see what you'd want with 'em, but whatever happened, she got 'em back. So what do you say we forget it."

Lucy took a sip of her coffee. "I guess that would be the best thing to do. I wish I could do somethin' to get her to like me. And there's Hattie. Sometimes I think she hates me."

"Don't worry, Lucy. Dovey'll come around. And as for Hattie, she's good at her little games, but she really is soft-hearted. Now tell me about this man that grabbed you. Is there somethin' you'd like to say to me that you didn't want to say in front of the young-uns? And who really shot the turkey?"

"I shot the turkey, but I said Arthur did because if he hadn't a-scared off the man, I couldn't have shot the turkey. Arthur's feeling pretty good about protecting me."

"I know. Guess I got me another man around here." Holman pushed back his chair and stood. "I'd better get ready to go look for that man. You sure there's not somethin' you can tell me that will help?"

"Don't know much, 'cept he came at me and grabbed me."

Holman thought about the day at the mill. Was that Herby Ledford up to something? "Did you know who this man was, Lucy?"

Lucy shook her head. Holman got the feeling she wasn't telling him all she knew, but he knew enough about her to know that she wasn't going to talk unless she wanted to. He laid an envelope down on the table. "I found this in the peddler's belongin's. I think it belongs to you. Thought you'd like to have it back."

Lucy searched for words. "I—I—was just curious about my ma's family. The peddler promised to find out somethin' for me and let me know when he came back."

"Guess you'll have to wait till spring. Hope you're not too let down." Holman turned toward the kitchen door. Let her go. He didn't need her. Dovey could forget that schooling and raise the young ones. As for him, well, he'd buried his dreams. A great loneliness washed over him as he closed the door.

≈ *10* ≈

Lucy took a deep breath of the cold December air. What was it about Christmas that made her feel a hush in her heart?

"Are you a-coming, Lucy?"

"I'm a-coming, John. Fast as I can." She bent down and tightened the strings that held Holman's oversized boots on her feet.

"We're over here," called Arthur. "Come see what you think about this tree."

Lucy hugged herself against the wind and trudged through the heavy snow to join the boys. She found Arthur standing next to a huge pine. "Sure is gonna look nice by our big old fireplace. Don't you think so, Lucy?"

She looked at Arthur and then at the tree. What about the children back at the house? They were busy making decorations for the tree. Would they be able to make enough for a tree *this* big? Arthur looked so happy. Telling him it was too big would wipe the smile from his face. He'd been so helpful since the turkey hunt. She'd just hurry home so she could help make more decorations. "It'll be just right, Arthur. Why don't you and John cut it down, and I'll head on home to see how the decorations are coming."

Back at the house, Lucy emptied her pockets on the kitchen table. "I found these little pine cones on the way home. There's some red yarn in the sewing basket. Thought maybe we could tie them on the tree."

Annie May picked up one of the cones and looked at it. "These will be pretty, and my teacher showed us how to make angels from paper. Can I make one for the tree top?"

Hattie brought the yarn and began to cut ties. "Who wants a old paper angel for a Christmas tree? The peddler had some tinsel angels. Wish we had one of them."

Dovey cleared a spot on the table. "Ma always said, 'if wishes was horses, beggars wouldn't walk,' Hattie. Come on, Annie May, you can work here, and I'll help you." Dovey set down a bowl of popcorn. "I hope Pa'll get home in time to go to church with us tonight."

Hattie tied a piece of yarn onto a pine cone. "He'll be here. He never misses seeing me be an angel. Are you coming, Lucy? Oh! I forgot you're a heathen."

Annie May asked, "Are you a heathen?"

Lucy looked down into her eyes, put an arm around her, and pulled her close. "No, I ain't a heathen. Where I come from, we just didn't have a church to go to, but my ma, she believed in God, and she told me lots of stories about him."

Annie May picked up a pencil and wrote on the back of the angel, To Ma, with love, from Annie May. "Good. So I guess you know the story of the birth of Jesus, and how he come down here to live on earth to save us from our sins. You can come with us tonight and watch the play. I'm gonna be Mary, Jesus's mother."

Hattie squeezed between Lucy and Annie May. "And the boys, too. They're shepherds and wise men."

"I see this is a family affair," said Lucy. She toyed with a rope of popcorn as she thought about what Annie May had just said. This Jesus person and sins. There was so much she didn't know. Maybe she'd start going to church even if Dovey didn't ask her. The kitchen door opened.

"The tree is outside," said John. "Where do you want me to put it?"

"In the front room where we always put it. The decorations are just about ready," said Dovey. "We'll be right in."

"All right," said John, "I just have to do a little bit of trimming on it and I'll bring it in."

Lucy helped the children gather up the decorations and carry them to the front room. Arthur was right. The tree fit perfectly in the corner by the fireplace. She watched the joy in their faces as they crowded around the tree. The younger children hung the decorations on the lower limbs. The older ones wrapped the tree with strings of popcorn and tied on the pine cones. It wasn't long until they were ready for the angel to be put on the top.

Hattie looked at the angel. "I sure liked the peddler's angel better. Do we have to use *that* old angel?"

"We sure do."

Everyone turned to see Holman standing in the doorway. He looked up at the tree top. "Annie May, why don't I hold you, and you can put your angel on the tree." He hoisted her up on his shoulder. Lucy gathered up bits and pieces of leftover Christmas decorations. Annie May sure looked happy. Was it because of Holman's help, or the angel she'd made?

Annie May put the angel in place then looked down into her pa's eyes. "You think Ma can see my angel, Pa?" Holman's eyes misted. Dovey wiped her eyes with her sleeve. "Think she can, Pa?"

Holman nodded and swallowed hard. He placed Annie May on the floor. "Now, let's hurry and get the chores done. It'll soon be time for church." He looked at Lucy. "You coming with us?"

"She's coming, Pa," said Annie May. "We've already asked her."

"Good."

Lucy smiled to herself as she swept up the pine needles. She knew part of Annie May's happiness was because of making the angel for her ma, but she couldn't help believing some of it was from her pa's attention. He'd not only made Annie May smile, but Lucy also liked the way he'd said the word *good*. It sounded like he meant it. Maybe he was beginning to appreciate her help.

Every pew in the little country church was packed. Holman and Lucy sat with the four youngest children in the second row from the front. From the corner of his eye, Holman watched Lucy shift uneasily in her seat. Maybe he shouldn't have brought her. The children said she'd never been to church. The last thing he wanted was to make her feel like she had to go places with him. He glanced around. A few of the women's heads were turned in their direction. Well, let the old biddies look. He didn't care. He'd done what he needed to to take care of his family. He was about to ask Lucy if she was all right when the organ began to play.

The music floated through the air. The little church became hushed. A feeling of expectancy filled the room. A young man stood up and began to read. "It came to pass in those days, that there went out a decree from Caesar Augustus, that all the world should be taxed. And Joseph with his espoused wife, Mary, went to be taxed." The reader paused and everyone turned toward the back of the church. Annie May was wearing a medium blue shawl around her shoulders. Richard Jones led her down the aisle toward Dovey and Will who were the innkeepers.

"I'm sorry. There's no room in our inn," said Will. Dovey arched an eyebrow at Will. Richard and Annie May turned away. The dejected look on Annie May's face brought tears to Holman's eyes.

"Wait!" The young couple stopped. Dovey turned to Will. "Please! Can't we find a room for them somewhere? See how tired she looks."

Will's eyes traveled down Annie May's body. "Well, . . . I . . . guess, we can try. There's the stable out back. At least it'll give them some protection from the cold."

"Thank you, sir! Thank you." Richard bowed and took Annie May by the arm.

"Wait. I'll find some bedding." Dovey moved toward the side door. "You can make a bed in the hay." They all followed her out the door.

"We will all sing 'It Came Upon the Midnight Clear'," said the reader. Holman's voice rose above the crowd's. He wasn't much on church, but one thing he did like was singing, especially at Christmas.

The next scene was a group of shepherds gathered on a hillside. "And suddenly the air was filled with a heavenly host." Hattie appeared through the side door carrying a lantern. The light cast a halo around her blond curls. Holman remembered the trouble she'd given Lucy. She was a little imp even if she looked like an angel.

Arthur whispered loudly to one of the other shepherds, "I can't believe that's my sister."

Holman smiled to himself. Yes, the children were growing up. And Arthur was right, Hattie was beautiful. Annie May, too, if only . . . Holman's thoughts returned to the play.

There was more singing, then more reading. From the side door, an old man staggered in. The lining hung from his coat. His pants legs were rolled up and lots of patches covered his clothes. He stopped and stared at Mary and baby Jesus. Annie May looked up and saw him. She motioned for him to come closer. With bowed head, he crossed to where the manger stood. He removed his old felt hat and made a low bow. The audience clapped.

Lucy leaned over to Holman. "Who's the old man?"

"That's Tilman. He's a little teched. He insists on being in the play so every year they let him come to pay his respects to the Christ Child."

When the audience was through clapping, an older gray-headed man stood up. "We sure would like to thank these young folks for their fine Christmas play. It has spoke to my heart, and I hope it has touched yours. We would also like to invite you out to Sunday service. We don't have a regular parson, but we praise the Lord the best we can on our own. The parson will be through here in the spring. We will have us a baptizing down in the river then. If you want to be baptized, you can just let me know. Now, let us pray."

The man's voice droned on. Holman thought about spring and what it would bring. Lucy probably wouldn't be here. She'd find a way to Cherokee by then, he was sure. A parson was coming. If Jake or some other peddler didn't come, she'd more than likely hitch a ride with the parson. That would mean Dovey would have to quit school. He hated that, but Dovey hadn't made things too easy for Lucy. He couldn't blame her for wanting to go.

≈　　≈　　≈

The young-uns were still in bed. Dovey set out all the Christmas presents. She held a doll close. "Ma," she whispered. "I done the best I could."

Her pa came in and took the doll from her. "Guess we'd better get everything under the tree. I see this doll is for Annie May. You know Hattie's gonna want a doll, too. What'll we tell her?"

Dovey snatched the doll from her pa. Tears filled her eyes and rolled down her cheeks. Hattie certainly wasn't going to get this doll! She'd had too hard a time getting enough eggs to pay for it with that Cow's Tail Lucy around. "Tell her she'll have her turn next year. By then Annie May will be too old for a doll." She rubbed her nose on her sleeve. "Pa, you don't know how it's been with that Lucy woman around here being so bossy. You'd think she'd *always* been here the

106

way she acts." She wiped at her eyes. "I know you don't like the way I've been treating her, but how would you like it if somebody tried to take *your* place?"

Pa pulled up a chair and sat down. "Come over here a minute, Dovey." He took both her hands in his. "I know it's been hard for you, but it sure ain't been easy for me. Sometimes I think . . ." His voice trailed off and he cleared his throat. "Maybe it would have been easier on you young-uns if it had been me instead of your ma."

Dovey dropped to her knees and threw her arms around him. "Don't say that, Pa. I wouldn't want to choose between you and Ma. I don't know what we'd do if somethin' happened to you, Pa." She buried her head in his lap.

He lifted her chin. "Dovey, ain't nothing gonna happen to me. I'm as healthy as a horse. Now come on, let's celebrate Christmas!"

"I s'pose you have somethin' for that Lucy woman, too."

"Yes, Dovey, I bought a little somethin' for her. Wouldn't want her to get nothing, seeing it's Christmas and all, would you?"

Dovey looked down. It wouldn't make any difference to her. It looked to her like she was getting her way around here. Wasn't that enough? She lifted her head and looked at her pa. "Guess not, Pa. Do what makes you happy." She watched him as he placed the gifts under the tree. Yes, let him do what he wanted to about Cow's Tail Lucy, but he need not expect her to try with this woman. Before the winter was over, she'd make her wish she'd never come here.

Holman looked around the room. "Don't you think we'd better get on with this Christmas?"

"The young-uns is still sleeping," said Dovey.

"Get 'em up. Don't want 'em to miss Santa."

Dovey went to get the little ones as Lucy entered the front room. Holman pulled a chair close to the fire and stuck out his hands in front of the blaze. "Sure is getting cold out. Afeared we're gonna have us a rough winter."

Lucy glanced at the mantel where thirteen socks with bulging toes hung in row. Yes, a long cold winter trapped here with all these children to watch over. She cleared her throat. "Could be worse. At least you have a nice tight house. I wonder how Pa'll . . ."

"Listen, Lucy, I knew you'd be worried about your pa, seeing it's Christmas and all. I . . ."

Lucy tilted her chin up and turned away from Holman. "Don't want to hear about him. If he loved me, he'd try to come to see me."

Holman touched her shoulder. "Lucy, it's not that . . ."

"Here's the littl'-uns," said Dovey.

Holman took his hand off Lucy's shoulder. "All right, young-uns. Time for presents. Socks first." He took down the socks in order and handed them out. Each sock had an apple, an orange, and two sticks of peppermint candy.

Hattie slung her sock on the floor. "I want a real present."

Mary picked it up. "If you don't want it, Hattie, can I have it?"

Hattie eyed the sock with disgust. Suddenly, she snatched it up. "No! It's mine."

"I believe you got up on the wrong side of the bed, Hattie," said Holman.

"Same side she always gets up on, Pa," said Dovey.

"Dovey, don't be so hard on your little sister," said Holman.

Hattie dropped her lower lip and crossed her arms on her chest as she slouched in her chair. "Everybody's picking on me."

"Come on, Hattie," said Holman. "Give us an angel smile. After all it's Christmas morning."

Hattie sat up in her chair and turned on her charm. "Can I help pass out the presents, Pa? Please? Can I?"

Holman pulled out an unwrapped gift. "Let's see. This says it's for a little girl named Mary. Here, Hattie. Give Mary this little broom."

Hattie carried the broom to Mary. "Wish Santa had left me one."

"I see Santa knows you have a hard time with your spelling, Hattie. He left you a dictionary," said Holman.

Hattie took the book and flipped through the pages. "It ain't got no pictures. I don't want no old book without pictures." She threw it back under the tree.

Holman reached for the doll. "Here, give this to Annie May."

Hattie grabbed the doll and backed away from her pa. "No! I want the doll. Ain't fair all I get is an old book with no pictures."

Annie May's eyes opened wide, looking at the dark ringlets that hung down the doll's back. "She's so beautiful! How come I get a doll and Hattie don't, Pa?"

"You'll have to ask Dovey. She was in charge of getting ahold of Santa."

Dovey shot her pa a quick glance. Well, he still gave her credit for being in charge of something around here, but if she didn't get rid of that Cow's Tail Lucy by next Christmas, *she'd* probably be saying who got what. Or worse yet, she wouldn't worry about saving the eggs to buy presents with, and nobody would get anything.

"Don't Santa want Hattie to have a doll, Dovey?" asked Annie May.

"Course he does, honey, but Ma let Santa know before she died that she wanted you to have one this year because you'd be too big next year. Hattie'll have her turn."

Hattie's face puckered into a half scowl. "You mean Ma wanted Annie May to have a doll and not me." She slung the doll toward Annie May. It hit the corner of the hearth and something cracked.

A strange quietness fell over the room. Everyone turned to stare at Hattie. She burst into tears and buried her face in her hands. Annie May rushed to pick up the doll. She brushed ashes from the doll's dress, turned her face up, and rubbed a spot of soot from her nose. "Hattie, she's all right. Here, why don't you hold her? I'm sure Ma'd want us to take turns."

Hattie rubbed the tears from her eyes with the back of her hand. "You mean she didn't break? What was that noise?"

Arthur held up two halves of a walnut. "Somebody left these walnuts too close to the fire. It'd been like the Fourth of July in here in a few minutes." He put the box of nuts near the door.

Hattie took the doll and sat down. Annie May sat down in front of her and patted the doll's foot.

Holman pulled a box from his pocket. "Before we look at any more gifts, I'd like to take this time to thank Lucy for all her help." He held the box out to her. "Merry Christmas, Lucy."

"But I didn't get nothing for you."

"That's all right. Just take this. You've earned it." Lucy took the box. She wanted to tell him she didn't expect any pay, that she was only keeping up her pa's end of their deal, but it was Christmas.

She'd just take the present and not raise a fuss. She lifted the lid. A shiny gold-colored chain nestled in one corner of the box. She picked it up and let it slide through her fingers. She felt the locket around her neck. It was a beautiful chain, but she'd have to take off her ma's old blue ribbon, and she didn't want to do that. Nodding to Holman, she dropped the chain back in the box.

≈ *11* ≈

Holman was right about it being a cold winter. January brought a deep freeze. It was too icy for the children to go to school. Just staying warm was an effort. Holman wasn't gone as much as usual. He spent most of his nights sleeping on his bedroll in front of the fireplace and keeping the fire burning. After the chores were done, they would all crowd around the fireplace. Some nights, a pile of potatoes was buried in the hot ashes to bake. Other nights, the corn popper was shaken over the blaze. The smell of popped corn lingered long into the night. Every night the children begged their pa for one of his stories.

Holman pulled his chair close to the fire. He stirred the ashes with the poker. He sure missed Mary. It had been over a year since she'd died. Life hadn't gotten any easier. His job was the only thing that helped fill the ache in his heart, and that was only because most of the time it kept him away from home. That didn't help the children much. He wondered if Dovey realized how lucky she was to be able to go to school. Spring would probably bring an end to that.

John tugged on his ear thoughtfully. "Pa, you know the story the peddler told us about seeing a haint over at Crying Rock? Do you think what he saw was some kind of warning to him?"

"What do you mean, son?"

"Well, Lucy said that she saw little girl right before her ma died that nobody else could see."

Holman looked over at Lucy. What would she think if she knew about her pa? Would that make her more superstitious? Well, he couldn't afford to upset her now. He needed her too much. "You think that was a warning to you that your ma was gonna die, Lucy?"

"Could have been. I don't really know. Just seems strange to me." Lucy pulled her shawl tighter around her.

"Did you ever have somethin' like that happen to you, Pa?" John leaned toward Holman as he waited for his answer. Holman tilted his cane-bottom chair against the wall, crossed his arms on his chest, and chewed on a wad of tobacco for a few minutes. Finally, he leaned forward and spit a stream of tobacco juice into the fire. The flames sizzled and devoured it. A smile played around his mouth.

Hattie moved closer to him. "Have you, Pa?"

Holman twisted his mustache. "You could say I've had my turn with these so-called haints."

Carl and Harley begged in unison, "Tell us about it, Pa!"

Holman looked uneasily at Lucy. "Well, it was when I was a-courting your ma."

Dovey sat straight in her chair. "I want to hear about you courting Ma."

Holman studied Lucy for a few minutes. Would talking about his late wife upset her too much? Maybe he shouldn't say any more. "It's all right with me, Holman," said Lucy.

"How did you first meet her?" asked Dovey.

"Luther Jones and me went to a barn dance over in her settlement. She was there with her four brothers. I couldn't take my eyes off her. Guess you could say she stole my heart that first night. Course, I kept going back. Your ma was the only girl in her family. Her brothers had a reputation for drinking and carousing. Didn't take nothing off nobody.

"They ganged up on me one Sunday night after I took your ma to church. Said they were tired of seeing me around, and that if their pa was still alive, he'd put a stop to it. One of her brothers said, 'Yeah, Carpenter. I wouldn't want to be in your shoes walking across that mountain in the dark!'"

"Did they believe in haints?" Hattie asked in a shaky voice.

Holman chuckled. "I doubt it, Hattie. One of them said, 'Some folks in these here parts believe that our pa was so mean that the devil wouldn't have his soul. Could be he's still roaming the mountains looking for a home!'" Holman paused and twisted his mustache for a moment.

"I'd heard rumors about her pa. Guess it didn't much matter to me, seeing he was dead. Didn't think much about what the boys said

112

till I got halfway up the mountain that night. It was pitch black. Clouds covered the moon. About halfway up I stopped to listen. I had a feeling I wasn't alone. I called, 'Anybody there?' No answer. I started down the other side. Sounded like footsteps beside me."

"What did you do, Pa?" asked Hattie as she edged closer to John.

"I stopped and the other footsteps stopped. Then I ran and the steps ran. I decided to take the shortcut through the church graveyard. I tripped and fell in a freshly dug grave. Crawled out with mud all over me. I think the fall knocked some sense into me."

"Grave!" exclaimed all the children at once.

"What do you think you heard?" asked Dovey.

"Pro'bly just heard my own heart beating." The children roared with laughter.

"When did you go calling on Ma again?" asked John.

"I went back the next Sunday, but I came home before it got dark. That was the Sunday I asked your ma to marry me. It wasn't long after that, maybe a year or so, I heard footsteps again."

Everyone looked surprised. Hattie crawled up in John's lap. "You mean the haint come back?"

Holman spit again. "No, Hattie. The way I see it, could be that your grandpa found him a home in the little feet that began to pitter-patter around here." The room echoed with memories of days gone by. The children inspected their feet as if they expected to find their grandfather's initials carved on the bottom of them.

Holman stood and stretched, bent over, and spit his wad of tobacco into the fire. He looked at Lucy. "Thanks for listening, Lucy. You know young-uns like to hear about the olden times."

"I understand, Holman. It's only fitting they hear stories about their ma."

Holman picked up another log and put it on the fire. He watched as Lucy straightened up the room. Whoever Lucy had run into on the mountain at Thanksgiving sure wasn't a haint or a ghost. He was very much alive. He sure hoped there'd be no more trouble.

"Pa?" They all turned toward the back of the room where Dovey stood with a Bible in her arms.

"What do you want, Dovey?" asked Holman.

"I was just a-wondering if you'd read us some out of Ma's Bible. She used to read to us before we went to bed."

"I'd be pleased to, Dovey. What do you want to hear?"

"I'd like to hear the part in the Bible that tells about what a good woman is. That part fitted Ma."

"I think you mean Proverbs Thirty-one." Holman opened the Bible and began to read. "Who can find a virtuous woman? For her price is far above rubies. The heart of her husband doth safely trust in her, so that . . ."

Lucy's thoughts wandered back to the day she'd gone to visit Bessie when they had sat at the kitchen table visiting and eating Bessie's chocolate cake. She had asked Bessie how Holman had met Mary. Bessie had been glad to tell her, but when she mentioned that Annie May must look like her ma, Bessie had started to say something but stopped. What had it been? It was easy to see that Holman and the children thought Mary was a good woman. And what about what the man on the mountain had said last summer? Could it be that the first missus wasn't as good as Holman thought?

The sound of Holman's voice cut into her thoughts, "Her children rise up and call her blessed; her husband also, and he praiseth her." Holman closed the Bible.

Dovey stood. "Ma always closed with the Lord's Prayer." She bowed her head and began to pray. "Our Father, who art in Heaven . . ." Lucy bowed her head also. If only she could read the Bible, she could find out more about this Lord they talked about. She looked from under half-closed eyelids and wondered about asking Holman if he'd help her learn to read. No, she didn't want him to know she couldn't read, and the children might tease her. ". . . Amen."

Lucy slipped from the room. She needed time alone. As she crawled into bed, the noises in the house faded away. Her mind began to fog with sleep. Like a flash of lightning, Bessie's name flickered across her mind. She was wide awake. That was it! Bessie. She was the answer to her problem. When the children went back to school, she'd go see her and ask her if she'd help her to learn reading and writing.

≈   ≈   ≈

The cold held. Lucy opened a trunk that held the family's supply of quilts. She found only one that wasn't in use, but at the bottom of the trunk were several quilt tops. She spread one of them on the bed. The pattern of Jacob's ladder wound its way from the foot of the bed to the head. She shook another free of its folds and laid it over the other one. Each block had a different family's last name on it. The one she picked up next took her breath. Circle after circle entwined each other in brilliant colors. This had to be a wedding ring. She'd heard her ma tell about the pattern, but she'd never seen one.

"What do you think you're doing?"

Lucy turned to face Dovey. "I was just thinking we're low on quilts, and there's all these quilt tops. The weather's so cold we can't do much—it would be a good time to quilt up some more."

Dovey ran to the bed and scooped up the quilt tops. "Ma made these here tops. They're for us young-uns, and you ain't gonna mess them up. I'm gonna tell Pa what you're fixing to do. Pa, come in here a minute."

"What's all the yelling going on in here?" asked Holman.

"I thought since the weather was so cold it would be a good time for us to quilt up some of these tops. Dovey seems to think I just want to mess them up because they're her ma's." Holman went over to Dovey, took the quilt tops, and spread them on the bed again.

"You ain't gonna let her quilt Ma's tops, are you, Pa?"

"Seems to me like it would be a good idea if they was worked up, and Lord knows we will need them if this cold weather holds."

Dovey grabbed the wedding ring top and hugged it to her breast. "Well, you can let her work on any of them but this one. Ma made it for me, and she ain't to touch it."

Holman picked up the friendship top. "This looks like a good one to get started on. I'll go out to the barn and get the quilting frames. Lucy, there's some wool rolled up and hanging in the loft where the boys sleep. I've got some feed sacks out in the barn. I'll bring them in tonight when I do the feeding. You can wash them out and sew them together."

"Doubt if she can sew a straight seam," mumbled Dovey. She rolled up her quilt top and stuck it under her straw mattress.

115

Holman ignored Dovey's remark. "The quilt will be ready to work on by tomorrow night, Dovey. Just see that you have your thimble and needle ready."

The next day Lucy washed and sewed the feed sack lining. Holman hung the quilting frames from the front room ceiling. He helped Lucy stretch the lining and tack it onto the frame. They unrolled the wool onto the lining. Next came the quilt top. It was also stretched tight and tacked in the frame. After dinner, Holman took the boys possum hunting, and Lucy gathered the girls around the quilt. She helped Mary, Fannie, and Nannie thread their needles and started each one on a block to quilt.

Everyone but Dovey seemed to be enjoying the quilting; she sewed in silence. A few times Lucy felt her eyes on her, but she pretended everything was normal and joined in the fun the others were having. "You know my ma had a special saying about new quilts."

"Tell us," urged Hattie.

"The rest of you interested?" asked Lucy.

Dovey never raised her head. "Ain't interested in superstitions."

"I'd like to hear," said Mary.

"She just used to say that if a young girl slept under a new quilt she would dream of the boy she would marry."

"See there, Dovey," said Hattie, "you should have let us work on your quilt. That way you'd know who you're gonna marry. Can I be the first to sleep under this quilt, Lucy? Please? Can I?"

"I told you, Hattie, I don't believe in them old wives tales," said Dovey.

"You heard her, Lucy. Is it all right if I sleep under it first? If I dream of Will, it'll just be Dovey's loss."

Lucy looked at the girls. Dovey looked worried. Hattie had tricked Dovey into giving her the first dance at the candy pulling, but she'd caught her at her little game. This young-un could still take some watching. It wouldn't be too smart to give her any leeway. "Let's wait till we get it done, Hattie. We'll decide who'll sleep under it first then."

"Ma saved the newest quilts for Sunday quilts," said Annie May. "I remember every Sunday morning, she'd take the newest quilts and put them on the beds. Said you never knew when somebody would drop by for a visit."

"That's true, but where I lived, we didn't have nobody to drop by," said Lucy.

"Must have been awful lonesome," said Hattie.

"Oh, sometimes it was, but for the most part it wasn't bad. The fire needs stirring. It's getting cold in here." Lucy poked at the logs in the fireplace. "It's getting late. Guess we'd better quit."

Everybody but Annie May moved closer to the fire to warm themselves. Lucy watched the girl as she stitched on her block. Maybe this would be a good one to replace the old ragged quilt she dragged around all the time. She gasped as Annie May pricked her finger, but Annie May didn't seem to notice. She was too lost in her work. Slowly, a drop of blood gathered on her finger and fell onto the quilt.

Lucy wiped at the spot. "Come on, Annie May. Let's quit for tonight. You can work on it again tomorrow."

Annie May's solemn little face turned to look up at Lucy. "But I need to get it done." Her nimble little fingers gathered a bunch of stitches onto her needle. Lucy tucked a black curl behind Annie May's ear. Yes, this quilt should go to her. She needed it to replace her old worn-out one.

≈   ≈   ≈

The cold finally broke and school reopened. Holman was gone again. Lucy wished she knew where he went and what he did. Maybe he'd tell her if she asked, but why should she? She'd lived with her pa all her life, and she'd never asked him where he went or what he did.

Lucy bundled up the three youngest and headed up the mountain to visit Bessie and Luther's widow. As Lucy entered the yard she noticed the chickens that had been running loose last spring were not there, but their droppings still littered the yard. An old speckled hound dog lay in front of the door. Lucy stopped at the top porch step. "Bessie, you home?"

The dog lifted his head. His eyelids drooped. He slowly raised himself on all fours and walked toward Lucy. Emily and Lou Ellen clung to her skirt. Martha squirmed in her arms and reached down toward the dog. Lucy started to back away when the front door opened.

"Get over here and lay down, Freckles. He won't hurt a flea. Just wants to be friends."

"You never know, Bessie. These young-uns ain't been around a dog much. Guess Holman thinks it's just one more mouth to feed."

"I can understand. This-un here don't get much to eat. Ain't too many table scraps." Lucy watched the dog walk to the other end of the porch and ease himself down. You could count his ribs. She was glad they didn't have a dog if it meant he'd look like this.

"Come on in. What brings you up the mountain, Lucy?"

"Well, I got cabin fever being cooped up with all the young-uns during the cold weather. Thought since the young-uns were back in school, I'd get the littl'-uns out for some fresh air and sunshine."

"Sure wish I could get Luther's missus out a little, but it's hard enough just to get her out of bed."

Lucy shook her head. "That's too bad. Is there somethin' I can do?"

"No, Lucy, she's the only one that can help. If she don't want to help herself, I don't see what we can do." Bessie wrung her large hands. "Sit down, Lucy. I'll fetch the coffee pot." Lucy unbundled the children and pulled a chair up in front of the fire. Bessie reappeared with the coffee pot.

"Where's your littl'-uns?"

"There's just two that's not in school and they're taking a nap with the missus. How about me fetching a quilt and making a pallet in the corner? Your littl'-uns can take a nap while we visit."

"Sounds good. The walk up the mountain tired 'em out." Bessie left and soon returned with a large quilt which she folded and put in the corner. Lucy placed the three little ones on it.

In the meantime, Bessie brought in coffee cups. "We'll have our coffee in here. Takes too much wood to keep two fires going."

"Here's just fine." Lucy sipped the black coffee. "I need your help, Bessie."

Bessie looked at the younger woman with questioning eyes. "How can I help you?"

"Bessie, can you read and write?" Bessie rose from her chair and walked to the fireplace. Lucy wondered what she was thinking.

Finally, she replied, "I can read enough to get by. Never liked school much."

Lucy lowered her eyes. "I never had a chance to go to school, so I can't read or write. I was a-wondering if you'd help me learn."

Bessie threw back her head and laughed. Lucy's face flushed. Why had she come here? She should have known she would be laughed at. "I'm sorry." She began to gather up the little ones' wraps. "I shouldn't have come."

Bessie laid her large work-worn hand on Lucy's shoulders. "I ain't laughing at you, dearie. I'm honored that you'd ask me."

"Well then, what's so funny?"

"The idea of me learning anybody somethin'. All I've ever done is hard work." Bessie sat down and sipped her coffee thoughtfully for a few minutes. "Come set down Lucy, and let's talk about this." She waited for Lucy to lay the wraps on a chair and sit down again. "Why do you want to learn to read and write, Lucy? Lots of people around here can't read or write."

"So I can read the Bible. I want to know more about Jesus the young-uns talked about at Christmastime."

The laugh lines in Bessie's face softened. "Lucy, I ain't much on this church stuff—just go when the young-uns have somethin' special." She was quiet for a few minutes. "Course that don't mean I don't believe in God. Do you believe, Lucy?"

"I never been to church 'cept at Christmas. My ma used to talk about God and heaven. She was half Indian so she had her own belief, but anyone that sees a sunrise knows there's someone that makes it happen."

"I see. Tell you what. I've got an old first grade reader in my trunk. I'll get it out and look it over. If the weather holds, I'll come down later on in the week."

"Oh, thank you, Bessie."

"Don't get too excited. I ain't promising you I can be of much help."

"Your trying is enough."

"Tell you what, Lucy. We'll work on your reading and writing a couple of times a week, but we'll allow some time for me to read some from the Bible. Can't promise you I can tell you much about what I read. Won't hurt me none neither, I s'pose."

When the little ones woke from their naps, Lucy gathered their wraps and bundled them up for the walk home. "Goodbye, Bessie, and thank you again." There was a spring to Lucy's step as she started home. Hope grew in her heart. She'd have to stay here all winter, but she'd learn reading and writing.

≈   ≈   ≈

Lucy hadn't been home long before the older children came home from school. Dovey dashed through the door first. "Guess what, Lucy! I have some good news." Lucy looked up, surprised at her excitement. "When will Pa be home?"

"In a day or two, Dovey, but I'd like to hear your good news."

"There's gonna be this district-wide spelling bee and I've been picked to go. Ain't that just great?" Dovey hugged herself and danced around in circles.

Lucy felt a quickening of her heart. Yes, it was nice, but it was nicer that Dovey had shared her good news with her. Maybe Holman was right. It did seem she was coming around. "I think you deserve it, Dovey. Your pa'll be mighty proud of you."

Dovey's expression changed from excitement to a kind of sadness. "Yeah, Pa'll be proud of me, but I won't get to go."

"That's nonsense, girl. Your pa'll want you to go."

"He'll want me to go, but where will he get the money?" Dovey's eyes narrowed. "It's all your fault that I won't get to go."

The girl who had entered the room a few minutes ago bursting with joy was now one filled with resentment. Lucy wanted to say, "You know if I hadn't been here to take care of the littl'-uns you wouldn't even be in school," but instead she said, "How do you figure that, Dovey?"

"If Pa hadn't bought you that chain for Christmas, he'd have the money."

"Dovey, what are you yelling at Lucy for now?" They both turned to find Holman standing in the door. Dovey's voice had been so intent that neither one had heard him come in.

"Pa, you're home!" Some of the joy returned to her face.

Holman ignored her. "S'pose you tell me what this is all about, Lucy."

"But Pa . . . !"

"Don't but me, Dovey. I've listened to your side of the story every time. Now I think it's Lucy's turn."

"Dovey has some good news, Holman. I think you should let her tell you."

"All right, Dovey, but there'd better be a good reason for your yelling at Lucy. I was hoping you'd come around to being nice to Lucy on your own. It's beginning to look like it's gonna take a trip out behind the barn to straighten you out."

Between stifled sobs, Dovey told her pa about the trip. Lucy watched with an ache in her heart. She didn't want her to get a whipping because of her. She thought about the chain that sat in its box with her belongings. She could offer it back to Holman if it meant Dovey's going. Dovey's voice interrupted her thoughts. "I know money's tight, but I want to go so bad, Pa."

"And I want you to go, Dovey, but you're right. Money's tight right now. Food's gonna have to come before trips. And I'm tired of you yelling at Lucy. If she wasn't here looking after the littl'-uns, you wouldn't even get to go to school, let alone a trip." Dovey looked at Lucy from lowered eyelids. "Don't you think you should tell her you're sorry for yelling at her? It's not her fault we don't have the money."

"I'm sorry, Lucy."

Lucy doubted there was one sorry bone in Dovey's whole body, but she had no intention of saying any more to her than she had to in front of Holman. "Dovey, I'm sorry that you can't go. Maybe somethin' will turn up so you can go. When is this trip?"

"The middle of March, but the teacher needs to know by the first week in March."

Holman twisted on his mustache. "That gives us a couple of weeks. Maybe somethin' will happen."

"I doubt it, Pa." She slammed the door as she left the room.

"I'm sorry she's giving you such a rough time, Lucy. I've tried to be patient with her. Don't look like it's done much good."

"I don't care how she acts or what she says. I let her know the first night I was here that I was going to do my job. I guess that's why she don't like me."

"I hope she changes. Don't like to whip my young-uns, but sometimes it's the only way. See you at supper, Lucy."

The door closed behind Holman, leaving Lucy alone with her thoughts. She knew what she had to do. She went into the bedroom, found the box Holman had given her, and opened it. She untied the ribbon and slipped the locket off. Then she took the shiny new chain and slid the locket through it. There! That looked a lot better. She smoothed the worn ribbon with her finger, folded it and placed it in the box, then closed the lid.

≈ *12* ≈

The March wind wrapped Lucy's dress tightly around her legs. She looked to see how fast the sun was setting and saw that shadows were already covering parts of the mountainside. She quickened her pace. Bessie had said the teacher usually stayed around the school for an hour or so to finish her work. She must hurry, or Dovey wouldn't be going on her trip.

Lucy fingered the thin chain that encircled her throat and followed the links until they came to rest on the locket. She clutched it firmly in her fist. She was about to part with the only treasure from her childhood. She let her forefinger slide over the inscription. It didn't matter. Love was never going to happen to her. The teacher's horse stood under a tree near the school. Good. She'd made it in time. She rushed up the steps and knocked on the door.

The teacher sat at her desk working on papers as the late afternoon sun reflected the red in her hair. She looked up as Lucy entered the room; she didn't seem surprised to see a visitor. A pleasant smile softened her face. "Yes, may I help you?"

Lucy searched for words. "Are you the teacher for the Carpenter young-uns?"

The woman came around to the front of her desk. "Yes, I am. May I ask who you are?"

Lucy didn't know how to act in front of her. She talked differently from anyone she'd ever met, but maybe that was because she was a teacher. "I'm the woman . . ."

"I know," broke in the teacher, "you are the new Mrs. Carpenter. The children told me they had a new mother. I must admit I didn't expect someone so young and . . ." She hesitated.

"You mean Indian-looking. Well, I *am* part Indian."

"No, Mrs. Carpenter, that wasn't what I was going to say. I was going to say you have a distinguished look about you."

Lucy thought of what the teacher had said. Distinguished. Was the teacher trying to say, in a nice way, there was something else wrong with her? "Well, Miz . . ."

"My name's Mrs. Allison."

"You might as well know, Miz Allison, I ain't got no learning so I don't know what your fancy words mean."

"Don't be embarrassed, Mrs. Carpenter. Lots of people around here don't have an education. And I meant you carry yourself with pride. You have a proud look about you. Please, Mrs. Carpenter, have a seat." She motioned to one of the children's desks.

Lucy squared her shoulders and sat. She lifted her chin slightly. "All Davenports are proud, Miz Allison."

Mrs. Allison smiled and sat down behind her desk.

"I've come about Dovey, Miz Allison."

"She's a wonderful child, Mrs. Carpenter. A little on the serious side but very bright."

"She don't like me. I can't much blame her. Don't know how I'd feel if I was in her place. She thinks I'm trying to be her ma. That's the last thing I want to do."

Lucy couldn't help noticing how soft and white Mrs. Allison's hands were as she folded them on her desk.

"I understand, Mrs. Carpenter. It's hard, but we have to keep trying."

Lucy thought about the peddler and his returning in the spring. He should be coming soon, and she planned to go with him. She was tired of trying.

". . . about Dovey," Mrs. Allison was saying.

Lucy forced her attention back to the teacher. "You see, Miz Allison, Holman and me both would like for Dovey to be in this spelling bee, but it's a bad time of the year, 'specially since we've had such a rough winter. Money's tight."

"I understand, Mrs. Carpenter. And putting your family in a bind is not what I want to do, but this is a real opportunity for Dovey, and it would make us all proud when she wins."

"You're that sure she'll win?"

"I'm positive. She has a natural ear for sounding out words."

Lucy reached behind her neck, unclasped the chain, leaned over, and dropped the locket on the desk. "Will this pay for Dovey's trip?"

Mrs. Allison picked up the locket and read the inscription. "Are you sure you want to part with this? It's valuable because it's gold. And besides, from the word inscribed on it, I'd say it means a lot to you."

"My ma gave me the locket, and Holman gave me the chain for Christmas."

"Here, take it," said Mrs. Allison. "I know how much it means to you." She touched a cross that hung around her neck. "My mother gave me this. I know what it means to me. I wouldn't want to part with it."

Lucy pushed the locket toward the teacher. "No, Miz Allison, I can't do that. If we can't pay, Dovey can't go."

Their eyes met across the desk. Finally, Mrs. Allison picked up the locket. "All right, Mrs. Carpenter. I'll take it. I can see this is important to you. I hope Dovey appreciates what you're doing."

"No, Miz Allison, Dovey can't know that I was the one to pay her way. Promise me you won't tell her."

"Why don't you want Dovey to know?"

"I told you, she don't like me. She'd never take somethin' from me."

The teacher hesitated for a moment before she leaned toward Lucy. "I'll tell her the School Board has provided for her to go."

"Do you think she'll believe you?"

"I don't see why not. It's not unusual for the board to help with something that will give credit to the school."

Lucy rose to leave. "Thank you for your help, Miz Allison."

"I'm glad I could help, and if there's anything I can do to help you, I'm here."

"I'll remember, Miz Allison, but I think I can get along all right on my own."

≈   ≈   ≈

Shadows had almost covered the mountains by the time Lucy started home. A chill in the late evening air nipped at her nose. She

125

pulled her shawl tight around her shoulders. Her throat felt bare. She laid her hand where the locket had hung. "Ma, I'm sorry, but I just had to see to it that Dovey goes on this trip."

A rain dove called in the distance. A lonesome feeling overwhelmed her. A teardrop ran down her cheek. She brushed at it with the back of her hand. "My throat may be bare, Ma, but my heart is full. I still have my memories." She moved her hand from her throat to her heart. "Anyway, that locket wasn't doing no good hanging round my neck. It'll do Dovey more good."

The shadows deepened. Lucy remembered all the stories she'd heard about boogers, witches, and haints. She wasn't sure if she believed them, but she didn't want to be caught out here in the dark by herself. She'd better hurry.

He was there before Lucy realized it. He blocked her path. That Herby Ledford—she'd know his ugly chuckle anywhere. "You still a-spying on me, girl?"

Lucy stepped to the other side of the trail. "No, I had me some business at the school to look after."

"So the new missus is trying to get herself educated, huh? Well, I'm gonna give you a different kind of education. One that will teach you to mind your own business."

If she ran, maybe the teacher would still be at the school. She dodged as Herby Ledford reached for her. She whirled in the road and headed back toward the school. Before she'd taken three steps, he had her by the nape of the neck.

He yanked her head backward. "When I finish with you, you ain't gonna be no better than Carpenter's first missus. Always a teasing the men with that flirty look of hern, but wouldn't put out. 'Cept maybe to one special man."

Lucy screamed as loud as she could. He capped his hand over her mouth. She bit down hard. The taste of blood filled her mouth. He jerked his hand free. "You little witch. Fight! I like my women to have some spirit."

She kicked at his groin. His grip loosened and he bent over in pain. She didn't lose a second. She had to hide! She could never outrun him. She darted into a laurel thicket. It smelled dank and musty. She shivered. She'd have to be quiet or he'd hear her. She edged her way to the center and sat huddled in the darkness, waiting.

Ledford swore and called out words that she'd never heard. She plugged her ears and tried to think of the prayer she'd heard Dovey pray. It wouldn't come. "God, I don't know any prayers, but help me anyhow, please!" Why didn't Holman come along or the teacher? She unplugged her ears and listened. She couldn't hear anything except Ledford's beating and thrashing of the bushes. Maybe God didn't hear Indian prayers. Suddenly from the distance, she heard hoofbeats. She waited breathlessly. The hoofbeats stopped and she heard the creak of leather as the rider dismounted.

"What's going on here? Did you lose somethin'?" Lucy heard the sheep-shearing voice she'd heard on the mountain.

"Thought I saw a bear in the bushes. Gonna shoot him if I can. Ain't had no bear meat at our house in a week of Sundays." Lucy could hear them thrashing through the bushes. "I don't see nothing over here. It's getting late. Let's go. We'll come back and look for his tracks tomorrow. Can't see nothing out here in the dark."

Lucy listened until the hoofbeats faded. She crawled from her hiding place. It was a good thing it was dark. She'd just slip into the house and maybe no one would notice her mussed up dress. The last thing she wanted was to have to answer a lot of questions. She'd stay closer to home from now on.

≈　≈　≈

The few days following Lucy's trip to see the teacher were busy ones. She didn't have much time to think about the loss of her locket or the man on the road. Bessie came often to help her learn. Her progress as a student was slow, but Bessie's teaching wouldn't take any prizes either. Bessie had kept her word about reading from the Bible, and Lucy enjoyed the stories.

Bessie was gathering her belongings to go home one afternoon as the children began to straggle through the door from school. "I'm going! I'm really going!" sang Dovey as she skipped into the kitchen.

"Going where?" asked Bessie.

"To Asheville to be in the spelling contest."

"You don't say so!" said Bessie. "Guess you'll have the big head—'specially if you win."

"You're just jealous because a Jones didn't get picked to go."

"Wouldn't have mattered. We can't buy groceries—don't see how we'd pay for a trip like that."

"Well, we ain't paying. Miz Allison said the School Board was giving a scholarship, and I've been chosen to go." Lucy dumped the leftover coffee into the slop bucket by the back door.

"No wonder that school is always wanting money," said Bessie, "wasting it on sending young-uns traipsing all over the country!"

Lucy kept her back to Bessie and Dovey. It still hurt whenever she thought about her locket. If they saw her face, they'd know for sure what she'd done.

"I'll see you next week, Lucy."

"All right, Bessie. And thanks for your help."

Dovey looked at Lucy. "What kinda help is she giving you?"

"Nothing special."

Dovey's eyes fell on her mother's Bible. The look on her face changed. "What's Ma's Bible doing out here on the table?" She grabbed the book and hugged it to her chest.

"Me and Bessie was just looking up somethin'."

Dovey's blue eyes snapped. "Well, if you and Bessie want to use a Bible, she'd better bring hers 'cause nobody uses Ma's Bible unless I say so."

Lucy wanted to slap her. She raised her hand but instead turned to the water bucket and began to fill the coffee pot. "When you've put the Bible away, we need some water from the spring."

"That's the boys' job."

Lucy didn't bother to answer. She heard the bedroom door open and then close behind Dovey. She sat down at the table and cupped her face in her hands. This was getting to be too much. Dovey wasn't getting any easier to live with and that Herby Ledford was still a problem. Why on earth was he still after her? She'd stayed close to home all winter. Why did he think she was spying on him? On the mountain the day of the turkey hunt, he'd warned her to forget what she'd heard. What had she heard? All she could remember about their first meeting was hoping she could get a ride off the mountain, and how scared she was of his voice. What had he said? If she could remember, then she'd know why he was worried about her.

"What are you thinking about?"

Lucy looked up. Holman stood on the other side of the table. She had been so deep in thought that she hadn't heard him come in. "I'm glad you're home, Holman."

"What's wrong?"

How much should she tell Holman about her attacker, or should she tell him anything? Thank God no one had seen her that night. And Dovey. She didn't want to get her into trouble. She was already hard enough to live with.

"From that worried look on your face, I'd say you've seen the man that was after you when you was turkey hunting."

She nodded as she watched Holman's eyes cloud with concern. She'd have to be careful how she told him. She didn't want him to go running off and get himself killed. Then she'd never get away from here. "No, he didn't hurt me. Just said a lot of nasty things."

Holman pounded his fist on the table. "If I ever get up with that varmint, I'm gonna teach him a lesson he'll never forget. Now, about Dovey. Has she given you any more trouble? I promised her a trip out behind the barn if she didn't straighten up."

"She ain't done nothing, but she has somethin' to tell you."

"I hope it's good. Ain't in no mood to fool around with somethin' that don't amount to a hill of beans."

"She's in the bedroom. You want me to fetch her?" She moved toward the door. "Dovey, your Pa's home." She turned back to Holman. "I'll leave you two alone. What she has to tell you is special."

"You don't have to go. You're part of this family."

"I know, but I think it's best." Dovey passed Lucy on her way out of the bedroom and gave her a dirty look.

"Is Dovey in some kind of trouble?" asked Hattie as Lucy entered the front room.

"No. Why do you ask?"

"I heard you call her, and usually when we see Pa alone, it means we're in trouble."

Lucy thought about the way Dovey had acted about the Bible. If she'd told Holman about it, there would have been trouble. She was glad she hadn't said anything.

"I heard her sass you. Did you tell Pa?"

"Ain't none of your business what I told your Pa, Hattie. And if you must know, Dovey's telling him about her trip."

"That's all we'll hear about till she goes. She thinks she's so smart. She ain't no smarter than me. Ain't my fault they don't have a spelling bee for ten year olds."

"You'll have your turn, Hattie. Now, it's Dovey's. Let's try and be happy for her."

Hattie tossed her head of blond curls. "Don't plan on making her feel no better than she already does. Seems to me somebody needs to bring Miss Smarty Pants down a little bit."

Lucy caught Hattie by the shoulders and shook her. "Remember our deal. If I catch you spying on Dovey or anyone else, I'm telling your pa what you've been up to."

Hattie's blue eyes widened in feigned innocence. "I ain't gonna do nothing, Lucy. Promise." She crossed her chest with her arms.

Lucy could see she had her fingers crossed under her left arm. "You'd better behave."

"I will." Hattie bounced out the front door.

"Where's Hattie going in such a hurry?" asked Holman as he and Dovey came out of the kitchen.

"Pro'bly out to play before it gets too dark."

"Or somebody asks her to do somethin'," said Harley from the front door.

"Since you're talking about doing somethin', Harley, Lucy needs the water buckets filled," said Holman.

"I just came in to tell you that the peddler is a-coming up the road."

Lucy's heart pounded. At last she would be leaving this place. Someone else could take care of these children. She was going to be free!

It didn't take long for the word to spread that the peddler was coming. Once again, the Carpenters gathered in the front yard to await his arrival. It seemed to Lucy as though the wagon would never make it up the long road to the house.

Hattie danced around in circles. "It's my turn to get somethin' from the peddler," she sang. The others ignored her.

Lucy took her by the arm and said in a low voice, "Hattie, didn't Fannie let you have her turn the last time?"

Hattie gave Lucy an innocent look. "Yeah, but . . ."

"No buts about it, Hattie. I think it's only fitting that you let Fannie have your turn this time."

Hattie pulled away from Lucy. "Fannie owes . . ." Hattie's voice broke.

Lucy glanced toward Holman. He hadn't caught Hattie's protest. "Remember our deal, Hattie. You'd be smart to do what I say." Hattie gave Lucy a dirty look and sauntered off toward where Fannie stood. Lucy watched as Fannie's eyes lit up. She nodded toward Hattie. Hattie stuck out her tongue and ran toward the house.

"Where's she going?" asked Holman as he came up behind Lucy.

"Don't know. She just told Fannie she could take her turn with the peddler."

Holman shook his head. "I don't understand that one. Just when I think there's no hope for her, she goes and does somethin' nice."

Lucy watched Holman as he twisted his mustache. He would know what Hattie was really like if he spent more time at home. He'd also know why she had to get away from here. "You can never tell what young-uns will do."

"Guess you're right, or grown-ups either. Take the peddler, I didn't expect to see him so soon. I thought it would be early summer before Jake was up and about."

The peddler's wagon pulled to a halt in front of the house. Annie May ran with open arms to greet him. Holman greeted him with an outstretched hand. "Glad to see you out and about so soon, Jake."

"You got any goodies for my animals this time?" asked Annie May.

"Ain't got goodies for anybody this time. Ain't gonna be a peddler any more."

A look of dismay swept over the upturned faces. "No goodies!" they all exclaimed at once. "How come?"

131

Lucy felt her legs grow weak. She had waited all winter to go with the peddler and now he wasn't going. Or maybe he was. Surely he hadn't come to stay in these parts, and if he didn't have peddling to do, he could take her straight to her ma's people.

"We'll never get nothing now," said Mary sadly.

"What're you gonna do?" several voices asked at once.

The peddler ran his hand through his dark curly hair. "Ain't rightly sure. Got a few leads on a job. Do you mind if I spend a couple of weeks in your barn loft?"

Holman rubbed his forehead with his left arm. His eyebrows were knit together. Lucy had learned that look meant he was worried. "Be glad to help you out as much as I can, Jake. I can give you a roof over your head and somethin' to eat for a few days."

"I'd sure appreciate that, Holman. I don't take something for nothing, so I'll help with the chores or anything else I can do."

Lucy stepped up beside Holman. "When Bessie was here the other day, she was a-saying she didn't know how they were gonna get spring planting done. Maybe he could get a job working for Bessie."

"I know they could use the help, but I don't know if they can hire a man. Jake, you remember the Joneses, don't you?"

Jake nodded. "Heard he was shot right before the last trip I made. I'd be happy to help them out any way I can."

Holman placed his hand on Lucy's shoulder. "Ain't such a bad idea, Lucy. Let's eat supper and get some sleep. Tomorrow morning we'll take Jake up and see what they have to say."

Lucy could still feel the weight of Holman's hand on her shoulder as she turned toward the house to start supper. His touch had the same kind of concern as she'd seen in his eyes earlier. Well, she couldn't afford to worry about his feelings now. She had to figure out a way to pay the peddler for taking her. If she was right about his kind, he wouldn't be staying around long.

≈   ≈   ≈

The next morning Holman reined the horse and wagon into the Joneses' yard. The peddler jumped down from the wagon seat, turned to Lucy, and offered her his arm. "Allow me, madam."

Lucy returned his steady gaze and smiled. She took his arm and stepped down. Wasn't any use acting like he bothered her. Maybe if she was extra nice to him, he'd take her to Cherokee without any pay.

Bessie stood on the porch with her hands on her hips. "Lawd me," she said, "if it ain't Jake the peddler!" She came down the porch steps and reached toward Jake with an outstretched hand. "How are you? Holman said at Thanksgiving you'd had a run of bad luck."

He took her hand in his and kissed it. "Could say that, Bessie, and don't seem like it's over yet. Seems things ain't been too good up here. Sorry to hear about your brother. If there's anything at all I can do, let me know."

"I'll do that, Jake, and thanks for your offer."

"How's Mrs. Jones doing?" asked Jake.

"Poor thing's a-wasting away. Just can't get her interested in much at all."

"Do you all need some farm help? I'm looking for a job. Sometimes it lifts a person's spirits seeing the work get done."

Bessie's face broke into a smile. "Could be. I have to admit it gets on a person's nerves when there's so much to do and no one to do it."

"Well, you see, since my run of bad luck last fall, I'm getting out of the peddling business. I'm going to be staying over at Holman's place for awhile. If you need any help, I'll be glad to lend you a hand."

"It's for sure there's plenty of work to be done, but ain't got no money to pay a hired hand."

"Ain't looking for pay, Bessie. Just be willing to help a friend out for a place to stay," said Jake.

"Now if that ain't right nice of you, Jake." She took him by the arm and they walked toward the porch steps. "Seeing how Lucy's got a man down at her place to watch out for her, why don't you come on up here and stay for awhile? I'd feel better if there was a man around, and I'm sure the missus would too. Ain't much to eat, but if it'll help you out, you're welcome to stay."

Jake put an arm around Bessie's shoulders and hugged her tight.

"Bessie, you've got a heart as big as all outdoors. I'd be happy to stay. Don't want you worrying about them haints."

"As I told Holman's family when you got beat up over at Crying Rock, I'm too big and ugly for the haints."

Jake kissed her on the cheek. "You're the best looking lady in these parts."

Bessie blushed. "Your sweet talking got you an apple pie for supper, but you'll have to bed down out in the hayloft."

"Get your stuff out of the wagon," said Holman. "I'll help you get settled in while the womenfolk visit."

Bessie waited for Holman and Jake to leave, then she turned to Lucy and placed an arm around her shoulders. "Come on in the kitchen, dearie. Coffee's made. Maybe we'll have time for you to show me how you're doing with writing your name."

They walked across the porch. Lucy looked for the old dog that had greeted her the last time she was here. He wasn't anywhere in sight, but the black cat lay stretched out on the porch rail, his long black tail swishing back and forth, waiting. She wrinkled up her nose. This place sure did smell like death!

≈ 13 ≈

The warm April sun brought new life to the mountains. The scent of flowering honeysuckle vines and freshly plowed earth filled the air. The children were eager to shed their shoes, but Dovey insisted they wear them until May. Her ma'd always told her that the weather would be warm enough by then to keep them from catching colds.

Lots of people had their potatoes planted. Thanks to the peddler, the Joneses weren't behind this spring. Jake spent most of his evenings on the Carpenter's front porch telling his ghost stories.

The day before Dovey was to leave for Asheville, she pressed her church dress and folded her good petticoat. Holman came in and handed her a box. "I thought since this was your first trip away from home, it would only be fitting that you have your first store-bought dress."

Dovey opened the box and lifted out the nicest pink dress she'd ever seen. "Pa, you didn't have to do this. How did you pay for it?"

"I ain't yet, but don't you worry none . . . things is gonna get better."

Dovey shook the dress and held it against herself. "Oh Pa, it's beautiful! Guess I'd better press out the wrinkles."

Hattie burst through the door with her usual impish expression. She stopped short at the sight of Dovey with the new dress. "Ain't fair that Dovey gets a new store-bought dress." She stuck out her tongue.

"When I get home from my trip, I'll let you wear it," called Dovey over her shoulder.

Hattie followed her into the kitchen. "You know I can't wear it. It's too big for me."

"Maybe we could take it up a little bit." Dovey remembered how it had hurt when she'd cut up her ma's dresses and sewed them into clothes for the little girls. It would be a lot easier to cut up her own.

135

She spread the dress on the table and spit on the flat iron. It was too hot. She'd have to let it cool while she packed the rest of her stuff in the box.

"Don't want to wear your old store-bought dress. Besides, Pa said I could have the new flour sack, and I'm gonna dye it red," Hattie taunted as she followed her back into the front room.

Dovey felt a tinge of sadness. She'd wanted to make Martha a dress from the flour sack. The day her pa had brought it home, she'd thought how she'd make it. "There ain't enough in that flour sack to make you nothing. Martha could get a new dress from it."

"Too bad—it's mine," Hattie threw over her shoulder as she headed back toward the kitchen.

Dovey shook her head. That young-un didn't have a unselfish bone in her body. Maybe she shouldn't take this trip. The little ones needed so much. She glanced over at Lucy, who was sewing a patch on a pair of Carl's overalls. And could she trust Cow's Tail Lucy while she was gone? She guessed it was too late to back out now. Mrs. Allison was counting on her. She shoved her long hair behind her ears and crinkled up her nose. "You smell somethin', Lucy?"

Lucy sniffed the air. "Smells like somebody's burning somethin'." She clinched a piece of thread between her teeth and bit. "Pro'bly somethin' outside." She reached for her needle.

Dovey sniffed again. "Smells more like it's coming from the kitchen."

The words were barely out of Dovey's mouth when Arthur appeared in the doorway. "Somebody's burning up a dress out here on the table."

Dovey gulped and pushed Arthur aside. "No! It can't be!"

Lucy and Arthur followed Dovey into the kitchen. The pink dress lay on the table with the flat iron sitting on the hem. Dovey raced over and grabbed the iron, then sank into a chair. "I was just gonna press out the wrinkles. I left the iron standing right here to cool a little bit." She pointed at a spot on the table.

"You sure you didn't forget and leave it setting down?" asked Lucy.

She glared at Lucy. Just like that Cow's Tail Lucy to blame her. "Now why would I do somethin' crazy like that!"

Arthur put his arms around his sister. She pushed him away. "Ain't my fault," she sobbed. Could Lucy somehow be to blame? No, she hadn't left the room, but it would be like her to mess up the only new dress she'd ever had. Maybe she'd gotten one of the children to do it. No, there wasn't any of them mean enough to do something like this. She guessed she'd have to make do with the dress she wore to church. It wasn't anything special, but at least it wasn't patched like the rest of her clothes.

"Nobody's saying it's your fault, Dovey. The iron pro'bly just got knocked over somehow." Lucy picked up the dress and looked at it.

"Can it be fixed?" asked Dovey.

"Ain't long enough to hem up again." Lucy brushed at the burned spot with her fingers.

Dovey buried her head in her arms and sobbed louder. "Ain't fair after I worked so hard for this trip."

Lucy laid the dress down. "Arthur, where's Hattie?"

"Out by the barn playing with the twins. Why?"

"I was just wondering if she'd let me use that flour sack of hers."

Dovey rubbed her nose on her sleeve and peeked at Lucy. What could Cow's Tail Lucy be up to now? "You know she'd never let you have that sack. Anyway, what do you want with it?"

"I was just thinking that maybe I could make a ruffle to put around the hem. You'd never be able to see the burnt spot then."

"Hattie'll never let you use it." Dovey rubbed her eyes with the back of her hand. It would be just like Lucy to mess up Hattie's sack, too. And besides, she had no business deciding how the dress would be fixed.

"You leave her to me," said Lucy. "Now take that flour sack and rinse it out so tonight after supper I can make your dress good as new."

Dovey took the sack from the shelf over the cook table and began to fill the dishpan with water. She hesitated and looked at Lucy. Was it possible this woman that rode around on a cow's tail would do something to help her go on her trip? She'd do what Lucy said and see what happened.

Arthur said, "I almost forgot. I just came in to let you both know the peddler's outside. Wants to know if he can borrow one of Pa's hoes. I'd ask John, but I can't find him."

"You wash the sack, Dovey. I need to have a word with Jake." Outside, Lucy found Jake sitting on the edge of the porch.

He looked up at Lucy. "I heard you arguing with Dovey. What was it all about?"

"Wasn't arguing. Somehow, Dovey's new dress got burnt. I'm gonna fix it with the flour sack she's washing out."

"You're always fixing something around here."

"I try and earn my keep."

"A good looking filly like yourself shouldn't find that hard to do."

Lucy felt her face grow warm. He had no right to call her a filly. And how she earned her keep was her business. Her black eyes softened. She had a reason for talking to him. Best not to get on his bad side, or he wouldn't let her have the combs. That is, if he still had them. "Remember last summer when you came around, and Dovey used her turn to buy cloth for the littl'-uns new dresses?"

"Yeah, for Dovey that wasn't unusual. She hardly ever got anything for herself."

"I know. I wish Hattie was a little like her. You remember those combs she looked at? The ones with the row of pearls on them?"

"Why yeah, in fact, I still have 'em."

"I was hoping so. Would there be a chance you'd let me have them for Dovey?"

The peddler ran his hand through his dark wavy hair and grinned up at Lucy. "Well, I guess I could, and I'm sure we can work out some way for you to pay for them before I leave."

Lucy's hand reached for her throat. Then she remembered. The locket was gone—gone to pay for a trip for an ungrateful young-un. And here she was trying again to fix things for her.

Jake's eyes twinkled. "Don't worry. Holman's credit is good."

The peddler was right. It was Holman's young-un, let him do the paying. Besides, she had to think of some way to get him to take her with him now that the locket was gone. She turned to go into the house. What did he mean by *before he left?* She hoped he didn't plan to leave soon. At least not until Dovey returned from her trip. She couldn't go off and leave the little ones without somebody to watch them.

Back in the kitchen, she found Hattie fuming. "What's my flour sack doing wet?"

"I had Dovey rinse it out."

"You had no right to do that, Lucy. It's my sack, and I'll do the washing."

"I'm gonna use your sack to mend Dovey's dress, Hattie."

"You're gonna do what?"

"You heard me, Hattie."

Hattie grabbed the wet sack. "You can't. It's mine. Pa said so!"

Lucy picked up the new pink dress. If her guess was right, Hattie probably had something to do with this. "Do you know anything about how this happened, Hattie?"

Hattie looked at the burned spot with surprise. Her eyes grew large as she backed away. "You . . . you think I'd burn a brand new store-bought dress? I might say mean stuff, but I'd never ruin Dovey's new dress."

"You just said the other night that she needed to be brought down a notch. You sure you didn't burn the dress?"

Once again Hattie crossed her heart with her arms, but this time her fingers weren't crossed. Lucy lowered her eyebrows and studied the expression on Hattie's face. Could she be misjudging this young-un? "Maybe you didn't, but I can see you ain't sorry it happened."

Hattie smiled. "Can't say as I am, but it ain't my fault, and that's all that matters."

Lucy set a chair next to the stove. Maybe it wasn't her fault, but her attitude was her fault or her pa's. She was a spoiled young-un that needed to learn to give. "I'm gonna use the sack to make a ruffle to cover the burnt spot."

"And I'll tell Pa."

"That's fine, Hattie, and I'll just have a little talk with him myself."

Hattie let her bottom lip drop. "Ain't fair at all."

"Maybe if you'd try being a little more giving, you wouldn't feel that way."

"Here, take the old flour sack. I don't care. Wasn't big enough to

139

make me nothing nohow." Hattie turned to leave the room. "When I went out earlier, I heard somethin' fall. I guess it could have been the iron. I didn't look back."

Lucy hung the flour sack over the chair to dry. So that was how the dress had got burned. Dovey had left the iron on the table to cool, and when Hattie went out, she probably slammed the door. That's when the iron fell on it. She had sensed Hattie was a little bit sorry. Maybe she'd been too hard on her. Could it be all this bright-eyed, curly-headed little girl needed was some extra attention? She vowed to try to give it to her while Dovey was away.

≈ ≈ ≈

Lucy shaded her eyes with her hand as she watched the wagon fade out of sight. Holman was on his way to take Dovey to meet Mrs. Allison. Dovey's hair was neatly held in place with the combs Lucy had given her. Also, the dress with the flour sack ruffle had been carefully folded and packed in her box. She would wear it tomorrow at the spelling bee.

"Are you ready?" asked Annie May.

"Ready for what, Annie May?"

"The peddler said he'd go with me to see the deer. You said you'd come, too. We need to hurry. The peddler will be waiting. He said he'd meet us on the trail."

Lucy looked toward the sinking sun. She remembered her promise to see that she gave Hattie more attention. Maybe this would be a good time to give Hattie some responsibility. She looked down at Annie May. "You sure we'll have time before it gets dark?"

"The best time to catch the deer is at dusk. It won't matter if it's dark on the way home. We'll take the lantern."

"Ain't sure I want to be out there in the dark with someone that tells haint stories."

"Come on, Lucy. You know there ain't nothing out there. Besides, I think it'll be fun."

Lucy went to get her shawl. "Hattie!"

Hattie poked her head around the kitchen door. "What do you want now?"

"I'm gonna go with Annie May to see the deer. Could you keep a eye on the littl'-uns while I'm gone?"

Hattie looked surprised. "You'd trust me to watch out for the littl'-uns?"

"Why not, Hattie? John's out in the barn if you need anything."

Hattie's face lit up. "Should I get them ready for bed?"

"That would be good, but if they give you too much trouble, just leave them, and I'll help you."

Hattie picked up Martha. "Have a good walk and don't worry. I can manage just fine."

Lucy gave Hattie a pat on the arm. She hadn't expected her to want to help. She'd start giving her more jobs, but how would Dovey like that? She'd have to be careful. Dovey had acted pleased that she'd fixed her dress. And the combs had put a big smile on her face. Still, she had a feeling her troubles with Dovey weren't over. She rushed out to catch up with Annie May. "Wait," she called.

Annie May stopped and looked back. "The peddler's waiting. I see him up yonder."

Lucy's heart quickened with her pace, but it wasn't all due to her rushing. There was something about this peddler man that made her feel light-headed.

"See, I brought the lantern," Annie May said as she handed it to Lucy.

Lucy took her free hand. "Having the lantern makes me feel better, Annie May, but you carry it."

"Hurry up, you two," called the peddler.

"We're coming." Annie May pulled free from Lucy and ran toward the peddler.

"What's the lantern for?"

"Lucy's afeared it'll get dark before we get home. Guess she's afeared of your haints."

The peddler chuckled. "Don't you trust me to keep the haints away, Lucy?"

"I'm more afeared of you being the haint."

"Would you listen to her, Annie May? You'd think I was the big bad wolf."

Annie May giggled and handed Jake the lantern. "Here, can you carry it, please? I want to look for wildflowers." Annie May ran ahead and soon came back clutching a fistful of purple violets. She looked toward the sinking sun and ran back to Lucy and Jake, pointing up at the sky. "Look up there! See the birds circling? What are they?"

The peddler shaded his eyes and looked up. "They're buzzards, Annie May. Must be something dead."

"Why's that?"

Jake looked at Annie May. "That's what buzzards feed off of."

"Ugh! How awful. I hope we don't see it. I don't like dead things, do you, Lucy?"

Lucy shook her head. "Nobody does, Annie May, but sometimes it happens." The ache she'd felt when her ma died settled over her as though it had never left. How could her pa send her away from the place where she felt closest to her ma?

They were almost at the clearing where the deer fed. Annie May ran ahead. Suddenly, she crumpled to the ground. Lucy ran to her. Her pale face looked even paler.

"What's wrong, honey?"

She pointed. "It's dead, Lucy. The baby deer is dead."

Lucy looked toward the clearing. A fawn lay on its side. The legs stuck out and its stomach was ripped open. Lucy felt sick. She gathered Annie May in her arms. "It's all right, Annie May. Just don't look."

The peddler inspected the fawn then came back to Lucy. "Looks like a hungry animal got him."

Lucy remembered the other night when she'd heard something that sounded like a panther screaming. Annie May pulled herself free from Lucy. "We just can't leave him out here for the other animals to eat."

"You're right, Annie May," said Jake. "We'll have to bury him, but we'll need a shovel. You wait here with Lucy, and I'll go get one."

"No! You wait with Lucy. I'll go for the shovel."

"No, you . . ." Lucy protested.

Jake put his hand on her arm. "I think that's a good idea, Annie May. You run along and get the shovel. Lucy and me will wait right here for you."

Annie May headed for the house running. Lucy turned to face Jake. "Why did you go and do that?"

"It's better that she goes for the shovel instead of sitting here looking at that dead fawn."

"I guess you're right." Lucy walked over to where the fawn lay. Yes, it was better that this pale-faced young-un that didn't like dead things be spared all the pain she could. "Life sure can be cruel, can't it?" She felt Jake's presence behind her, but he didn't answer her question. The sun sank behind the mountains. The shadows moved across them as silently as the ghosts he told stories about. In the distance, the frogs sang in unison. Lucy quivered.

"Are you cold?"

"No, just . . ." Her long black hair fell over her shoulders. Jake had removed the pins that held it in place.

She felt his cold hand beneath her hair as it touched her warm neck. The hand slid down to her shoulder and turned her to face him. Their lips came together. Jake's arms encircled her waist. He pulled her close.

Lucy could feel the hardness of his body against hers. Her mind whirled. No, this wasn't right. She was a married woman. She brought her hands up and pushed against him. "No!" she gasped and turned away.

He took her by the shoulders and turned her around. "Look at me, Lucy."

She looked up. There was a hurt look in his blue eyes. No, maybe it was more of a 'I-need-to-know' look.

"You've never . . . you know, been with a man, have you?" She blushed and looked away. Wasn't none of his business. "Then what you told me last spring about your marriage to Holman ain't changed?"

"That's right." She stepped back. "He just needed someone to care for the littl'-uns so the older young-uns could go back to school."

"Don't be ashamed." He reached for her again. "Let me be the one to teach you."

Lucy took another step back. "Jake, no matter why I'm here, I'm still a married woman."

"Come on, Lucy, you've known there's something between us—has been since the minute we first saw each other. All you mean to Holman is someone to take care of that bunch of young-uns."

"You're right. I ain't never slept with a man."

"Well then . . ."

She turned around and sat down on a stump. "It's like this, Jake. When I sleep with a man, I'm not only gonna be married to him, but I'm gonna love him."

Jake put his right foot up on another stump and studied Lucy's face for a few minutes. As he started to speak, Annie May called, "It took me a little while. I had to find the shovel."

Lucy stood and quickly pinned up her hair. She noticed Annie May had her old tattered quilt tucked under her arm. Why did this young-un have to drag that old quilt around with her all the time? It sure was dirty. Maybe she'd wash it the next wash day. "I should have told you to look where Harley was digging for fishing worms." She reached her hand out to Annie May.

Jake took the shovel, moved to the edge of the woods, and began to dig. The earth was loose, and it didn't take him long to dig a shallow grave. "I think we're going to need the light to finish by." He took the lantern Lucy handed him and lit it. "Here, you hold the light, Lucy. I'll get the deer."

Annie May hid her face in Lucy's skirt as Jake dragged the fawn to the grave and rolled him in. "Now, we need to cover him up."

Annie May peeked from behind the folds of Lucy's skirt. She took a step forward. "Wait!" She held out the tattered quilt. "Put my quilt over him so he won't be cold." Tears welled up in Lucy's eyes. So much for the washing! There was always the new quilt. As soon as she finished hemming it, she'd give it to her.

Jake took the quilt, folded it, and draped it over the deer. Without saying any more, he began to shovel dirt into the grave. Lucy bit her lower lip to hold back the sobs that rose in her throat. She felt Annie May's tears as they splashed on her hand. Somehow, she knew this wasn't the end of their heartaches.

≈   ≈   ≈

Lucy picked up the bunch of wilted violets at the edge of the clearing. Annie May had dropped them there last evening. She walked over to the fresh mound of earth, bent, and placed them on it. She could still feel the warmth of Annie May's tears on her hand. The heaviness she felt in her heart was still there. She sensed Jake's presence before he spoke.

"It's over, Lucy. Let it be."

She turned. "Then why do I feel that it's just the beginning?"

Jake shrugged his shoulders and walked toward her. Her heart didn't race the way it had yesterday. He pulled her into his arms and buried his face in her hair. She felt her body grow warm against his. He tilted her head and kissed her on the throat. He worked his way up till their lips touched, and for that moment, the only world that existed was theirs.

Lucy pulled away. "Jake, we've got to talk."

"I know, Lucy." He reached for her again.

Lucy watched the muscle in his jaw work up and down. There must be something awfully wrong with him from the look in his eyes. She'd just get on back to the house. The last thing she needed was to bother with somebody with troubles. She had enough of her own. She started toward the path.

"Come back here. I'll tell you anything you want to know."

"You can't be from around here, 'cause you don't talk like mountain people do. Whereabouts you from?"

"From down around the ocean. Used to work on ships. That was before my wife died."

Lucy kicked a loose clump of dirt. So that was what she had seen in his eyes. He'd loved and lost. "How did she die?"

Jake sat down on a stump. "Trying to give me a child. Doctors told us it would kill her and it did . . ." His voice broke, and he stared off into the distance. Lucy sensed he was in another world. She touched his shoulder and waited for him to return.

Jake shook his head as though to clear away his thoughts. "After my wife died, I lived in a daze for months. Then I started my peddling business. It was kind of nice traveling around and meeting all sorts of people. I soon learned I wasn't the only one hurting. Seemed like about every family I come upon had some sort of problem."

"And the Carpenters. What kind of problem did you find here?"

Jake turned his face up toward hers. "Why do you think I found problems here?"

Lucy remembered her talk with Bessie. *Annie May!* Could it be possible Jake was her pa? Should she ask? "I was a-wondering about Annie May. She seems so fond of you, and she don't look like the other young-uns."

Jake turned from her. For a long while, the only sound in the clearing was the occasional chirp of a bird. Had she spoken too soon? Would he leave? And maybe she wouldn't get to go with him. She touched her throat. Her locket was gone, and now she was gonna lose her chance to go away with Jake. She watched his slouched shoulders. She did feel something about him. She even thought it might be love, but that wasn't going to be any help if he didn't feel the same way about her. Slowly, Jake turned. His eyes still had a faraway look about them. She was sure he wasn't going to answer her question.

His face relaxed, and the Jake she knew returned. "Are you trying to ask me if she belongs to me?"

Lucy nodded. At least he wasn't going to walk away.

"I've wondered about that. For one reason . . . her name . . . my wife's name was Annie May."

Lucy pushed back the urge to laugh. "Mary had pro'bly run out of names."

Jake raised an eyebrow. "No, Mary wasn't like that. All her young-uns were special to her."

Lucy could tell from the tone of Jake's voice that whatever had happened between him and Holman's wife, he didn't think badly of her. "Jake, she was a happily married woman with young-uns. You was a-taking another man's *real* wife."

"Happily married, you say. Life, married or not, ain't that simple. Mary was a beautiful, loving woman who found herself trapped out here in these mountains with a husband who was gone most of the time. I'm not saying she didn't love him. I know for a fact Holman worshiped her. I'm not trying to find excuses for her or me, but

146

loneliness can make a person do things they wished . . ." His voice trailed off.

". . . they hadn't." Lucy finished his sentence. "I guess I've been alone so much I wouldn't know."

Jake walked to Lucy, put his arms around her, and pulled her close. "I want to change that for you, Lucy. I want to take care of you, always."

Lucy pushed him away. "Jake, I need time to think. This is happening too quickly."

"You wanted to get away from here, didn't you? I can do that for you, Lucy. There's a whole world waiting out there. I'll give you a little time if that's what you want." He bent and kissed her on the cheek. "Don't take too long, though. And don't think too badly of Mary. Loneliness can cause people to do foolish things."

"You sure it ain't that loneliness you're feeling again?"

"No, Lucy, I've been in love. I know what I'm feeling for you."

There was a long silence in the clearing. In the distance the frogs began to croak. Shadows cut a path across the mountains. Lucy nodded, then disappeared into the gathering dusk.

~ *14* ~

Sunday dinner turned out to be a celebration. Dovey was home, and she'd won the spelling bee. Her brothers and sisters crowded around her to see the blue ribbon she'd won.

Lucy felt a tightness in her throat. She went to the window and looked out. She was sure her ma'd understand she'd found a man to love—a man who wanted to take her away from here. Seemed to her like there wasn't any use taking any more time thinking over what Jake had said. She'd been waiting all winter to get away from here. Besides, he loved her. And she *must* love him. At least it felt like love. If it wasn't love, she was sure it would turn into love. Then she'd have a good-looking husband and a whole passel of children of her own. She'd just go with Jake and get married again and this time it would be for real. She touched the bare spot on her neck. She'd done all she could for the young-uns. Now it was her time.

A chair scraped against the floor. Lucy turned from the window and saw Annie May's pale face staring across the table as she gripped the back of her chair. "I got somethin' to say to everybody."

"Go ahead, Annie May. We're listening," said Holman.

"Well, I just wanted you to know that at church this morning I asked Jesus to live in my heart. When the parson comes around, I'm gonna be baptized."

Dovey put her arms around Annie May and hugged her. "Ma'd be so happy, Annie May, and we'll all be there to see you be baptized, won't we, Pa?"

Holman nodded his head. "That's what families are for."

Annie May looked at Lucy. "Will you come?"

Lucy bowed her head. She wasn't sure what to say. She'd been wanting a reason to go to church, but would Jake stay around long enough? And how would Dovey feel about her going? She looked up to find Dovey glaring at her across the table. That did it. She'd go.

Surely, Jake would wait on her. "Course I will, Annie May, and I'll make you a new dress out of the scraps I've been saving."

Annie May clasped her hands. "Really, Lucy? You'd do that for me?"

"I'd be happy to."

Annie May turned toward her pa. "Pa, can I ask the peddler?"

"I think that he'd like that very much. Why don't you ask him the next time he comes down?" Holman pushed back his chair and stood. "I've got to tend to some chores out in the barn."

Lucy wondered if she dared go to the clearing with Holman home, but Jake would be waiting for her. She'd give Holman time to get to the barn and then she'd leave. Wasn't any of his business what she did. She was taking good care of his children, and that was all that should matter to him. "Dovey, you and the girls can do the dishes this evening. I'm gonna go for a little walk." She was surprised that neither Dovey nor Hattie had anything to say about her going.

As Lucy entered the clearing, no one was there. She wanted to call out Jake's name but thought better of it. What if some of the young-uns had followed her? She scouted the edge of the woods looking for him, then sat down on her stump to wait. She must be early. A faint rustling of dead leaves caused her to sit up straight. She listened. The rustling grew louder. She jumped up and started toward the path. What if it was that mean old Mr. Ledford? Suddenly she wanted to run, but her feet were glued to the ground. It could be the animal that had killed the fawn. It was more of a thrashing sound now. She saw a shadow and opened her mouth to scream, but no words came. The shadow emerged from behind a tree and there stood Holman.

"Lucy, what're you doing out here?"

"Just came to make sure nothing had dug up the fawn that Jake buried out here Friday evening. What're you doing here? I thought you had chores to do back at the barn."

"Annie May just told me about the fawn. I came out to see if there was any sign of a wild animal. Thought maybe if I came up through the woods, I'd see tracks, but I didn't see anything."

"What do you think it was, Holman?"

"It could've been a panther. Thought I heard one screaming the

149

other night. I'm gonna take the boys out hunting tomorrow. Might ask Jake to come. Maybe we can see some sign of it. Can't have wild animals so close. Ain't safe."

Lucy shivered and wrapped her arms around herself. Wild animals weren't the only reason to be afraid out here. A two-legged animal by the name of Herby Ledford was scary, too.

"Don't you guess we'd better be getting on back to the house? It's getting late."

Lucy scanned the edge of the clearing. "You looking for somethin', Lucy?"

"Not really. I was just a-wondering what was out there in the woods."

"Well, whatever's out there, let's leave it to another day. Come on. Let's get going."

She had to go with him, even though it meant not seeing Jake. What would he think when he came and didn't find her here? As they turned onto the path leading to the house, she saw something move in the bushes.

≈   ≈   ≈

The next morning Holman and the boys left to go hunting. School was out for spring planting. After breakfast Lucy said, "Dovey, you can take care of the dishes. I'm going up and visit with Bessie for a spell."

"You're getting awfully friendly with her."

"That's my business, Dovey. You just see that you take care of things here." She took a clean apron and tied it around her waist. This girl was going to be the death of her yet. Well, with the way things were going with the peddler, maybe not. Maybe she'd be gone from here soon.

She had reached a spot in the trail where the road turned off to the clearing. She stopped and looked up the path to where the trees began to thin. Why not? It would only take a few minutes. She moved swiftly up the trail as though something called to her.

The first thing she saw when she reached the clearing was the fresh mound of earth. The same sadness she'd felt the night they had

150

found the fawn returned. The earth had already begun to sink. She knelt and patted the ground. Tears splashed on the back of her hand. They felt warm, but inside she felt cold. The tears rolled off her hand and melted into the ground. A shadow moved in front of her. Herby Ledford—he was after her again. Before she could move, strong arms lifted her to her feet. She turned to face Jake.

"I hoped you'd be here," he whispered and drew her close. The warmth and tenderness Lucy had felt before returned. Her body relaxed against his. He tilted her face and kissed her.

A slow warmth crept up her throat. "I came the other evening, Jake, but Holman showed up and I had to go home with him. I was afeared you'd think I hadn't come."

Jake tightened his arms around her. "I saw what happened. When I got here, Holman had just stepped into the clearing. I waited. By the way, you did just fine."

"What do you mean, Jake?"

"The way you explained your being here and all."

"I was plenty scared, but I was more scared you wouldn't be back."

"Don't want to act too friendly around you. Can't have Holman getting any ideas. Why did you come here this morning?"

"I don't rightly know. I started up to visit with Bessie. When I got to the fork in the road, somethin' just drew me here."

"You know, I was starting up the mountain to find Holman and the boys. Suddenly, I had an urge to come by the clearing," Jake said as he ran his hand through his hair.

Lucy traced the outline of his face with her forefinger. Love. Was there something about it that drew people together? If there was, then she'd done right deciding to go with him. "Ain't no use wasting more time, Jake. You might as well know, right now, I decided to go away with you. We can get married and I can be a *real* wife. There's just one thing we have to wait for. Annie May's gonna be baptized. She's been a-waiting to ask you to come. She was disappointed you didn't come down last night."

Lucy felt Jake's body tense. "What's wrong, Jake? You'll come, won't you?"

"I hate to hurt that little girl, Lucy, but I ain't much on church."

"Will you just think about it? It would mean a lot to her."

Jake's face showed no reaction. "I'm not making any promises. I got to be going. Holman'll be wondering what happened to me."

"Ain't you forgetting somethin'?" Lucy asked playfully. Jake turned back with a grin and bent to kiss her. "No, not that, silly. Your gun! Can't hunt without a gun."

Jake picked up the gun where he'd dropped it. Lucy turned to go. "You'll think about what I asked you?"

"Yes, Lucy, but I'm only making you one promise."

"What's that?"

"When this panther business is over, we're making some plans for getting away from here." He kissed her lightly on the cheek. "I have to be going now. Holman'll be looking for me."

Lucy watched him vanish into the woods. She felt warm and good inside. Maybe Jake would decide to come to Annie May's baptizing, but most of all, he was really falling in love with her. It had been so long since she'd felt any kind of love. She missed her ma, missed her pa . . . missed her mountain, but if Jake really loved her, there'd be someone else to hold her, someone else to care. The sun broke through the clouds. Lucy smiled and headed down the path.

≈　　≈　　≈

Holman slammed the barn loft door. The hunt for the panther had not been successful. He'd had more reason for going hunting than looking for a panther though. He'd been looking for that two-legged varmint that had been pestering Lucy. And Jake wasn't hanging around these parts for nothing either. Could it be he was helping with this illegal business? He'd hoped to find out, but Jake hadn't done much talking. Well, he'd have to leave the panther hunting to the neighbor men. He had to get back to work.

He started toward the house. He supposed Lucy wouldn't be too happy about him leaving again with the panther still on the loose. He stepped inside. "Lucy, I have to go away for a week or so."

She looked surprised. "Won't you stay till you kill the panther?"

"I'd planned on it, but with Annie May's baptizing in a couple of weeks, I need to go now so I can be back."

152

Lucy nodded in agreement. "What about the panther? I don't want the boys out looking for him."

"I took care of that. Herby Ledford said he'd take some of the neighbors and go out looking for him." Lucy lowered her head and said nothing. "Don't look so worried, Lucy. He's the best hunter around here." Holman had an urge to reach out and touch her, to comfort her, but that was not in their bargain. He'd have to watch his feelings. Mary was his only love. "Somethin' else, Lucy. If I was you, I wouldn't be out after dark and please keep the young-uns close to the house."

Lucy looked startled. "Why? Are you afeared the panther will come around the house?"

"If it gets hungry enough, it might just do that. So keep an eye on things. I'll be back as soon as I can."

Lucy raised the firebox door and shoved in a stick of wood. Holman studied her. She sure was a mighty fine-looking woman—one who wasn't afraid of doing what she thought was right no matter what. It gave him a good feeling to be able to go off and not have to worry about things at home. It was too bad Dovey didn't realize how lucky she was to have someone like Lucy here to look after the little ones. He shook his head again. Yes, a fine-looking woman! He slipped from the kitchen, saddled up his horse, and rode away.

Lucy had just finished the dishes when Bessie knocked on the door. "Come on in, Bessie."

"Where's Holman off to? I just seen him ride away."

"Said he had some business to care for, and he had to do it this week before Annie May's baptizing."

"What about the panther?"

"Said Mr. Ledford would hunt for him. You know Bessie, the panther ain't the only thing we've got to be worried about."

"What're you trying to tell me, Lucy?"

"Well, I didn't say nothing about this earlier, seeing how there wasn't any need to be out and about much. Remember the man that was after me on the mountain at Thanksgiving?"

Bessie nodded and furrows lined her forehead. "Has there been more trouble, Lucy?"

"Back awhile, the same man gave me a good scare on the trail going to the school. I think there's more going on round here than we know."

Bessie rubbed the lines in her forehead with the back of her hand. "You could be right, Lucy. Wonder if it has somethin' to do with Luther's shooting?"

"Bessie, I've had a feeling ever since the night of the wake that there was a lot you ain't saying."

"Well, like I said that day, there's some things better not talked about."

"Holman's gone most of the time. You *do* have Jake."

"At least Jake's there part of the time, but he spends an awful lot of time somewhere else."

"Do you know if he will be down here tonight?"

"Pro'bly will. He goes somewhere about every night. If he don't come here, I don't know where he goes. Do you, Lucy?"

Lucy felt her pulse quicken. Could it be that Bessie knew about her and Jake? No, there was no way she could know. She felt her face grow warm as she thought about what Bessie would think about her when she left with Jake. She pushed the thought out of her mind and said, "I ain't Jake's keeper. Why'd you ask me?"

"I was just a-wondering. He's different lately."

"What do you mean, different?"

"I don't know. Seems like a man in love."

Lucy turned her back to Bessie. She had to give her friend credit for being able to read people's feelings. If she'd had any doubts about Jake's feelings, they were gone now. "I wouldn't know about that. He comes down here once in awhile to tell the young-uns his haint stories. Anyway, Annie May has been waiting for him to come so she can ask him to her baptizing. That's the only reason I asked if he was coming down tonight."

"When's Annie May gonna be baptized?"

"In a couple of weeks when the parson comes."

Bessie leaned back in her chair. "You going?"

"Wouldn't miss it." Lucy pulled out a chair and sat down at the table with Bessie. No, she wouldn't want to miss Annie May's baptizing. It would be the last thing she'd be able to do for the child.

Bessie opened the lesson book. "I ain't much on church, but I usually go to the baptizing and funerals. Most everyone does. Now let's get down to your lesson. You know, you're learning real good."

Lucy worked on her writing, wondering where Jake went every night. He sure didn't come here, and she didn't meet him after dark. Maybe he was out with that Herby Ledford looking for the panther or seeing about a job somewhere.

≈　　≈　　≈

A few days later, Lucy tied her bonnet on and started up the mountain. She felt lighthearted as she turned onto the path that led to the clearing. She heard footsteps behind her. All she needed was one of the little ones tagging along. She turned to see Jake strolling toward her with a broad grin on his face. "If I was a superstitious man, I'd think you could read my thoughts, Lucy Carpenter. You sure you don't have a little witchcraft in you?"

Lucy grinned. "Don't you wish you knew?"

Jake's voice grew serious. "I hope to find that out."

Lucy slipped her hand in his, and they walked the rest of the way in silence. When they reached the clearing, she pulled her hand away and rushed over to the grave. "Look how much the dirt has sunk. I wish I'd brought a shovel to fill it in."

"It'll be all right, Lucy. It's not a human's grave, you know. Come sit over here. We need to talk."

Lucy sat down on a stump. "I can't stay. I told Dovey I wouldn't be long, so someone might come looking for me. Where have you been all week? Annie May's been waiting to ask you to come to her baptizing."

"Bessie's been keeping me busy. She's been acting kind of strange towards me."

The talk she'd had with Bessie rushed back to her mind. Something was wrong here. She felt it in her bones. Could Jake be a part of it? No, he'd been on the road then with his peddling business. Whatever was happening on this mountain didn't have anything to do with Jake. Maybe she ought to ask him where he went every night.

No, if she loved him, she had to trust him. Besides, he was a man and men didn't want women to know about their business. "Bessie was down to the house the other day. She was asking me questions about you."

"What kind of questions?"

"She said you acted like a man in love. She asked me if I knew where you went most every night."

"What did you say?"

"I said you spent some nights on our porch telling haint stories."

"Well, that's no lie."

"I know, but you don't come *every* night."

Jake shrugged his shoulders. "I don't much care what she thinks. Ain't important to me. It's what *you* think that's important."

"It really matters to you about what I feel and think?"

Jake pulled her to her feet, crushing her to him. "For the first time since my wife died, I feel alive. Yes, you do matter. In fact, you're the only one that matters." He kissed her.

Lucy was taken by surprise. It was not the same sweet kiss he usually gave her. What was happening? She didn't know kissing could be like this. She felt her face grow warm and pulled away. Now was not the time to start something she had no intention of finishing. "I have to get going. The young-uns might come looking for me."

"When are we gonna talk and make plans? I've been thinking about leaving the day after Annie May's baptizing."

"Leaving!" Lucy felt her heart leap in her chest. "That's so soon, but Annie May will be glad we'll be here for her baptizing. Why don't you come down to the house in the morning? We can talk while everyone's at church. Even if Holman comes home, he won't think nothing about you being at the house."

Jake nodded as Lucy started toward the path. He called after her, "I'll be down tonight to tell Annie May I'm coming to the baptizing."

Lucy's heart raced with excitement. Jake had said they'd be leaving the day after the baptizing. She'd soon be leaving here! And she'd have a whole new life with Jake.

≈ ≈ ≈

156

Annie May's face had glowed when Jake told her he'd come to her baptizing. Lucy had never seen her look happier, and this morning she was singing as she left for church.

Lucy stacked the dishes and made a fresh pot of coffee. Jake would soon be here. She picked up the fly brush and shooed the flies away from the table. They were worse this spring than they were last year. Of course, the weather was much hotter this spring. If it stayed this hot, and the rains came hard, they'd have more worries than a panther. They'd have to worry about typhoid fever. She set two coffee cups on the table.

"Hello, dearie. Did you see me coming?"

Lucy looked up to find Bessie filling the doorway. Her heart sank. This meant she wouldn't get a chance to talk with Jake. She forced a smile and hoped Bessie wouldn't notice. "Come set and have a cup of coffee. I've just made some fresh. It's a good time to visit while the young-uns are at church."

Bessie pulled out a chair and sat down. "That's what I thought. If you'd like, we could get in a lesson."

"I don't much feel like a lesson this morning, Bessie."

Bessie looked at Lucy a little closer. "You not feeling well, Lucy?"

"I'm not sick—just ain't in the mood for lessons."

Bessie shook her head. "Somethin' must be bothering you for you not to want to study."

There was a knock at the door. Lucy saw Jake standing in the door. She set another cup on the table. "Come on in and have a cup of coffee with us, Jake."

Jake never glanced at her, but instead, he looked directly at Bessie. "No thank you, Mrs. Carpenter. I just came by to tell Bessie I'm going to go look for sassafras. It'll be late when I get back."

"I ain't never heard you say nothing about liking sassafras tea."

"One of my favorite teas, Bessie."

Lucy poured Bessie's coffee, and without looking at Jake said, "Where you gonna go?"

"Thought I'd go up to the top of Chimney Knob and work my way back down to the clearing. I seen some up there the other day."

Lucy looked at him. She knew he was trying to let her know where he'd be later, but that didn't replace the disappointment of not being able to spend the morning with him. "The clearing where the fawn is buried?"

Bessie spooned sugar into her coffee. Jake winked at Lucy. "That's the one. Should make it there around dusk. Bessie, you can have Richard start the chores without me, can't you?"

Bessie never looked up from stirring her coffee. "All right Jake, and we won't wait supper on you either. Sure is a good thing I'm not paying you, the way you've been gone lately."

Jake gave Lucy another wink. "See you all later." Lucy wanted to run after him. It sure would be nice if she could spend her day tramping through the mountains with him looking for young sassafras roots.

Bessie sipped her coffee. "That is a strange one. Seems like he spends a lot of time off by himself." She tipped up her cup and drained the last of the coffee. "If you don't want a lesson, I think I'll get on back home and see how the missus is doing."

"We'll work on my lessons later in the week. Maybe I'll be more in the mood," said Lucy.

"You better get some rest. You know this ain't a good time of the year to get run down. If it rains with the weather this hot, we could have a bout of the fever."

"I'll be fine, Bessie. Don't you worry about me. You have enough worry with your family."

Lucy washed the dishes and put on Sunday dinner. It wouldn't be long till the young-uns were home from church. She felt lonesome. She'd been wanting to go to church with them. She should have gone this morning. She could've talked to Jake later.

≈   ≈   ≈

Lucy disliked Sunday afternoons. They were so quiet. Dovey had some fool notion that you weren't supposed to work on Sunday. She dumped the dishwater into the slop bucket, then slipped out of the kitchen and headed up the path toward the clearing. She wondered where in the world Jake could be. She lowered her body onto a moss-covered spot under an old oak tree and ran her fingertips across the

158

soft moss. Her eyes drifted upward. Light fluffy clouds floated overhead. She made pictures out of them. Soon her eyelids grew heavy and she slept.

Startled, she sat up. Shadows were creeping over the mountains. The chirping of frogs filled the air. Jake was nowhere in sight. She stood up and began to pace.

"You been waiting long?"

Lucy turned to find Jake standing at the edge of the clearing. She took a step toward him. "I went to sleep waiting for you. I don't want to be out after dark. I'm scared of that panther."

Jake walked toward her. "Don't worry, Lucy. That's why I brought this lantern along. Panthers won't bother you if you have a light."

Lucy shuddered. "I hope you're right, but I don't want to find out. We won't be around here much longer."

Jake pulled her into his arms. "I said *I* was leaving."

Lucy backed away from him. "But . . . you asked me if I wanted to get away from here with you."

Jake reached for her again. "I remember, and I meant it. The way I see it is that I need to get myself a real job so I can take care of a wife." Lucy looked up at him with a question in her eyes. "I'm going to find a job and get us a place to live. Then I'm coming back for you, Lucy."

Lucy's arms tightened around his neck. "I don't want you to go without me. I don't see how I can stay here now."

Jake kissed her on the cheek. "I won't be long. I promise. Just give me a couple of months to get on my feet."

Lucy pulled his head down toward her. Their lips touched. The shadows deepened as Jake tightened his arms around her. His lips begged for more. More than she wanted or could give him right now. He'd asked her to wait for him to come back. If that was the way it was going to be, then he could just wait, too. A lone star winked down at her. She broke away. Somehow she knew if she didn't go home right now, she'd give more than she'd planned to. She turned toward the path.

"Wait," called Jake, "I'll light the lantern and walk with you to the fork in the road."

Lucy watched as he raised the globe and lit the wick. The flame flickered and then caught. A soft glow encircled them as they walked down the trail. She knew in her heart that the flame of love had caught.

The dark made Lucy feel uneasy. As she hurried down the trail toward home, she was glad Jake had given her the lantern. A whining noise near the trail caused her to stop and listen. It sounded like a baby crying. This had to be the panther. She fled down the trail. When her feet hit the first kitchen step, the air filled with a blood-cuddling scream. It sounded like a woman screaming for help. Thirteen pairs of large eyes greeted her in the kitchen. "John, is the front door open?"

"It was a few minutes ago."

"Hurry! Close it." She turned to Dovey. "Fetch all the oil lamps to the kitchen. Arthur, you fetch the oil from the shelf over there!"

"I closed the front door, Lucy." John said. "You think it's the panther?"

"I'm sure it is, John. Start a little fire in the fireplace. Quick! Don't need much. Just enough to get some smoke up the chimney."

"We ain't got but three lamps, Lucy," said Dovey.

"That's better than none. Arthur, fill them with oil. Dovey, you and Annie May put one in each window in the front room. Hurry. Close the shutters in the bedroom, Harley."

Arthur tilted the oil can as he finished the second lamp. "Lucy, we ain't got no more oil."

Lucy picked up the lantern and shook it. "We'll set this out here in the kitchen."

Arthur capped the oil can and set it on the shelf. "What're we gonna do if we run out of oil?"

John grabbed some wood from behind the cookstove. "We've got plenty of wood. The smoke will keep him away."

The young-uns huddled together, big-eyed, in front of the fireplace. No one asked for ghost stories tonight. The hours ticked by. Outside, it was very quiet. Lucy brought quilts and covered the little ones who had fallen asleep on the floor. The lights from the lamps were growing dim. John added more wood to the fire.

Lucy cocked her head to one side. "Listen. Sounds like scratching on the roof."

"He's right over the fireplace," said John. "The smoke ain't gonna keep him out." He ran over to the fireplace, snatched the shotgun from the rack, and shoved in a shell. Crouching in front of the fireplace, he waited.

The pawing grew louder.

Hattie screamed, "He's coming down the chimney, Lucy! Do somethin'—you're s'posed to take care of us!"

A louder scream pierced the night air. A heavy rock fell, splashing ashes, soot, and sparks into the room. The fire was gone. The last lamp sputtered and went out. The room was dark.

The panther screamed again. This time a loud blast followed the scream. No one made a move. There were footsteps on the porch. They waited. The front door swung open. A lantern flickered on the porch and there stood Holman. In the yard lay a huge black panther.

≈ 15 ≈

Lucy looked over the crowded church yard. She didn't see Jake anyplace, but there stood Bessie on the top church step. Bessie waved and called out, "How you doing, dearie?"

Heads turned. Lucy waved back. Why did Bessie have to be so loud? Be just like her to blurt out something about her lessons right here in front of all these people.

Bessie wormed her way through the crowd toward Lucy and Holman. By the time she reached them, sweat dripped from her chin. "I seen you looking and thought you was looking for me. Want to go in and see if we can find a seat?" said Bessie.

Lucy glanced toward the church and wondered how a body would breathe in there. Looked to her like there was half a dozen children hanging from every window. "No, Bessie, I think I'll stay out here where I can get some fresh air." Anyway, the parson's voice sounded like thunder. She wondered if God would be that loud if he were here.

Bessie wiped her forehead with her arm. "It's plenty hot. Guess we'd smother in there." She looked up toward a pile of angry thunderclouds behind the church. "I think we'll get some rain before the day's over. Hope we get to have dinner first."

"Me, too. I'd hate not to get to enjoy the fried chicken we brought."

Bessie finally mopped her chin with the tail of her good apron. "You brought fried chicken? We did, too."

Lucy gulped. How could she eat theirs after seeing that bunch of half-feathered chickens in their yard? And that smell—it was enough to turn a body's stomach! Well, she'd have to make sure she didn't get any of theirs. "How long before the baptizing?"

Bessie sauntered over to a tree and leaned against it. "Should be soon. It'll be before we eat."

162

The organ began to play. The crowd in the yard joined in the singing. Lucy looked at the dark clouds that filled the sky. Bessie was right. It looked like it was going to rain, but most of the planting was done. Bessie had said with hot weather like this, and now with the rain, they'd have to watch out for typhoid fever. She shuddered at the thought.

Bessie craned her neck. "Here they come." A group of mostly young people emerged from the church with the parson following them.

"Bessie, ain't I seen that old man somewhere before?" asked Lucy. "Wonder why he's got his britches rolled up like that? And where are his shoes?"

Bessie chuckled. "Yeah, that's Tilman, all right. See, he's come to be baptized again."

"What do you mean, again?" asked Lucy.

"You know he's a little strange, don't you? Ain't quite right. Every year he comes to be baptized, but he's never made it yet."

"Why?"

"Last year the parson led him out in the water and was just getting ready to dip him when he begin to stutter and point. Nobody could understand what he was trying to say. The parson tried to dip him, and he got real mad. Finally, he got out what he wanted to say."

"What was it?"

"He said 'Da-m-n it. There's a sna-a-a-ake in the water.'"

"What did the parson do?"

"He just led him out of the water. Wouldn't baptize him because he swore."

The crowd moved toward the back of the church yard. Lucy could hear the rushing of the nearby creek. She wiped the sweat from her brow. She wished she could splash the cool water on her face. Bessie nudged her. "Look at Tilman. He's always the last in line. Bet he finds a way out of this."

The parson removed his socks and shoes, rolled up his pants legs, and turned toward Annie May. She motioned for him to bend down and then whispered into his ear.

Lucy shaded her eyes with her hand. "Wonder what she's a-saying."

163

Before Bessie could answer, Annie May withdrew her hand from the parson's and ran toward the back of the line.

"Lawd a mercy!" said Bessie. "What's that child a-doing?"

"I know. Sh-h-h-! Be quiet." She watched in awe as Annie May reached out her hand toward Tilman. The expression on his face looked like that of a frightened animal. Annie May said something and moved closer. Tilman's hands hung limp at his side. She touched his gnarled hand with the tips of her small white fingers. Slowly, her hand clasped his. The frightened look disappeared as he gazed into her radiant face. They turned back toward the river bank. He stumbled. Annie May leaned down and put her arms around him. He pulled himself up, this time reaching for her hand.

"Lawd a mercy," said Bessie. "The Good Lord can clean up his heart, but it's gonna take a bar of hard lye soap to clean up his feet." Lucy motioned for her to be quiet again.

Annie May placed Tilman's hand in the parson's. The crowd held its breath. The parson's voice broke the silence. "I baptize you, Tilman, in the name of the Father, the Son and the Holy Ghost." At that moment he dipped him under the water. A low muttering spread through the crowd.

Bessie slowly let out her breath. "And a little child shall lead them."

A cool breeze stirred. Lucy remembered her ma quoting that scripture. She swallowed a lump that crowded its way up into her throat. "Amen," came a voice from behind her. Lucy turned to find Jake standing behind her.

The parson's voice rose again. "I baptize you, Annie May, in the name of the Father, the Son, and the Holy Ghost."

Annie May rose from the water and waved in their direction. She took Tilman by the hand and walked toward the bank.

After the baptism ceremony and the blessing, the dinner began. The long tables were laden with platters of fried chicken, bowls of green beans, boiled corn on the cob, and sweet potato pie.

Annie May heaped a tin plate with food and carried it to Tilman, who sat in the sun. Lucy saw him shiver as Annie May handed him the plate. That was odd. It was too hot to be cold, even with being so wet.

Others filled their plates and gathered in small groups under the shade trees to eat. Lucy ate and fed Martha from her plate. She wondered where Dovey was. Most of the time she still wouldn't let her take care of the baby. By the time she finished eating, Martha was beginning to fuss. "Bessie, I'm gonna take the baby home to take her nap. If Holman asks where I went, tell him I'll be back later."

"Get yourself a nap, too. Your face looks a little flushed."

"It's just the heat. I'm fine."

Lucy passed by Tilman. His chin rested on his chest. He looked as though he was half asleep. She started to speak. No, it would be better to let him rest. She moved on toward the path that led home. She glanced over her shoulder. Jake stared after her. She hurried out of sight. She didn't want him watching her with so many people around.

≈   ≈   ≈

Martha was sleeping by the time Lucy reached the house. She placed her in the cradle. The baby gave a deep sigh and turned over. Lucy pushed the damp curls from her face.

"You'll make a wonderful mother."

Lucy turned to find Jake standing in the doorway. "What are you doing here? Thought you'd stayed at the church."

"I saw you leave and I asked Bessie where you were going. She said you came home to let Martha take her nap. Thought it'd be a good time for you and me to say our goodbyes."

"Did Bessie see you leave?"

Jake pulled her into his arms. "I don't care if she did. I ain't here to talk about Bessie."

"What if Holman or some of the young-uns come home?"

Jake pushed the bedroom door closed with the toe of his boot. "They'd knock, wouldn't they? Now give me a kiss."

Their lips met. A warm blush crept up Lucy's neck. When the kiss ended, she started to speak. "Jake, . . ."

He reached for her again. "This is not the time for talking." He kissed her neck.

Goosebumps ran up Lucy's spine as Jake lowered her onto the big

165

brass bed. Why did his kisses make her lose her senses? Make her feel all mushy inside, like she was light as a feather? A part of her knew she wasn't doing what was right, but that didn't seem to make any difference. She felt his hand fumble with the buttons on her dress. She quivered when his fingers touched her bare skin. Just then a soft knock came at the bedroom door. "Lucy, are you in there?"

Lucy's mind snapped back to reality, and she pushed Jake away. She jumped from the bed, buttoned her dress, and smoothed her skirt as she tried to steady her voice by taking deep breaths. "Yes, Holman, I'm here."

"Are you all right? Bessie said you'd come home."

"I'm fine. Just brought Martha home to take her nap. Thought I'd rest for a few minutes."

By now Jake was on his feet. He slipped out through the door that led to the kitchen.

"I wanted to be sure you wasn't sick. Bessie said you looked tired."

Lucy straightened the covers on the bed, smoothed her hair with her hands, and opened the door. She motioned for Holman to be quiet as she pulled the door shut behind her. They walked outside, and Lucy sat down on the porch swing.

Holman spoke first. "Lucy, I've been a-thinking . . ."

"Yes, Holman?" she answered in a slow, even tone. He sat down on the swing beside her. She scooted over to the other side.

"I don't know how you feel about me, Lucy. Lord knows I ain't much to look at."

Lucy's eyes moved over her husband. He sure wasn't a good-looking man like Jake. Sweat glistened on the muscles in his arms. They were strong arms, but they'd never held her tight like Jake's had. If he ever held her tight, would it make her heart beat fast? And if he kissed her, what would it feel like? Wonder if he'd even want to kiss her.

Holman looked at her a little sheepishly. "A man gets awful lonesome out here, Lucy." Holman cleared his throat. "You have the young-uns. I can see they're getting fond of you, 'specially Annie May. Martha, too. You're the only ma she'll know. Mary's been dead over a year now. Her memory's getting dim. Sometimes at night I lay awake trying to remember her touch, a smile, just somethin' to ease

166

the loneliness." His voice faltered for a minute and his eyes misted.

Lucy lowered her head. Was he going to cry? She sure wasn't up to dealing with a blubbering man. She glanced up in time to see him take a deep breath. "I was just a-wondering if I could, you know, kinda court you?"

Lucy couldn't believe her ears. She'd expected him to try to be a real husband to her, but not this way. Before she could recover from the shock, a man's voice interrupted. "Anybody home?"

Holman turned around in the swing. "Why howdy, Jake. Come on around and have a seat."

Holman stood up, took a chair that leaned up against the wall, and offered it to Jake. He put his right foot up on the bottom step and leaned forward. Lucy felt her cheeks flush. She looked away from Jake and Holman.

"No thank you, Holman. I just came by to say my goodbyes."

Holman sat down on the chair he'd just offered Jake. "Where you going? Ain't you happy at the Joneses?"

"There's no future for me there."

"What're you gonna do?" asked Holman.

"Going on into town and see if I can find myself some kind of work. Some of the store owners might need help."

Holman twisted his mustache. "Could be. We'll miss you around here—'specially the young-uns. They love your haint stories."

"And I love to tell them, but I can't make a living telling haint stories."

Holman rose and offered Jake his hand. "Well, I wish you luck. And remember, you're always welcome here."

From the house they heard Martha start to cry. Lucy rose and started toward the door. Holman motioned for her to sit back down. "I'll fetch her. You stay right here and rest."

As soon as they were alone Jake said, "I won't be gone long, Lucy. I promise."

Lucy stood and moved toward the steps. "I'll walk you to the front gate." They started down the path. "You'd better come back soon. Holman just asked me if he could court me."

Jake grinned down at her. "And you said what?"

"I didn't have time to answer. You showed up just in time."

Jake's face grew serious. "You just remember I love you, and I'll be back for you soon."

"I promise, Jake. I'll remember."

At the gate she looked back toward the house. Holman sat in the swing with Martha. The little girl waved to her. A warm feeling filled her heart. She'd sure miss that little one when she left.

≈   ≈   ≈

Bessie was right about the rain. It had started on Sunday night and rained all week. It was hot and the flies swarmed. Lucy waved her hand at a bunch settled on the table. She couldn't remember them ever being so bad. They stuck to everything. Holman came in with two buckets of water. "I think it would be a good idea if we started boiling our water."

Lucy frowned. "Why's that, Holman?"

"With all this rain, everything is flooded. Things are just right for the fever."

"You mean typhoid?"

Holman nodded. "I'm afeared so. I remember back when I was a boy we had weather like this and there was an epidemic."

Lucy shooed the flies away from the table with a wave of her hand. "The flies are bad. They can carry the fever, too."

"I know. Just try to keep all the food covered and be careful with the milk. Germs grow fast in milk."

Lucy shooed away another swarm of flies with a tree brush. Holman turned to leave the kitchen. The sound of the church bell tolling floated through the open window. The bell tolled on and on. Finally, it stopped. Holman broke the silence that followed. "Must have been somebody old that died."

"Who'd you think it is?"

"Could be any number of people. There's several old people in the community, but I don't know of anybody that's sick."

John rushed through the back door. "Pa, there's a rider coming up the road."

"Maybe it's somebody to tell us who died."

168

Lucy followed Holman and John outside. Holman squinted and shaded his eyes with his hand. Lucy strained to see. "Can you tell who it is, Holman?"

"Looks like Doc Rogers. Wonder what he's doing out here. John, go get his horse and give it some water." John went toward the doctor, took his horse, and led it to the barn. Holman and Lucy walked down to the gate to meet the doctor. Holman reached out his hand. "Howdy, Doc. It's been awhile."

The doctor tugged at his beard and thought a minute. "Let's see, I've not been out this way since Mary . . ." He looked away and shuffled his feet.

"That's all right, Doc. Mary's gone. Can't say I don't still miss her, but we're managing." Holman gave Lucy a sideways glance. "What brings you out here, Doc?"

"One of the Ledford young-uns don't feel too well. I hate to say it, but looks like it could be the fever."

Holman cleared his throat. "I was afeared of somethin' like that. Just told Lucy here we'd better start boiling the water." The doctor's eyes moved over Lucy as his brow arched in a question. "Doc, this is my new wife, Lucy."

The doctor smiled and bowed. "I'm pleased to make your acquaintance."

She smiled at him. Was he studying her to see if she was pregnant? "I'm glad to meet you, Doctor, but I'm a-hoping we won't be a-needing you around here."

Holman cleared his throat again. "Doc, the church bell was tolling. You have any notion who died?"

The doctor shifted his eyes from Lucy to Holman. "That's why I stopped by, Holman. Someone found Tilman dead in his shack late this afternoon. Thought maybe you'd ride up there with me. There'll need to be arrangements made. Seeing he has no family, it'll be up to the community to bury him."

Sadness filled Lucy's heart. He'd looked so happy at his baptizing Sunday. Why hadn't she made some effort to make friends with him? There'd been time during dinner, but she'd been too busy to bother.

Holman turned to her. "I won't be long, Lucy. Why don't you get the boys to bring up some more water? It looks like we're gonna get more rain tonight. It wouldn't hurt to get started with the boiling."

Lucy watched them ride away, then started toward the house. She looked down. Soggy earthworms covered the ground. The air felt hot and muggy. Not only was it muggy, it had a funny smell, a sickening smell. She shivered in the heat. Typhoid fever—that was a scary thought. She wished Jake could be here to hold her in his arms.

≈ 16 ≈

The fever raged. It had been two weeks since Tilman's death. The doctor was sure he'd died of typhoid. After he was buried, some of the men burned his shack. The rain had stopped and the heat had let up some, but the flies still swarmed. The church bell was often heard tolling out its mournful message over the valley.

Dovey and Fannie washed the breakfast dishes. Lucy boiled the water for the day. "When you girls finish the dishes, you can get on outside and help watch the littl'-uns. Bessie's coming to have coffee with me this morning."

Dovey slung her dishrag down on the table. "That woman comes down here an awful lot. What do you and her talk about?"

Lucy felt the heat rise to her face. "Just woman stuff. Nothing you'd like to hear."

Fannie wiped her hands on the tail of her dress. "Come on, Dovey. Let's go find the rest of the young-uns before she finds us another job."

The two girls went outside. Lucy heard Dovey say to Fannie, "I know Lucy and Bessie are up to somethin', and I aim to find out what it is."

Lucy pulled out a chair and sat down. Maybe when Bessie came today, they'd just have coffee and visit a spell. Her lessons could wait till school started again. That way, Dovey wouldn't find out Bessie was helping her learn reading and writing. A knock came at the kitchen door. "Come on in, Bessie."

"It's me, Miz Carpenter, Richard Jones."

"Oh! I was expecting Bessie."

"That's why I've come, Miz Carpenter. I come to tell you she wouldn't be down today. Ma's purty bad sick. I'm on my way to fetch the doc."

"Sure hope it's not the fever."

171

"We hope it ain't either, but Aunt Bessie's real worried. You know Ma ain't been well since Pa was killed."

Lucy stood. "I know she ain't, Richard. That was too bad about your pa."

A shadow passed over Richard's face. "If I ever find out who shot him, he's gonna pay—the lousy polecat!"

Lucy studied the boy's face for a second. He was too young to be without a pa. Too young to have to take on the care of a whole family. "I can understand how you feel, son. I've been reading some in the Bible, and it tells us to love our enemy. Hate don't help none."

"He'll pay," muttered Richard as he turned and started for the door.

"I hope you find the doc. There's so much fever, no telling where he's at."

Richard called over his shoulder. "Thought I'd stop at the Ledford's. I heard another one of their young-uns came down with it."

Lucy followed Richard into the yard. "That makes the third one, don't it?"

"I think so."

Lucy straightened her apron. Too bad it wasn't that mean old Herby that was sick. Wasn't fair at all that it was one of the young-uns. She remembered what she'd just told Richard about loving your enemy. She had to agree with him. It wasn't all that easy. "I hope all eight of them don't have it. They've been lucky 'cause nobody's died. If you can't find the doc, tell Bessie that good nursing is about all you can do for the fever."

"Thanks, Miz Carpenter, I'll tell her."

John rushed in from the barn. "Lucy, Annie May's gone. I can't find her nowhere's. I should have told you this morning that she'd been talking about going to find the peddler. I never thought she'd really do it."

Lucy patted John on the shoulder. "Calm down. We'll find her." That foolish girl! She hoped she didn't get hurt or something. The church bell tolled again. She wondered who the bell was tolling for now. The way it had been ringing, must be lots of folks dying from

172

the fever. "You watch after the young-uns, John. I believe I might know where Annie May's gone."

John tugged nervously at his ear. "Now Lucy, don't you go running off and get lost, too. I remember when you went looking for somebody that was shooting on the mountain. I had to come looking for you."

How well she remembered. That had been the start of all the crazy business that had happened since. Maybe John was right. She could tell him where to look. No, if Annie May was in the clearing, *she* wanted to bring her home. "You stay here, John, and don't go nowhere till I come back."

Lucy hurried up the trail, a trail that she had gotten to know well. She could almost follow it with her eyes closed. So much had happened in the clearing. Maybe Annie May had come here hoping she'd find Jake.

Lucy slowed her pace as she approached the clearing. She didn't want to rush in because Annie May could be praying or something. What she found was not a child praying but Holman and Jake. She slipped into the growth of trees. She could tell the way Holman held his head that he was angry. Jake sure didn't look like the Jake that she'd come to love. She crept behind some bushes, edging her way around the clearing, until she could hear what they were saying.

"You used me, Jake. Friends don't do that. You came back here under the pretense of looking for work, and you was a-working all the time—working for him. How could you? You know it's against the law."

An ugly grin twisted Jake's face. "Holman, you're fighting a losing battle. You know as long as them Indians want to buy there'll be somebody who'll sell to them. Why don't you help us? There's money to be made."

Holman clenched and unclenched his fist. "I don't want money that's illegal. This whole nasty business is what got my friend Luther shot. It looks like it's gonna cost me two more friends."

Jake's face relaxed, and he looked more like the Jake Lucy knew. "It don't have to, Holman. It's your choice."

Holman moved toward Jake. Was there going to be a fight? Before

Lucy could move, Annie May darted into the clearing and ran toward Jake calling, "You can't go away. Please don't!"

Lucy took a step forward. She'd have to stop her. She didn't want her to get hurt. "Annie May," she called, "it's Lucy. Come, let's go look for deer. Your pa and Jake has business."

The little girl halted and turned to look at Lucy. Her eyes were filled with tears. Her face, which was usually so white, looked flushed. She looked from Jake to Lucy. "Lucy, make him stay. Don't let him go away."

Lucy stepped closer. "Honey, it's his choice. We all do what we have to. Let's you and me go for a walk and leave your pa and Jake to finish up their business." Her eyes met Jake's. He'd told her he was going to go away to look for work. Looked like he already had a job. A job against the law. She sure would like him to do some explaining, but now wasn't the time. Annie May didn't look too good. She needed to get her out of here. She put her arms around Annie May and pulled her close. As her face touched Annie May's, she looked quickly toward Holman. "This child is burning up with fever." Before Holman could reach her, she crumpled in Lucy's arms.

Jake took her from Lucy and rocked her back and forth. "Annie May. My Annie May. *Mary's* Annie May . . . please, don't leave me."

Holman stepped back, his face ashen, and turned from Jake. His arms hung limp, empty. Lucy knew from the look on Holman's face that now he knew the truth about Annie May.

He turned back to confront Jake. "You give me my daughter, you dirty . . . ! I raised her. And get out of here—now!—or I'll blow your brains out!"

"You coming with me, Lucy?" asked Jake.

Lucy reached her arms out for Annie May. "No, I'm staying with Annie May. She's the only one that needs me now." Annie May had been special to her from the start. Always wanting to go for walks to see the deer. It wasn't fair she'd be the young-un to get sick, but then she was the puny one. Lucy looked at Holman. "Are you just gonna stand there? Go for the doctor. She's a mighty sick girl."

≈   ≈   ≈

Holman made Annie May a bed in the hayloft. Between him and Lucy, they kept a constant vigil by her bedside. This was the seventh day since she'd come down with the fever. In the late afternoon, Lucy sat by the bed bathing Annie May's head with cold water. The little girl called for her ma from time to time. Suddenly, she opened her eyes and looked at Lucy. "Am I gonna die?"

Lucy smoothed the sheet around her. "No, honey. The doc says there's no reason you shouldn't be fine in a few weeks if we take real good care of you."

Annie May tried to sit up. "I don't like dead things, Lucy. I'm afeared."

Lucy cradled the child in her arms. "I know you don't, baby. I don't like dead things either. Please don't worry. Your pa and me are gonna take real good care of you. Here, let me fluff up your pillow."

Annie May settled back down. "I've been dreaming about Ma."

Lucy held her hand. "You've been calling her in your sleep, too."

Annie May smiled, her lips quivering around the corners. "I was dreaming that she was an angel. If I could be a beautiful angel like her . . ." Her voice trailed off.

Lucy squeezed her hand. "You're our beautiful angel. Now try to rest. I'll bring you out somethin' to eat. I want you to try to eat a little bit." Angels. Her ma had liked angels, too. She'd have to try to find some way to get her ma a tombstone with angels on it. Her locket was gone. Maybe she should have used it to buy a tombstone instead of paying for that trip for Dovey, but even if Dovey knew she used it, she probably wouldn't feel any differently about her. Well, it looked like her and Dovey was going to have to learn to put up with each other for a little while, or at least till she could find her another way to get to Cherokee. She was sure Jake wouldn't be back now. And even if he did come back, she wasn't sure . . .

Annie May's eyes closed. Lucy touched the fluttering in Annie May's neck. It was going real fast, like hummingbird's wings. She had to bend close to tell if she was breathing. Doc Rogers had said her fever would last until the typhoid ran its course.

Holman came up the ladder and looked over at Annie May. "How's she doing?"

"Come outside where we can talk. She'll be all right for a few minutes."

Outside, Holman stood with his back to Lucy for a few seconds thinking about Annie May. She was his young-un. He didn't care what Jake thought. She was his. He'd kill Jake without a second thought if he ever showed his face around here again.

Lucy waited quietly for Holman's attention. Finally she spoke. "She just asked me if she was gonna die."

"What did you say to her?"

"I told her that we was gonna take real good care of her and not to worry. She also said she dreamed about her ma and that her ma was an angel. I told her *she* was our angel."

Holman frowned and wiped his face with his arm. Lucy hadn't been a *real* wife like Mary, but in so many ways, she's been more like a wife. And a real ma. He liked a woman who knew her mind. Maybe with a little courting, he could make her his real wife. He took a step closer. "I don't know how we'd manage without you, Lucy."

Before Lucy could respond, the church bell began to toll.

"Lucy, I forgot to tell you Effie Jones died." Holman watched her face for some kind of reaction. Lucy slumped forward. Wasn't fair! Now Bessie would be so busy that she wouldn't have a friend at all. Maybe if Mary had had a friend like Bessie, . . . but Mary wasn't the neighboring kind. Guess Holman hadn't known Mary as well as he thought he had. He'd never thought she could be untrue to him.

Holman reached out to steady her. "You all right?"

"I'm fine. Just upset about Miz Jones. Poor Bessie! How's she gonna manage?"

Holman guided her over to a huge rock. What would he do if Lucy got sick? How would he make it without her? "Here, sit down. Don't worry about Bessie. She's a strong woman and she'll be fine. I want you to get on in the house. Try to rest. Nannie has the littl'-uns out playing, and all the others are hoeing corn."

Lucy stood up. "Dovey could probably use some help with supper."

Holman watched her start for the house. Why couldn't Dovey at least give her a chance? He'd have to see what he could do about that. "Dovey can manage," he called. "You rest."

176

Lucy looked back over her shoulder. "I'll try, but first I need to look in the trunk for more sheets."

In the house Dovey stirred a big pot of mush. As soon as it was done, she'd take some out to Annie May. Maybe she'd take her doll to her. She'd taken such good care of it. That Cow's Tail Lucy had probably not thought of what she could eat. Mush would be good and nourishing.

The door opened and Lucy came in. "Howdy, Dovey. You doing all right?"

"How's Annie May?"

Lucy cleared her throat. "Not good. Your pa says he may have to send for the doc again. I told her I'd be bringing her out somethin' to eat."

Dovey reached for her spoon. "I just fixed her some mush. I'll take it out."

"No, Dovey, I'll take it out. We can't have all of you getting the fever. That's why we put her in the hayloft." Lucy turned to leave. "A little snakeroot wouldn't hurt her, either."

Snakeroot! Dovey glared at Lucy as she disappeared through the door. She sure wasn't going to fix any of that Indian poison for Annie May. And she wasn't going to let that Cow's Tail Lucy do it either if she could help it. She'd just talk to her pa and make sure he didn't let her do it. Pa was home now, and it was up to him to stop this woman. They had enough trouble without some Indian cure.

Lucy went on into the bedroom and shut the door behind her. She was so tired—tired of young-uns, tired of men, tired of sickness, but most of all, she was tired of not having a place to call her own.

She sat down on the feather bed and felt it caress her tired bones. It'd only been a short time ago that Jake had held her here on this same bed. She'd been too busy with Annie May to think about him much. Her body shivered at the thought of Jake's touch. She couldn't imagine Holman making her feel that way. Her mind grew fuzzy with sleep but awoke suddenly when she remembered the sheets. She forced herself to stand and raise the lid of the trunk. There weren't any sheets. She'd have to use some of the quilt tops. Dovey would

177

be upset, but it couldn't be helped. She wouldn't use the wedding ring one. She folded it carefully and started to lay it in the trunk.

A faded tablet in the bottom of the trunk caught her eye. She picked it up and flipped it open. Was it a letter to somebody? A page dropped out. She bent and picked it up. Jake's name was at the top. What could this be? Well, now wasn't the time to read it, that was, if she could read it. She slipped it into her pocket and put the quilt tops she didn't need back in the trunk.

She listened. Dovey must have gone outside. She'd sure like to know what was in that letter. Since she was alone, she guessed now was as good a time as any to try to read it. She unfolded the paper. From what she could read, it looked like a letter to Jake from Mary. One she'd never mailed. Sure enough! Mary had believed Jake was Annie May's father. Carefully, Lucy folded the letter and slipped it back into her pocket.

≈   ≈   ≈

Annie May's condition worsened. She lay on her makeshift bed gasping for breath. Her glazed eyes stared straight ahead. Occasionally, a soft moan would escape from her. Sometimes she would mumble and then call for her ma. Holman bathed her face. "Lucy, I'm worried. I'm afeared she's not gonna make it."

Lucy touched Holman's arm. "I didn't realize you cared so much. You've never paid much attention to her."

Holman rubbed his eyes with the back of his hand. He should have shown Annie May more attention. It was probably too late now. "I don't want to lose Annie May. I loved Mary so much, and I lost her. If the good Lord just gives me another chance . . ." He looked up at Lucy.

She patted his shoulder. "Ma used to say faith and snakeroot would do wonders. We've got to believe she's gonna make it. Would you mind if I fixed some snakeroot and tried giving her a little?"

Holman frowned. Dovey wouldn't like it too much if he let Lucy give Annie May her Indian medicine. "You and your ma's Indian remedies!" He looked at Annie May. "I guess the snakeroot or somethin' helped Martha, and the way I see it, we don't have anything to lose. You go ahead. I'll sit with her and try to pray. I never been much of a praying man, but . . ." Lucy was gone before he finished. Dovey would be mad, but he'd take care of her later. He couldn't just sit here and let Annie May die.

In the kitchen Lucy found Dovey and Hattie talking. They looked up when she came in. "How's Annie May doing?" asked Dovey.

Lucy took a pot, filled it with water, and set it on the stove. Should she tell Dovey she was fixing to make her some snakeroot tea? "She ain't good. Your pa's real worried."

Dovey picked up wood and put it into the stove. "What does the doc say?"

"Said he's done all he could. We'll just have to wait and see." She might as well tell her what she was doing. Can't keep a secret around here. "I'm gonna fix her some snakeroot and put it in a little moonshine. Ma said that was a good remedy for the fever."

Dovey's blue eyes snapped. She slammed the stove door shut. "And Pa's gonna let you doctor her with your Indian poison?"

"Your pa says we have to try, Dovey. He's so afeared he's gonna lose her."

"Well! When he has to bury her because of you, maybe then he'll run you off. That's what he should have done a long time ago." Dovey wheeled and left the room.

Lucy took a jar from the cook table. If Annie May died, Holman wouldn't have to run her off. There would be no reason to stay. There wasn't any use arguing with Dovey.

"Don't worry about her, Lucy," said Hattie. "She's just jealous of you. You know, she's the one that's been taking care of us." Hattie's voice grew softer. "Lucy, you really think Annie May's gonna die?"

Lucy hugged the girl. Hattie'd changed so much since Dovey's trip. She still had her moments, but there had been a change. She wondered if it was because she'd been treating her more like a grown-up. "I don't know that, Hattie. We'll just have to pray that she'll be all right."

Hattie's face lit up. "You're right, Lucy. And that's what I'm gonna do." She ran from the room.

Lucy finished making her tea and started to the hayloft. As she rounded the corner of the house, she heard Hattie say, "The reason that I've gathered you-uns here on the porch is so we can pray for Annie May not to die. The only prayer I know is the Lord's Prayer so we're gonna pray it together."

Lucy listened as the late afternoon air filled with the echo of twelve young voices praying. She bowed her head and moved her lips with the words Hattie was saying.

She slipped by the children and went to the barn. She climbed the ladder to the hayloft where she found Holman trying to change dirty sheets. She set the jar of tea down. "Here, let me help you do that."

When the bed was done, Lucy spooned some tea into Annie May's mouth. It dribbled out of the corners of her lips. Holman dabbed at it with a rag. "Ain't gonna do no good, Lucy. She can't swallow."

Lucy took another spoonful. "We just have to keep trying. Maybe some will run down her throat."

Annie May turned and moaned. "You hear that, Lucy? She made a sound."

Lucy wiped Annie May's face. "Annie May, this is Lucy. Can you hear me?"

"Ma, you look so pretty."

"Annie May, it's Lucy, not your ma," said Holman.

A smile flickered across her face. "Ma! The Lord's Prayer. Do you hear it?"

Lucy remembered the crowd of young-uns she'd left on the front porch praying. She listened. She couldn't hear their prayers. Was it possible? How could she hear them? "Annie May, can you hear me?" The only answer she got was another moan. "Holman, if you can set with her a little while, I'd like to go for a walk."

Holman looked up at her. "You feeling all right, Lucy?"

She started down the ladder. "I'm fine. Just need some fresh air and some time to think."

"You sure you want to go alone? It's getting late."

"I ain't afeared. I just want to be alone for a little while. I'll be back before dark."

"Well, you be careful. Don't know how we'd manage if somethin' happened to you now."

Lucy left without answering. Jake! Where had he gone? Would he be back? She felt the letter in her pocket. She wondered if she should try to get it to Jake. No, Mary was Holman's wife. By all rights, he should have it. Then she remembered the pain she'd seen on his face when he'd learned the truth about Annie May. That settled it. She'd burn it the first chance she got.

Instinctively she had come to the clearing. She looked around. A shadow moved on the other side. Her heart leaped. Maybe Ledford was waiting out here for her, or could it be Jake? He'd lied to her. He'd lied to Holman. And Annie May? Did he really care for her? It didn't make much difference to her anymore. She'd lost everything.

A squirrel scurried away through the underbrush. A heaviness settled around her heart. She looked for the mound of earth where the deer had been buried. All she found was a sunken spot. She knelt and patted the ground. "Ma, everything's gone wrong. Life's sinking just like this grave has," she whispered as she brushed at her eyes, "but Ma, I can fix the grave." She pawed at the loose, black earth.

"Lucy," called a voice urgently.

She jumped to her feet and turned to face John. "Is she gone?" The question hung in the space between them.

"No, Lucy, but she's bad. Pa wants me to go for the doc again."

Lucy brushed the dirt from her hands. "Look, John!" She grabbed him by the sleeve. "See that little girl over there?"

"Where, Lucy? I don't see no little girl. Come on, let's go. You're just tired. Pa said you was wore out."

"She's over there by that big sassafras tree. I saw the same little girl when Ma died. It's a sign, John. I know Annie May's not gonna be here in the morning."

"Come on, Lucy. Let's go."

It didn't take long to reach the barn. Holman paced the floor. Annie May lay still. She was dead. She just knew it. If she was dead, she'd get on in the house and get her belongings and leave. "Holman, is she . . . ?"

"No, but I don't think she'll make it much longer."

Lucy felt her forehead. "She's burning up with fever. We're gonna have to get it down."

Holman banged his fist against a post. "I've been a-trying, but it ain't doing no good."

Lucy picked up a sheet. "You dig out that jug of yours and then go in the house and make me some more snakeroot tea."

Holman jammed his hands in his pockets. "If we can't get food down her, how are we gonna get snakeroot down her?"

Lucy ripped the sheet into pieces. "Get me the jug!"

Holman fished under a pile of straw, pulled out his jug and handed it to Lucy. She took out the cork and soaked the rags with the moonshine. "Go make the tea, Holman!"

Holman disappeared down the ladder. Lucy threw back the sheets and began to rub Annie May down with the rags. Darkness oozed its way through the cracks in the hayloft. She stopped long enough to light a lantern and hang it near the bed. She soaked her rags and rubbed Annie May again. A mouse scampered across the loft. Lucy watched him stop, stand on his hind feet, sniff the air, and disappear through a hole in the floor. She soaked the pieces of sheet again and covered Annie May with them. She picked up the jar containing the little bit of snakeroot tea that was left and spooned more into her mouth, but it dribbled out.

Holman came up the ladder with more snakeroot tea. Without looking up, Lucy said, "We've got to get her to swallow."

Holman handed Lucy the tea. "When baby lambs won't eat, you rub their throats and make them swallow."

"I know this tea will bring her fever down. Let's pretend she's a lamb. I'll spoon in the tea and you rub her throat. Maybe a little will run down."

Holman looked at her. "You just won't give up, will you?"

Lucy filled her spoon with tea. "Not as long as there's life."

Holman rubbed. Lucy spooned. The tea dribbled from Annie May's mouth. Holman lifted his head. "I hear a rider coming. Maybe it's the doc."

Lucy dabbed at Annie May's mouth. "Don't see what he can do that we ain't doing."

John called from the opening in the floor. "How's she doing, Pa?"

"She ain't no better, son. Did you find the doc?"

"Yeah, Pa, but he said he couldn't get here before morning. Is there somethin' you want me to do?"

"Naw, son, you get on in the house and get some rest."

"Holman, look! The tea—ain't as much running out her mouth."

Holman bent over the little girl. "I think you're right, Lucy. Spoon in some more and I'll rub her throat." He began to stroke her throat. "I felt a little movement. Put in some more."

Lucy put in another spoonful. "I think it's going down. Look! There ain't no dribbles. Now if we can just get enough down her to do some good."

A half hour later, Holman and Lucy had succeeded in getting part of a cup of tea into Annie May. "Her breathing is more even," said Lucy. "and I think she feels cooler." She laid down the spoon and pulled up the sheet to cover Annie May.

Holman straightened up and stretched. "Let's rest a few minutes and see what happens. I'll set with her, and you try to get some sleep."

Lucy rubbed the back of her neck. "I won't be able to sleep till she's out of danger." She walked over to the other side of the hayloft and peered out the cracks. Soft moonlight bathed the yard and a breeze rippled through the pines. The house loomed dark against the hillside. An unnatural silence hovered between earth and sky. Annie May stirred and moaned. As Lucy started to turn toward her, a shadow drew her attention back to the yard. It moved like a ghost between the barn and the house and then faded into the trees.

"Lucy, I think she's coming round."

Lucy leaned over the girl. "Can you hear me, Annie May? It's Lucy." She touched her forehead. "I think her fever's gone."

Annie May's eyelids flickered and then opened. "Where'd Ma go, Lucy? She was just here."

"You've been very sick, honey. I'm sure you've just been dreaming."

"No, Lucy! Ma was here."

"I believe you, Annie May, but right now you need to rest. I want you to drink some of this tea. After you've had a nap, we'll talk about your ma's visit." She picked up the snakeroot and held it to Annie May's lips.

183

She drank a couple of swallows and pushed it away. "I'm so tired." Her eyes closed and she was asleep, but this time it was a more natural sleep.

~ ~ ~

Three days had passed since Annie May had regained consciousness. Lucy lit the lantern and hung it above her bed and its light cast a soft glow around her head. She sure looked like an angel. Lucy sat down and took Annie May's frail hand into hers. Annie May gazed up at her with her sober blue eyes. Lucy wiped her face. "Maybe we can move you back into the house soon."

Annie May pulled her hand from Lucy's and crossed her arms on her chest. "Ain't going nowhere 'cept with Ma."

Lucy took a deep breath and started to speak, but before she could get the words out, Annie May spoke again. "Ma said she was coming back for me. Ma never did lie to me when she was living. Why would she now?"

Lucy studied the girl's face. She could tell that whatever she'd seen or heard, she believed it to be real. She reached over and smoothed the black curls from her face. "Your ma wouldn't lie to you, honey. I believe you. Now try to get some sleep. Maybe your ma will come to you in your dreams."

Annie May reached up and gave her a hug. Lucy kissed the girl on the cheek. "I'm sure your ma will know what's best for you."

Annie May picked up the doll and studied its face for a few minutes. "Lucy, will you take my doll and give it to Hattie?"

Lucy took the doll. "Course I will. Now don't you fret. Just get better." Soon Annie May slept.

Holman appeared at the top of the ladder. "How's she doing?"

"Fretful, but I got her to sleep. Maybe she'll sleep for awhile."

Holman picked up a straw and picked at his teeth. "How did you do that?"

Lucy stood and smoothed out her apron. "I told her maybe she'd dream about her ma and that pleased her."

Holman took a step toward her. "I don't know how you do it, Lucy, but you always know just what to do."

Lucy stepped back. She couldn't let Holman care for her now. It looked like Annie May was going to be all right, and as soon as she was sure, she was leaving here. Somehow, she was going to find her ma's people, find a place she could call home. "Just what did the doc say about her? Is she really gonna be all right?"

Holman cleared his throat and sat down on a crate as he twisted his mustache.

"Well?" said Lucy.

Holman sighed. "He didn't say much. Just that if there were no complications, she'd be fine."

"What kind of complications?"

"He said pneumonia can still set in because she ain't moving much. He's also worried about her heart."

The lines in Lucy's forehead deepened. "Guess that's why he's always feeling her pulse when he's here."

Holman threw down his toothpick. "Could be. He says her heart's never been good. We just need to keep her quiet till she mends."

Lucy touched the girl's forehead. Why hadn't she guessed that there was something wrong with her? Every time they'd gone for a walk she'd been exhausted. "That's gonna take some doing. She's gonna want to be up and about. You know how she likes watching the deer."

Holman stepped to the bed. "I'm a-counting on you and the young-uns to do it."

Lucy yawned. "We'll try. Think we'd better set up with her tonight?"

Holman nodded. "You try to get some sleep and I'll set with her for awhile." Lucy leaned back into a pile of straw and closed her eyes. Time moved on toward midnight. Holman kept his vigil by the sleeping child.

Suddenly Annie May sat up. "Ma!"

Lucy sprang to her feet. Holman tried to calm Annie May. Lucy knelt by the bed. "Did you dream of your ma?"

Annie May nodded. Lucy thought her eyes looked larger than usual. "She's in heaven. I saw her, Lucy."

Lucy hugged the girl. "I believe you, honey. Now just lay back down. Tomorrow we're gonna move you back in the house."

Annie May yawned and closed her eyes. Holman stood and stretched, then pulled out his pocket watch. "It's almost midnight."

"I'll set with her," said Lucy. "You've had a turn."

"She rests better with you." Holman lay down on the pile of straw.

Lucy sat down by Annie May. A shadow slid through a crack in the boards of the barn. As silent as a ghost, it moved toward Annie May's bed. It hovered over the bed for a few seconds then floated toward the roof. Annie May gave a soft moan. Holman rushed to her side. Lucy picked up the child's limp hand. Holman grabbed the lantern and held it up to her face. The girl's blue eyes stared up at him. The presence of death filled the hayloft.

≈ *17* ≈

Silence filled the Carpenter house. Alice Jones had taken Martha to their house for the day. Holman had gone to town to have a coffin made for Annie May. Hattie huddled behind the cookstove with Annie May's doll clutched to her chest.

Dovey wiped the breakfast dishes with a vengeance. Her sister was dead, and that Cow's Tail Lucy had killed her. What in the world had her pa been thinking about? She must have some kind of Indian power over him, or he would have already run her off.

"Thought you might need some help laying out the body."

Dovey looked up to find Bessie standing in the doorway. "If it weren't for Lucy giving her poison, we wouldn't need no help."

Bessie placed her hands on her hips and confronted Dovey. "Now you listen here, girl. I'll have you know what Lucy gave Annie May is the best medicine in the world for the fever. And somethin' else, young lady—Lucy is the best thing that could've happened to this family."

"You think so, huh. Well, you should try to live here. The only thing she ain't took over is sleeping with Pa in Ma's bed, and I ain't gonna let that happen."

Bessie never let her eyes leave Dovey's face. "If I know your pa, young-un, he'll sleep where he wants when he wants. He won't go a-asking you." She walked past Dovey. "Now what can I do to help? Where's Lucy? And where's Annie May at?"

"Thanks for coming, Bessie," Lucy said from the doorway. "Holman's got Annie May all laid out in here."

"Hope he closed her eyes. You know they have to be closed right away."

"Holman put some dimes on them right after he carried her in."

"That's good." Bessie said as she gently guided Lucy back into the front room.

187

"This ain't gonna be easy." Lucy mopped at her brow and wished the heat would break. She wasn't ready to lay out the dead. She remembered how Annie May had insisted that Jake use her quilt to cover up the deer. Now here she was covered up with a sheet. This couldn't be happening. She felt her knees shake, and Bessie's arms holding her. Sobs shook her whole body. After a while, Lucy's tears ceased. She wiped her eyes with the back of her hand. "Come on, Bessie. We've got a job to do."

Bessie wiped her own eyes with her apron. "A good cry is good for the soul. Revives it like a warm spring rain brings out the flowers."

Lucy put her arms around Bessie and gave her a hug. "You've been a real good friend. Don't know how I could've made it through the winter without you."

"What do you think friends are for? Come on, let's wash and dress Annie May so she'll be ready when Holman gets back with the coffin. You fetch some warm water and soap. I'll get a towel and washcloth."

"I've got the water." They turned to find Dovey behind them with a pan. She handed it to Bessie. "Take this, and I'll fetch a towel and washcloth."

"Fetch us another pail of warm water, too," said Bessie. "We'll need to wash her hair."

Lucy lifted the sheet. How in the world was she going to do this? No, she wouldn't think about it. She'd always done what she had to and now was no time to stop. She'd let this bunch of young-uns take over her life. She hadn't meant for it to be that way. It seemed as though she'd gotten lost in all the happenings. Dovey could be in charge as soon as Annie May was buried. She'd sure messed up enough. Could it be that somehow she was to blame? If only she'd watched out for Annie May more. There was one thing for sure, as soon as this funeral was over, she'd take her belongings and leave, even if it was still hot and rainy. Then she'd have plenty of time to think about herself.

Bessie quietly washed Annie May's body, then began to comb her hair. The knots were too tight. "I think we're gonna have to cut the lumps out." She laid down the comb.

188

Lucy picked it up and looked down at the hair. She remembered how those dark curls had bounced in the moonlight the first time the peddler had told his ghost stories. Who'd ever have thought things would turn out this way? "I hate to cut it," said Lucy.

Bessie smoothed Annie May's hair. "I think we'll be able to keep it long around her face, but this here in the back we'll just have to cut. It won't show."

Dovey came in with another pail of water. "What're you gonna cut?"

Bessie took the scissors from a sewing basket near the fireplace. "Her hair, Dovey. It's so matted we can't comb it."

Dovey reached for the scissors. "Can I please cut it?"

Lucy couldn't believe what she was hearing. Had Bessie's little speech gotten through to Dovey? Maybe she should have asked her for help with Dovey a long time ago, but Dovey had made it clear she was in charge here.

Bessie took the comb from Lucy and gave it to Dovey. "Why, Dovey, I'd appreciate that. You can cut her hair while Lucy and me fix her somethin' to wear." The two women watched as Dovey gently clipped clumps from the hair.

Bessie asked Lucy what Annie May should wear and Lucy shook her head sadly. "A young-un is usually buried in a white dress but she ain't got one. She's got the dress she was baptized in. I made it for her out of different colored scraps."

Bessie picked up some of the clumps of hair from the floor. "You have any yard goods we could make a shroud out of?"

Lucy took the hair from Bessie and put it in her pocket. "No, there ain't even any flour sacks. I used the last one to mend Dovey's dress that she wore to the spelling bee." She touched the bulge in her pocket. The letter. She had to remember to burn it, and later she'd bury the hair under a rock. Her ma'd always said never to burn hair.

"Do you have any dresses we could use?"

"We can use the dress I was married in." She went into the bedroom and returned with the blue dress. "Will this do?"

Bessie took the dress and shook it free of wrinkles. "This will do just fine. We'll make do the best we can."

189

The women worked in silence, each lost in her own grief. Lucy wondered what had happened to Jake. How would he feel when he learned of Annie May's death? She didn't know what her feelings were for Jake now. She was too hurt about Annie May dying to feel very much of anything, and she didn't want to hurt Holman any more than he'd already been hurt. The silence was broken by the tolling of the church bell. All three stopped and listened. One, two, three, . . . eleven. All was quiet.

≈   ≈   ≈

The next morning Annie May's black hair covered the pillow in the coffin. A sheet hung over the fireplace behind the coffin. Lucy would never have guessed Bessie's big hands could make such a beautiful shroud.

Family members filled some of the chairs and a few neighbors had come to help with the burying, since the fever had made a church funeral impossible.

Lucy tried to listen to the parson's words, but she felt so cold. Could she be getting sick, or was it just nerves? She looked at Holman. He rubbed his eyes with the back of his hand.

The parson opened his Bible and began to read. "The Lord is my shepherd; I shall not want. He maketh me to lie down in green pastures: He leadeth me beside the still waters. He restoreth my soul; He leadeth me in the paths of righteousness for His name's sake. Yea, though I walk through the valley of the shadow of death . . ."

Lucy straightened in her chair and looked at Parson Long. What was he saying about shadows? Had he said the Bible called death a shadow? There had been a strange shadow in the yard the night Annie May woke from the fever, and there was the shadow that hovered over the bed the night she died. A chill traveled up her spine. Her thoughts were interrupted with the parson's "Amen."

A neighbor lady went to the pump organ in the far corner of the room and began to play. The family moved toward the coffin in single file, the older young-uns carrying the littler ones.

Lucy followed at the end of the line. She'd try to not look at the others. She couldn't bear to see them cry. When she reached the coffin, she bent and kissed the little girl on the forehead. Annie May felt so cold. She hadn't liked the cold. She'd had Jake cover the fawn with her tattered quilt.

The parson took Lucy by the arm. "It's time, my dear. Just have a seat over here."

Lucy looked up at him. "Please wait a minute. I have to fetch somethin'!" She ran from the room and soon returned carrying the quilt the family had made last winter. She spread it over Annie May and smoothed it out. "There! Now you won't be cold." She grasped the edge of the coffin as she sank to the floor.

≈   ≈   ≈

The darkness that swallowed Lucy at Annie May's funeral wouldn't let go. For two weeks she struggled to surface from a bottomless pit. Her eyelids fluttered as she tried to focus. She tried to sit up. Annie May! It must be my time to sit with Annie May!

Holman eased her back on the bed. "You rest, Lucy. The doc will be here soon. He'll be pleased to see you're doing so much better."

Doc? Why did she need the doctor? She couldn't be sick. She remembered the way the doc's eyes had traveled over her. "I've got to take care of Annie May!" Her lips moved, but no sound came.

A voice called from the top of the ladder. "Here's the cold water you wanted, Pa. John just fetched it from the spring. Hope you don't think I'm gonna keep on running out here all the time. I've got the young-uns to take care of."

Lucy turned her head. Dovey stood near the opening in the floor. Holman took the water from her. "Here. Take this rag and wipe the sweat from Lucy's face while I mix up this powder the doc left. Hope he gets here soon. This is the last bit of medicine."

Dovey set down the bucket of water and took the rag from her pa. "You could always give her some of the poison she give Annie May. Then we could bury her, too!"

Holman gave her a stern look. "Dovey, I won't listen to that kind of talk. Do as you're told and keep quiet."

Images flashed across Lucy's mind. A white sheet . . . black strands of hair on the floor . . . a blue dress . . . a casket . . . the parson's voice. The last thing she remembered, before darkness swallowed her again, was the quilt she'd pulled over Annie May.

A few minutes later, the touch of the cold cloth brought her thoughts back to the present. Dovey stood over her. Lucy could see the steel blue of her eyes peering at her through the blond strands of hair. She tried to speak again. Still no words came. She tried to lift her arm to brush away the hair from Dovey's face, but she was too weak.

Dovey unbuttoned the collar of Lucy's nightgown and hesitated. "Pa, look here."

Holman came over and looked at Lucy. "I don't see nothing."

Dovey rubbed her neck with the rag. "That's just it, Pa. Her locket. It's gone."

Holman twisted his mustache thoughtfully. "Maybe it's in her belongin's back in the house."

Dovey handed him the rag. "I'll look for it when I go back." Lucy cringed at the thought of Dovey digging through her belongings. Fear gripped her. The letter! What if she found it? She'd planned to burn it, but she couldn't remember if she had. Her eyes felt heavy. She slipped back into a world of darkness.

Voices drifted in and out of Lucy's dreams. She couldn't tell which ones were real and which ones were from her dreams. She thought for sure she heard the doctor tell Holman she'd be all right. Jake's voice called to her from the clearing. She saw him holding his arms out to her, his eyes begging her to come to him.

She tried to sit up but fell back. Another voice hovered over her. A hand smoothed her hair. The dreams vanished, and she looked into the gentle blue eyes of Holman.

The dream of Jake's begging eyes flashed before her. Her face felt hot. She tossed her head, hoping to cool the heat. Flames leaped before her eyes. She heard the sizzle of burning paper. The letter! She remembered. She'd burned it the morning of Annie May's funeral. Weakness crept over her. The heat in her body turned to a clammy sweat, and she slept again.

≈   ≈   ≈

A few days later Lucy felt much better. She pushed herself up on her elbow. The late August sun filtered through the cracks and streamed across the bed. Holman mixed the powdery medicine in a glass and stirred it with a spoon. Lucy felt a gagging sensation at the thought of having to swallow one more mouthful of that horrible stuff. Holman offered her the glass. She wrinkled her nose. "Do I have to take any more of that medicine?"

Holman looked at the glass he held in his hand, then back at Lucy. "Well, this is the last dose, and you're just about better. The doc said you could sit up for awhile tomorrow. I guess it's more important that you rest than to get you all riled up over medicine."

Lucy sank back into her pillows with a smile. Holman set the glass down. "You try to get some more sleep while I check on how the young-uns are doing."

Lucy closed her eyes. She was glad to be left alone. She'd had enough of Holman shoving medicine down her throat. She traced the patterns the sun made on the quilt with her fingertip. There was so much to do. Summer was about gone. She wondered if Dovey had done any canning. She shuddered when she remembered the funeral. It seemed so long ago. She'd have to go to the churchyard and see to Annie May's grave when she was able. She didn't want it to sink like the fawn's grave had. When she was feeling lots better, she'd see about finding a way to go to Cherokee.

Voices from the barnyard drifted through the cracks in the loft. She strained to hear. "I've come to pay my respects," came the voice of a woman. The voice sounded familiar, but she didn't recognize it. She peered through the barn loft cracks. Why, it was Mrs. Allison, and she was talking to Dovey. Lucy heard her say, "I've been on a trip to see my sister out east. When I arrived home, I heard about Annie May's death. I wanted to tell you all how sorry I am and see if I can help in any way."

Lucy watched Dovey kick at a rock with her bare toes. "My pa just went in the house, and Lucy, she's in the loft. She's just getting over the fever."

The teacher took a step back from Dovey. "Your stepmother, Mrs. Carpenter? She has typhoid? Is she going to be all right?"

Dovey looked up toward the loft. "Don't know." Lucy watched as Mrs. Allison took another step backward. And she probably don't care, she thought.

"That's too bad. She is such a nice lady. I'll never forget the day she came to school and gave me the lock . . ." She clapped her hand over her mouth. "Oh, dear. I forgot—I have an appointment. I have to go. Please tell Mrs. Carpenter I hope she recovers soon."

Lucy turned over on her back and felt her bare neck. She wished that the teacher hadn't said anything about the locket. Maybe Dovey hadn't known what the woman was talking about. She heard Dovey's shrill voice at the foot of the ladder.

"Pa, she sold that necklace! I know she did. She used it to pay for my trip."

At first Lucy couldn't understand Holman's answer. His voice rose. "Now Dovey, if that's what Lucy did, she did it because she loves you, and you should be grateful."

"Why? She's not my ma! I don't want her doing nothing for me."

By now they were in the loft. Dovey ran to the bed and snatched Lucy's hands from her throat. "You sold it, didn't you? You sold the locket!" She clenched her fist. Her body grew rigid with anger. Her eyes looked wild. "You sold it so I could go to the spelling bee. You sold it so I could win." Her lips trembled. She stood silent for a few moments. Slowly, she spoke. "And . . . I . . . did . . . win." Her fist unclenched. Her body loosened. "I won all because of you." Tears streamed down her cheeks. "And . . . you . . . did . . . it all for me." She fell on her knees and threw her arms around Lucy.

Lucy smoothed the girl's hair. She knew Dovey was crying for all she'd lost: her ma, Annie May, and for the many months she'd fought her over the young-uns. All her hurt was coming out with her tears. Now her heart would be ready for love.

~ *18* ~

Fall came quickly, crisp, red, and golden. Lucy's recovery came as quickly. The children were back in school. Her afternoons were filled with sewing and late canning. She sat on the front porch swing, patching Holman's overalls. The rattle of a wagon caused her to look up. Richard Jones was here to help Holman get ready for the syrup making. Bessie had been the one to drive the old wagon last year, but with Effie dead, she had her hands full at home with the children.

Lucy breathed a heavy sigh. So many of the neighbors now rested in the church graveyard. A few days ago she'd gone to put the last of the fall flowers on Annie May's grave. As she held her needle up to the light to thread it, she saw Holman and Richard stacking cane in a neat pile. It looked like Richard had more than last year. Of course, Jake had been there to help with the planting, so they'd planted more. What had happened to Jake? She felt his lips on hers. Her skin grew hot at the thought of his touch. It seemed like his eyes called to her. She jabbed hard at the patch. Blood oozed from her finger. She dropped the overalls, and her finger flew to her mouth. "Ouch!" It was all Jake's fault.

"Loo-ou-cy!"

She pressed her finger with the corner of her apron. "What do you want, Holman?"

"Would you bring us a bucket of cold water from the spring?"

She sighed and rose. She swung the wooden bucket in the air as she crossed the yard. Seemed like all she'd ever done was to take care of menfolk's needs. The memory of her pa's voice cut through the brisk autumn air. "Girl, have my supper ready tonight!" She gave another deep sigh as she dipped the water from the spring and headed back up the path. "Now see to it, girl," came her pa's voice again. She wondered who was taking care of him now. Probably some

195

poor mountain woman. As she neared where the men stacked empty barrels, she could hear them talking.

"How's your family doing, Richard?" asked Holman.

Richard heaved the last barrel onto the stack, wiped his hands on his overalls, and sat down on the back of the empty wagon. "I'll tell you, Mr. Carpenter, it's rough with no money coming in. Aunt Bessie used to sell a few eggs, but for some reason, the chickens have been dying off." Lucy caught her breath. Death! It had even affected the chickens.

Richard's voice broke. "Since Ma's passing, there ain't much worth working for. Maybe she'd still be here if Pa were alive. If I ever find the polecat that shot my pa, I'll take care of him all right."

Holman brushed his hands together. "I'm sorry about your folks, Richard, but there's the littl'-uns to work for. You're the man of the house now."

Richard shrugged. "I guess so. That's why I've been thinking about looking for public work."

Holman smiled. "I guess you're getting old enough to work a public job. And your brother Joe, he's a strong young man. I know he's still in school, but most boys his age are ready to quit. John's saying he's not a-going back after syrup making."

"He wouldn't quit. He can't," said Lucy. "John has to go to school."

Holman ignored her as he reached for the dipper and took a long slow drink. When he finished, he filled the dipper and handed it to Richard. "Where are you thinking about looking for a job?"

Lucy sighed. Holman didn't pay her any mind either, just like her pa'd always done. Guess it didn't matter much when it came to a woman's needs. Even Jake wasn't thinking about what *she* wanted when he was making his plans.

A shy smile crossed Richard's face. He took a drink, tossed the rest of the water on the ground, and handed the dipper to Lucy. She picked up the bucket and started toward the house. She heard Richard say, "I was thinking since you worked at a public job you could help get me one."

The silence that followed stopped Lucy and she turned around.

Holman dug the toe of his boot into the hard clay and studied the ground for a few moments. Lucy watched Richard's face. He looked down at his own bare, dusty feet and nudged a piece of cane with his big toe. Bees swarmed in the air. Lucy stood motionless. Why didn't Holman say something? She'd never seen him without words. Why did he hesitate? Why was his face so white?

Richard broke the silence. "I'm sorry, Mr. Carpenter. I didn't mean to . . ."

Holman held up his hand. "That's all right, Richard, but I just can't do that."

Richard crawled onto the seat of the wagon. "You don't need to say no more, Mr. Carpenter. I understand. I didn't have a right to ask." He picked up the reins and tapped the two gray mules. The wagon lunged forward.

For a moment Lucy thought Holman was going to run after him, but instead he turned and banged his fist against a barrel. "Damn this nasty business. If it weren't for my family starving, I'd quit." Lucy hurried back to the house. Holman sure was angry. She'd never seen him so mad except at Jake in the clearing that day.

Steam rose from the kettle of squirrel stew boiling on the stove. Lucy hurried to get the table set. Holman would be hungry after stacking barrels and getting the mill ready.

Holman stuck his head in the kitchen door. "Smells good."

Lucy turned to look at him. She didn't see any sign of him being mad now. "Arthur shot some squirrels, and I made some stew. Call the young-uns. It's time to eat."

Soon the kitchen was full. Hattie squeezed ahead of the little ones to get to the table. She clutched Annie May's doll next to her chest. Lucy waited for all of them to be seated as she watched Hattie. She wedged the doll between her knees and reached for the cornbread. Mary reached for it at the same time. Hattie drew back. Hattie still had that devilish look in her blue eyes, but before Annie May died, she would never have waited for anyone else to go first.

Dovey poured milk in each of the thick mugs as she smiled at Lucy. "Why don't you have a seat there next to Pa, Lucy? I'll get the vittles."

Holman pulled out a chair and patted it. "Come on, Lucy. You need to rest more. I'm worried about you doing too much. It takes time to get over typhoid. It leaves a body mighty weak." Lucy sat down. Why hadn't he thought of that earlier when he sent her for water? He was right, though. She did feel tired by the end of the day.

Dovey placed the large kettle of squirrel stew in front of Holman and picked up Martha from the bench. Holman dished out the savory stew onto each plate as they were passed. When all the children's plates were filled, he filled Lucy's plate. "Lucy, here's a good helping of this stew. It will put the bloom back in your cheeks."

John reached for the cornbread. "Pa, I told Miz Allison I wasn't gonna come back to school after syrup making."

The twin boys' hands shot up. Harley said, "If John quits, I don't see why we can't quit."

Mary wrinkled up her nose. "I don't like school either. Can I quit, too?"

Holman ruffled Mary's blond hair. "You've just started. It'll get better. And what do you think you'd do if you quit school, Harley?"

Harley pulled up his shoulder and pushed out his chest. "I could squirrel hunt. Bet I could kill as many as Arthur does."

"Me too," said Carl.

Arthur leaned back in his chair. "If anybody quits school to do the hunting, it ought to be me. I'm the best shot."

"That's just because you shot the turkey for Thanksgiving last year. Ever since then, we don't get a chance to learn because you've always got the gun," Harley complained. Arthur bowed his head and began to sop up the stew on his plate.

Lucy took a bite. She sure was glad the boys didn't know who shot the turkey at Thanksgiving. That would be awful hard on Arthur, especially with Holman treating him like a man now. Holman rapped on the table. "Now wait a minute, young-uns. You'll quit school when you're needed. Not before! John here can help with the hog killing. I've got to go away again after we kill hogs. Somebody's gonna have to get the wood in for winter. Besides, most boys John's age has already quit."

Lucy licked her fork. "I don't see no need for anybody to quit. I'm getting my strength back, so there ain't any reason I can't get the wood myself. *I* can't go to school." A wistful look crossed her face.

Holman touched her hand. "Ain't having no woman of mine out getting in wood when I have a house full of boys. The boys can get the wood on Saturdays if John wants to keep up his studies."

Dovey wiped Martha's mouth. "Well, I ain't gonna quit. Someday I'm gonna be a teacher like Miz Allison."

Lucy's face beamed with pride. Dovey sure was taking this schooling mighty seriously. She was sure she'd make a mighty fine teacher.

Lou Ellen crawled down from the bench. "Ain't nothing for me to do. Everybody goes off to school, and even Pa goes away somewhere all the time."

Lucy turned to Holman. "I heard you and Richard talking about him getting a public job. What kind of job is that?"

Holman scraped the last of the squirrel gravy from the kettle to his plate. "See there? That's why you need to go to school. Anybody knows a public job is one you have to go away from home to work."

Lucy's face grew bright red. Dovey set Martha down from the table. "Ain't no reason Lucy should know that, Pa. She said there wasn't many people where she lived."

Lucy was so glad Dovey had changed since she'd found out about the locket, 'specially since she didn't feel up to going away yet. "My pa went somewhere to work every day, but he came home at night."

Holman laid down his fork and looked at Lucy. "Lucy, you're sure a mighty purty woman when you get het up about somethin'." Lucy blushed even a shade deeper. She began to clear the table, thinking about her lessons. With Effie Jones dead, there wouldn't be any time for Bessie to help her with reading and writing. Maybe if she and Dovey became better friends, Dovey would help her. Dovey stacked the children's empty plates and passed them to Lucy. Holman scraped the last of the stew from his plate.

Lucy turned to Holman. "Bessie told me you were a good handyman. Is that what this public job is?"

Holman rose from the table. "Lucy, you ask too many gol-darn fool questions. Some things ain't fitting for a woman to know. Ain't for womenfolks to know how a man makes a living." He slammed his chair against the table and stormed out the door. The boys followed.

Dovey took the dishpans and set them on the table. "Hattie, you and the twins get the littl'-uns ready for bed. Me and Lucy will do the dishes."

Lucy reached for the lye soap and made a lather in the dishwater. The suds crackled and disappeared as the greasy plates were lowered into them. Dovey took the teakettle from the stove and poured steaming water into the rinse pan. She set the kettle down with a bang. "Men! Always putting womenfolks down."

Lucy scrubbed the stew pot. "Now Dovey, don't be too harsh on your pa. I ask too many questions anyhow."

Dovey poured more hot water over the plates. "No, you don't. You have a right to ask questions. Ain't no man gonna ever talk to me that way."

Lucy emptied the dishwater into the slop bucket, wiped the pan, and hung it on a nail near the stove. She turned to Dovey and smiled. "Well, Dovey, there ain't been no beaus come a-calling on you yet."

Dovey giggled. "It could be that'll change before long." Her smile disappeared and she looked sheepishly at Lucy. "Could we talk for a minute?"

Lucy pulled out a chair and sat down. Dovey slid onto the bench behind the table. "You know Will Ledford is sweet on me, and I kinda like him, too. I think he's gonna ask Pa if he can come a-calling soon. Do you think Pa'll let him?"

Lucy studied the girl's face for a moment. She knew this meant a lot to her. "Well, Dovey. I know Holman thinks Will's a fine young man. Would you like for me to talk to him about this?"

Dovey's face lit up. "Would you, Lucy? Would you do that for me?"

"Of course I would."

Dovey came around the table and gave her a hug. "Lucy, I miss Ma, but since we can't have her we're lucky to have you."

Lucy pushed back the girl's hair. "I've tried the best I know how to be a ma to you young-uns. I'm glad you're getting to go to school. I hope you'll get to be a teacher. I wish . . ."

"You wish what, Lucy?"

"Nothing."

Dovey picked up a stick of wood. She poked the fire in the cookstove. "Lucy, I've been watching you. You can't read or write much, can you?"

Lucy blushed. "Bessie was helping me learn when the fever hit. And now with Miz Jones gone, she ain't got the time."

The room was quiet. Dovey sat down opposite Lucy. A spark from the fire in the stove broke the silence. Then Dovey spoke. "I'll help you. I ain't a teacher, but I could get Miz Allison to show me how to teach you."

Lucy reached for her hand across the table. Dovey clasped it. "We'll start tomorrow night."

Lucy nodded. A tear slid down her face. The fire crackled again, and the flames licked at the firebox door. A fire had not only been rekindled in the stove, but also in Lucy's heart.

≈   ≈   ≈

Black smoke bellowed from under the big black washpot. Lucy dumped two buckets of water into a washtub. The crisp November air bit at her nose. She set down the buckets and stretched out her hands to the fire. When they were warm, she cupped them over her face to warm her nose.

"You want me to fetch some water, Lucy?"

"Thought you was down at the pigpen with your pa, John."

John dropped his head. "I was, but I told Pa you'd need some help with the water. Takes lots of hot water to scald hogs."

Lucy handed him the buckets. John was such a soft-hearted young man. He'd make some lucky girl a good husband. "It'll only take a couple more trips to fill this pot. While you're doing that, I'll clean out the washtubs. We'll need them to put the meat in."

"Who's gonna kill the hogs?" asked Lucy.

"Pa'll do it."

Two rapid shots rang out. They echoed from the opposite side of the mountain. She straightened from cleaning the tubs. "John, you look a little pale."

John's face flushed. "I'll never be as good at killing as Pa is. Guess I'm more like Annie May was."

"Yeah, I remember." Wilted violets . . . a tattered quilt . . . a fresh mound of earth flashed across her mind. There was so much a person couldn't change. All you could do was try to make the best out of what happens to you. That was what she was trying to do. At least she and Dovey had become friends. She reached over and gave John a pat on the shoulder. "The world needs all kinds of people, son." John sighed and started for the branch with the water buckets.

"I don't like killing either." Lucy turned to find Richard Jones standing against the old walnut tree that shaded the wash place. "Bessie said you-uns would need my help today."

"Thanks, Richard. We can always use an extra pair of hands," said Lucy.

Holman came toward her. The mule pulled a sled that carried two hogs. Lucy threw back her shoulders. Well, the way things looked she'd be here for the winter. She'd make Holman know she planned on carrying her share of the work around here. Couldn't say a Davenport didn't earn their keep. "We're all ready, Holman. Water's hot. Tubs are clean for the meat."

Holman heaved the hogs over onto some boards. Will Ledford came from the barn with an armload of tow sacks. He dumped them on the ground.

Holman shook the feed out of a few and laid them over the hogs. "Hurry up, John. We need the buckets to scald the hog hides." John emptied the water into one of the pots and refilled them with hot water from the other pot. He handed them to Holman. Holman poured the water over the tow sacks. Lucy gasped and took a few steps back as the steaming, sickening stench of hog penetrated her nostrils.

"Richard, you keep the sacks hot. John, you keep the pots filled." Holman handed John one of the buckets. The hot steam continued to rise from the hogs. Soon they were scraping bristles. "Bring me that chain over here, Richard. We have this hog ready to hang and cut up."

"I'll get the chain, Mr. Carpenter," said Will. "Richard is still scraping on his hog."

"Thanks, Will. A boy like you would be welcome in this family.

Bring me that sharp butcher knife." With one swift stroke Holman split the hog's belly, loosened the entrails, and pulled them out. They fell into a large tub under the hog. Will hauled it away. "Get the liver out and give it to Lucy, Will. She can take it to the house for Bessie and Dovey to fry for dinner."

Will fished into the tub of entrails and lifted out a large blob of dark red, steaming liver. Lucy held out a dishpan. Richard cut the liver free and dropped it into the pan. The thought of fresh liver frying made her hungry. "I'll get on in the house and help Dovey and Bessie fry up some of this for dinner."

"That'll be good," said Will. "Ain't nothing better than fresh pork liver."

Lucy pushed open the back door with her foot and set the pan on the cook table. "Guess you all want this fried up for dinner," said Bessie.

"Yeah, the men are getting hungry."

"I figured they would be. Dovey's got the taters peeled."

Lucy turned to Dovey. "I'm glad you were willing to stay home and help Bessie today. I know how you like school, but this hog killing's a lot of work."

"Miz Allison insisted I stay and help you. She's worried about you. I am, too. You need to take it easy for awhile. You know the fever takes a lot out of a body."

Lucy took the pot of potatoes from Dovey and set them on the stove. "You run on out and see if you can help your pa and the boys. I'll help Bessie fry the liver. It won't take long so tell them to get washed up as soon as they can."

Bessie sliced liver. Lucy dredged the pieces in flour and began to drop them into the skillet of hot grease. Before the last piece was dropped in, Dovey burst through the door. "Lucy, guess . . ." She glanced toward Bessie and lowered her eyes.

Lucy's hand stopped in midair, the liver slice dangling from her fingers. Dovey moved closer to Lucy and whispered, "I just heard Will ask Pa if he could come a-calling on me." Lucy wondered what it would be like to have somebody call on her. For a moment Jake was in the room with her. The tingle of his lips on hers caused her cheeks to burn. The liver fell into the pan and hot grease splashed onto the stove. "Ain't you happy for me, Lucy?"

Lucy wiped her sticky fingers on her apron and put her arms around the girl. "I'm glad, Dovey. Will's a nice boy, and more than that, I'm happy you wanted to tell me."

"Who else am I gonna tell? You're my ma now."

"The men are coming," said Bessie. "Better get dinner on the table."

Holman entered the kitchen, took off his hat and coat, and hung them on the hook by the door. "That liver sure does smell good," he said with a grin. His thinning hair and large red ears replaced the picture of Jake in Lucy's mind. Wonder what it would be like if Holman kissed her! Not as long as she could remember the touch of Jake's lips. She knew Jake and Holman had had a falling out. Wasn't anything she could do about that, but that didn't change how she felt. Oh well, Jake would never come back for her now. No man was going to ever love her.

≈   ≈   ≈

When the sun set in the mountains, darkness soon followed. Shadows were already moving in—shadows that were ghostly.

Hickory smoke oozed through the cracks of the smokehouse. A dim light glowed inside. Lucy shifted the weight of the pan to her other hip and rushed toward the light. She had worked hard to get the last bit of sausage stuffed into the cleaned guts. She wanted to get it hung before dark.

"Holman, that you?"

"Yeah, just finishing hanging up the hams." He reached for the pan. His fingers closed over hers. The hickory chips stewed and spit in the gathering dusk. A field mouse scampered across the dirt floor.

Lucy glanced down at the sticky fingers closed over hers. Was it the time of day? The day's work they'd done together? Or could it be . . . ? She shoved the pan toward him. No! It couldn't be. This wasn't Jake. This was Holman. She turned to leave.

"We ain't hung the sausage yet."

She reached for the pan. "I'll hand them to you and you can hang them."

Holman stepped up on a bench. For a while they worked in silence. Then Holman spoke. "Will Ledford asked me today if he could come a-calling on Dovey."

"I know. She told me. Made me feel good. Like a *real* ma."

"In a way you are a *real* . . ."

"I got to get back and get supper on."

Holman stepped down from the bench. "Supper can wait, Lucy. You and me need to talk. Will asking me if he could come calling on Dovey made me realize my young-uns is a-growing up. I ain't getting any younger either, so I got to thinking about you and me."

"What about you and me?"

"Dovey might be thinking about you like a ma, but I've been a-thinking about you like a . . . a . . . woman."

"Well, I *am* a woman, Holman."

Holman spit into the hickory chips. "Shoot fire, Lucy! You know what I mean. I'm tired of sleeping in the hayloft by myself. I got to go away again tomorrow. When I come home, we're gonna have to settle some things." He stomped out of the smokehouse. Lucy sat with her head in her hands and stared into the smoking chips. Jake? Wife? Mother? Where did she belong?

~ 19 ~

Lucy took the popcorn from a shelf over the cook table and poured some into the popper. It was Christmas Eve day, and no one had mentioned putting up a tree. She'd pop the corn and string it. Then maybe it would seem more like Christmas. Dovey came into the kitchen and sat down at the table. "What're you doing, Lucy?"

"Thought I'd pop the corn for the tree."

"I don't feel like having a tree this year. Ain't gonna be no fun with Annie May gone."

"Annie May would want us to have a tree. Remember last year how much fun she had making the angel for the top of it?"

"I remember," said Hattie from the doorway. "I remember because I was so nasty to her. All I could think about was that we didn't have a tinsel angel for our tree. Can I hang Annie May's angel on the tree this year, Lucy?"

"I think it would be nice for you to put the angel on the tree. Now why don't you go find a couple of the boys to fetch it. Dovey and me will get the decorations ready."

Before long the Carpenter house buzzed with the excitement of Christmas preparations. Lucy popped the corn and the twins strung it into long ropes. Dovey helped the little ones make paper decorations. The ones they'd made last year were laid out on the kitchen table.

Hattie picked up the paper angel and gently unfolded it. She read, "To ma, with love, from Annie May." Tears rolled down her cheeks. "You think love can come from heaven, Lucy?"

"Course I do, honey. Where else would it come from? I'm sure your ma and Annie May send their love for this Christmas." Lucy felt a familiar loneliness wrap its icy fingers around her heart. For a moment it overwhelmed her. A noise outside interrupted her thoughts.

Hattie ran to the door. "It's the boys. They're back with the tree."

Everyone raced for the yard, leaving Lucy alone in the kitchen. She picked up the angel and pressed it to her breast. "Ma, I still miss you so much. I wish I could visit my spot on the mountain. I need to feel you near to me. Jake's gone and he won't be back. Annie May died. I loved her so much, Ma. Guess I'm really beginning to feel like I belong here. Dovey's treating me like a real ma, and even Hattie ain't being such a troublemaker. And Holman, Ma, sometimes I think he thinks of me as a real woman. If it hadn't been for his good care, I might not have got over the fever." Lucy laid down the angel and wiped her eyes. "And there's Pa, Ma. I wonder how he is. I wouldn't be surprised if he don't have a mountain woman to care for his needs."

Hattie came to the door. "Lucy, come see the tree. It's the prettiest tree we've ever had."

Lucy stepped into the yard. "It's perfect, John. Where'd you find it?"

"Up by the clearing. Just on the other side where the fawn was buried."

Lucy closed her eyes tight. She felt the emptiness of the clearing . . . heard the frogs croaking . . . smelled the damp earth. A warm hand touched hers. "You all right, Ma?"

Lucy opened her eyes half expecting to see Annie May, but instead Dovey peered at her from behind her stringy hair. Lucy reached out and pushed the girl's hair back. "I'm fine, but we're gonna have to do somethin' about your hair before Will comes a-calling tonight."

Dovey blushed. "He's just gonna walk me to church for the Christmas program. You think Pa'll be home to go to church with us?"

"He don't ever miss seeing me be an angel," said Hattie, "but I ain't gonna be an angel this year."

"You ain't! Why not?" asked Lucy.

"The Sunday school teacher decided Mary would make a better angel. Anyway, I'm getting too big for that kinda stuff. I'm gonna be Jesus's mother Mary this year."

"That's the part Annie May played last year, ain't it?"

Hattie looked up at Lucy and smiled. "Yeah, and we're gonna use the doll she gave me for baby Jesus."

Lucy gave her a hug. Even Hattie was growing up. Time did go on, no matter what. That's what she'd do—go on right here with the young-uns. Jake wasn't coming back, and she didn't have anywhere else to go.

"Time to put the tree up," called John. It didn't take long to get the children involved. Some strung popcorn ropes around the tree. Others hung paper decorations. Hattie picked up the angel and looked up at the top of the tree. "I wish Pa was here to hold me up so I could reach the top."

"Well, I ain't Pa, but I'll be glad to hold you." John hoisted her up onto his shoulder.

Hattie leaned over and tied the angel to the treetop. Her face beamed with pride. "There, Annie May, I've put your angel where it belongs, and tonight at church, me and your doll are gonna do your part in the Christmas play, too."

John set her down again and Dovey handed her a broom. "Let's hurry and get cleaned up. It won't be long till it's time for church."

Lucy put on her shawl and started for the barn. The warmth of the children's laughter followed her into the cold. She sniffed the sweet smell of cured hay as she climbed the ladder to the hayloft. The late afternoon sun seeped through the cracks, making long shadows across the hay. She remembered the weeks she'd nursed Annie May here on a bed of straw. These same shadows had taken her life. Then there were the long weeks Holman had taken care of her. It all seemed so long ago. And Jake—had he ever been real? Holman had said it was hard to remember his wife Mary. Time *did* make a difference. She reached down and felt under a pile of straw. The things she'd made for the young-uns were still where she'd hid them.

"Can't a man have a place to call his own?"

"Oh, Holman, I'm sorry! I just come up to see if the young-uns had got into the presents I made for them."

Holman threw down his bedroll. "Sorry! That ain't what I need to hear." He jerked the tie loose on the bedroll and started to spread it out.

Lucy watched him and anger sparked deep inside her. As she watched, the spark grew. Who'd he think he was talking to? She wasn't one of the young-uns who needed to be scolded. She swallowed, hoping to push the feeling away. "Holman, the young-uns will be glad you're home. They've been hoping that you'd be here in time to go to the Christmas play."

Holman took off his coat and slung it up over a rafter. "That ain't what I need to hear, either! They know that I wouldn't miss their play."

Lucy brushed a loose strand of hair from her face. *Needs!* That was all she ever heard. Her pa's needs . . . Holman's needs . . . the young-uns' needs. Needs was why she was here. Her hand moved to her throat. Need had taken her precious locket. Her cheeks felt burning hot. Her head hurt. *"Needs!"* she suddenly said aloud.

Holman dropped his bedroll and turned to stare at her.

"I'm tired of everybody else's needs! I got needs, too!" She pressed her temples. Blood pounded through her veins. "I'm a person, not a dream. I'm a real live person, and I need a place same as you!"

Holman moved toward her, reaching out to her. Her eyes searched his. A softness she had never seen before caressed the corners of his eyes. "Lucy, I didn't know . . . I didn't know how you felt . . . I didn't . . ."

Something deep within her wanted to erase all the hurt he'd ever known. "It's not all your fault, Holman."

"Needs . . . places . . . faults. The way I see it, it don't make much difference now." His fingertips brushed her cheeks as he reached for a piece of straw that hung from her hair. "Remember last year, Lucy, when I told you how I couldn't remember Mary anymore? Truth is, I was thinking about you."

Lucy blushed and looked away. Holman gently cupped her face in his hands and turned her toward him. "Don't you know I'm in love with you, Lucy? I tried to tell you that day in the smokehouse. I need a wife as much as the young-uns need a ma."

". . . and I need a . . . a . . ." Lucy stuttered.

"Do you need a husband, Lucy, as well as a place?"

Lucy nodded. Holman's hands moved from her face to her neck.

Lucy felt a throb in her throat. It quickened and raced with a new kind of energy—a kind that she hadn't felt with Jake. Holman's hands slid around to the back of her neck. He undid her hairpins and ran his fingers through the thickness of her long black hair.

Need! A sweet tingling need tore through her body. Holman's lips touched the place on her neck that throbbed. A need to be loved, and even more, a need to love, filled her. Her arms twined around him as she pulled him closer.

Her woolen shawl dropped to the floor. Holman fumbled with the buttons on her blouse. She felt the firmness of her breast against his chest. Her body, as well as her soul, was ready for this union. Goosebumps raced up her spine as Holman's rough hands caressed her soft breast. His mouth found hers and gently kissed her. It was a slow, burning kiss. She pressed her body closer to his.

Holman looked down into her eyes. "Are you sure, Lucy? Are you sure this is what you want?" She nodded and buried her face in his shirt. Holman lowered her into a soft mound of hay. She shivered, but it wasn't from the cold. Holman's mouth found hers again. This time he kissed like a man that hadn't had a meal in a week, but even with his hunger came gentleness. The soft dusk folded around them like a blessing. Soon, Lucy knew her needs had been met.

≈ ≈ ≈

Si-i-lent night. Ho-o-ly night. As the congregation sang, the air filled with a soft melody. The cast took its place on stage to prepare for a final bow. Lucy didn't even try to mouth the words of the carol. She gazed through the window. Soft moonlight bathed the church grave-yard. The mica in Annie May's homemade tombstone glistened. A lump moved up from the pit of Lucy's stomach to her throat. She swallowed. Annie May was buried! It didn't seem real. She brushed at her eyes with her hand. So much had changed since she'd come here.

A shadow moved across the graveyard. Lucy half expected to see Jake step from behind a headstone. That was where memories of him belonged—buried, like Annie May. In her mind she'd almost buried what the letter had said, too. They'd all suffered enough. And that mean old Herby Ledford—she hadn't seen him around lately, not even at the syrup making. Holman's hand touched hers. She smiled up at him. Yes, she'd finally found her place. This was real. The silence brought her thoughts back to the play. The cast bowed and the audience clapped.

The church rang with the joy of the season as friends and neighbors wished each other a merry Christmas. Lucy slipped her hand into Holman's, and in her heart sprang her own joy.

Bessie pushed her way toward them. "Howdy, dearie. You sure look pretty tonight. Somehow you look different. Your eyes are sparkling like a firecracker on the Fourth of July."

Lucy studied the middle-aged, plump woman in front of her. She looked more tired than usual. Her hands were rough and red. A large patch covered the front of her Sunday dress. Lucy glanced down. Bessie's shoes were the same ones that she'd had on when Lucy first met her, scuffed, unpolished, and rundown at the heels. Lucy smiled at Holman. She felt so young and yet so grown up!

Hattie tugged on Holman's coat. "Can't we go, Pa? We got to get all the young-uns in bed so Santa can come."

"That's a good idea, Hattie. You round up the littl'-uns and head them for the door. You about ready to go, Lucy?"

Lucy pulled her shawl tighter. She reached out and gave Bessie a quick hug. "I'll come up for coffee soon, and we'll have a good visit."

Hattie ushered the little ones toward the door. Lucy took Holman's arm and followed. In the yard Holman turned to Dovey. "You'd better run along with Hattie and help get the littl'-uns to bed."

Dovey glanced toward the shadows where Will waited. "Pa, do I have to? Hattie's big enough to take care of them."

Lucy squeezed Holman's arm. "Hattie can manage. Dovey wants to walk home with Will."

"Oh?"

Lucy jabbed his ribs with her elbow. "Hattie, you go ahead. Dovey'll be along soon."

"Oh?"

"Don't sound so innocent with your oh's, Holman. You know Dovey's growing up."

Will stepped up beside Dovey. "Thank you, Miz Carpenter." Will took Dovey's hand and they headed down the path.

A warm, sweet tenderness quivered in Lucy's chest. "Holman, why don't you have one of the boys run on ahead and move the big bed back to the front room?"

"Oh?"

"You know—the big brass bedstead, the one I sleep in."

"Oh?"

"I think the boys are still here," said Lucy. "There they are, talking to Richard Jones."

"John," called Holman. "Come here a minute."

The boys said their goodbyes, and John joined Holman and Lucy. "What do you want, Pa?"

"When you get home, will you see to it that Lucy's bed is moved back to the front room?"

"Sure, Pa. I'll see to it."

By now the church was dark. Lucy looked up at the stars. They seemed so close she felt she could pluck a handful. "Holman, could we stop at Annie May's grave just a minute?"

Lucy heard him give a heavy sigh as he guided her toward the graveyard. At Annie May's tombstone, neither one spoke. Buried; yes, it had all been buried. Now it was time to live. She touched her husband on the cheek. "It's good to have you home, Holman."

Holman pulled her close. "It's been a long time since I've been home, really home!"

~ *20* ~

The warm April rain splashed against the window. Lucy peered through it. Holman should have been here last night.

"Who're you looking for, Lucy?"

She turned to find John standing behind her. "Your pa. He said that he'd be home in time for my birthday today."

"You know Pa. He ain't like you, doing things on time." John eyed the table. "You always have the meals on time."

Lucy set a pitcher of sorghum across from a steaming platter of buttermilk biscuits. Then she poured a huge bowl of gravy and set it in the middle of the table. She scooted a jar of jelly over to make room for the homemade sausage and souse meat.

"John, why don't you run out to the springhouse and get us some more butter. Make sure to get one of the molds with a print of wheat on top. It needs to be used first. Got plenty of biscuits and gravy, but there ain't any eggs. Too many old setting hens."

John turned to leave. "Don't worry about Pa, Lucy. He'll be here before the day's over."

Hattie stumbled into the kitchen as she rubbed sleep from her eyes. She yawned and slid onto the bench behind the table. She took a biscuit and broke it open, then reached for the butter. "Ain't no butter on the table, Lucy."

"John's gone for the butter, Hattie. And put that biscuit down. Wait for the rest. I ain't raising no young-un without manners."

Hattie's blue eyes flashed. For a moment Lucy thought she was going to get some backtalk, but Hattie's face softened. A smile played around the corners of her lips, and she laid down the biscuit. Lucy realized how far she'd come from her first morning in this kitchen. It was good to joke and tease with the young-uns now. And a year ago she would've been dreading Holman's coming home.

Arthur appeared at the door. "Breakfast ready?"

The back door slammed. "Course breakfast's ready. By now you ought to know Lucy ain't never late with a meal." John set the mold of butter on the table.

Dovey came in carrying Martha. In one hand she held a hairbrush that had half its bristles out. The rest of the young-uns followed her. Mary's face was streaked with tears.

Lucy pulled out a chair and sat down. "What's wrong, Mary?"

"Dovey's been a-trying to pull my hair out by the roots."

"Well, if you'd let some of us comb it for you, it wouldn't look like a mop," said Dovey.

Hattie reached for the butter. "Ain't no wonder you can't get the tangles out with that brush. Looks like Pa's bald head."

Lucy glanced at the brush Dovey held. "We're gonna have to see about getting you young-uns a different brush, but get that one away from the table."

Dovey tucked the brush under her skirt. "That's gonna be hard with no peddler coming around."

Lucy passed the plate of biscuits to Dovey. "I'll speak to your pa and see what he can do about getting one."

Dovey flipped her hand under her long, straight hair. "I hope you can do somethin'. Will says when I brush my hair it makes it shine like the sun."

Harley chuckled. "We ain't had sun for a week. Will must be feeding you a line."

John cut a large hunk of butter, taking part of the wheat design. "You do have to watch out, Dovey. Sometimes boys say things just to get . . ."

Dovey cut him short. "Was that a line you was giving Alice out behind the church the other night? Looked more like a kiss to me."

John pushed back his chair as he reached for another biscuit. He winked at Dovey. "You sure you don't need glasses? Too bad the peddler ain't coming around no more. You could get some of the magnifying glasses he carried." He shoved the last of his first biscuit into his mouth.

Dovey set Martha down and wiped her hands and face with the dishrag. "I don't need glasses. I know what I seen."

Lucy picked up the half-bald hairbrush from the bench and stuck it into her apron pocket. When Holman came home, she'd show it to him. Holman! Her pulse quickened. Surely he'd be home before supper.

"Out there's Will Ledford in the yard," said John. "I'll go see what he wants."

Dovey set the dishpans down on the corner of the table. "The next time you see Richard Jones, you gonna tell him that you've been sweet-talking his sister out behind the church?"

"Well," said John. "It won't matter if the sun don't shine today. We'll have your head to light up the . . ."

Dovey gave him a warning glance and followed him to the door. "Dummy," she whispered, "you almost gave it away."

"What're you two whispering about?" asked Lucy.

Dovey looked up innocently. "Whispering? Who's whispering? Did you see anybody whispering, Hattie?"

Hattie cupped her hands over her mouth and snickered. "I didn't see nothing."

Lucy poured hot water from a big iron kettle over the clean dishes. Hattie and Dovey worked without speaking. Lucy felt the same kind of excitement in the air as she felt at Christmas. She wondered if it could be because she was expecting Holman to come home. Or could it be the whispering that still lingered in the air?

≈   ≈   ≈

By afternoon the rain had stopped. The sun played hide and seek from behind the clouds that lingered. Lucy threw a shovel of cow manure into a hole, then covered it with dirt. With her forefinger, she made a hole and dropped in two cucumber seeds. She raked warm earth over the seeds with her hand.

Conditions were right for planting. With the rain there'd be no need to water, and the afternoon sun would cause the seeds to sprout. Lucy bent to plant more seeds. The strong odor of manure gagged her and her stomach boiled. The seeds fell to the ground. She held her stomach and bent over as the vomit came. When her stomach felt empty, she eased herself down under the shade of an apple tree.

It must have been the souse meat she ate this morning. Maybe she'd put in too much pepper when she made it.

"Lucy, you about through out there?" John asked as he came across the yard. "You all right? You look a little green around the gills."

Lucy mopped her face with her apron. "My stomach don't feel too good. Must have been that souse meat I ate this morning."

John picked up the hoe. "Come on in the house. You can lay down. I'll take the hoe and wheelbarrow back to the barn."

"Think I will. You coming back to the house?"

John started for the barn. "I'll be right along."

Lucy walked toward the house holding her stomach. It seemed unusually quiet, and the door was closed. She reached for the knob just as the door opened. "Happy Birthday!" rose a chorus of voices.

Lucy caught her breath and took a step backwards. John came up behind her and took her by the shoulders. "You surprised, Lucy?"

"Is this why you insisted the cucumbers get planted this afternoon, John?"

John gave her a hug. "Had to get you out of here some way."

Hattie pushed her way through the crowd. "Come on, Lucy. Come to the kitchen and see your cake."

In the kitchen Lucy found Bessie behind the long kitchen table, grinning from ear to ear. In the middle of the table stood one of her chocolate cakes.

"Bessie, you shouldn't have. I know things are tight this year for you."

Bessie picked up a long knife. "I should have, and it didn't hurt us none. Dovey brought up the stuff for the cakes. All I did was bake them."

"Them?"

Bessie cut a slice of cake. "There's another one over there under the dishpan. Didn't think one would feed all this crowd, did you? My young-uns wouldn't ever miss a birthday party."

Lucy scanned the group. Alice had found John, and she was cuddling up to him. The little ones were crowded around the table hoping for a chance to stick their fingers into the chocolate frosting. "I don't see Richard."

216

Bessie passed her a piece of cake. "Richard's gone off and got him a public job."

Lucy took the cake. "What kinda public job?"

Bessie picked up her slice of cake and sat down. "Don't know. Just left the first of the week. Don't know when he'll be back." Bessie squinted at Lucy. "Why ain't you eating your cake, Lucy? Don't you like it?"

"The cake's fine. My stomach don't feel too good."

Bessie reached for the plate. "Why don't I put it over here under the pan, and you go rest for a spell. You do look a little peaked."

Dovey stepped up to the table. "Before you go lay down, Lucy, I have a present for you."

Lucy blushed again. "That ain't necessary. What you did, taking the stuff to Bessie for the cake, was present enough." She reached out to give Dovey a hug, but Dovey had already stepped behind her.

"Close your eyes tight, Lucy, and don't open them till I say so." Lucy's eyelids quivered as she squeezed them together. She felt Dovey's hand touch her shoulder. "Now promise you won't open your eyes till I say so."

Lucy swallowed. "I promise, but hurry. My stomach ain't feeling too good." She felt the touch of cold metal around her neck. Her hand went to her throat just in time to catch something. Her locket! She let her thumb rub across the letters. Yes, her ma'd been right. She had found love, and she'd found that it was more than a word on a piece of jewelry.

Dovey walked around in front of her. "You can open your eyes now." Tears filled Lucy's eyes and ran down her cheeks. She didn't trust her voice to speak. "I helped Miz Allison with some of the slower young-uns. She paid me with the locket that you gave her to pay for my trip."

Lucy placed her free hand on Dovey's arm as she cleared her throat. "I never thought that I'd see my locket again."

"I knew you didn't. After I found out what you did, I talked to Miz Allison. She told me she hadn't wanted to take it, but you'd insisted."

Lucy gave her a hug. "And you've been working all year just to get it back for me."

Now it was Dovey's turn to blush. "It was somethin' that I wanted to do for you. I knew how much it meant to you."

"Dovey, no matter what, even if I have young-uns of my own, you'll always be a special daughter." She glanced around the room at all the young-uns. "All of you have a special place in my heart." She felt dizzy. The floor rose to meet her as arms closed around her. The next thing she knew she was being lowered onto her bed. Someone placed a cold cloth on her forehead. She tried to sit up but fell back against the pillows. She could hear whispering, then the room grew quiet. Slowly she opened her eyes. Bessie sat on the edge of the bed. "What happened to me?"

Bessie looked down at her lap. "You can answer that question better than me."

Lucy took the cloth from her forehead and wiped her face. "Guess I just overworked in the garden."

Bessie looked her in the eyes. "That could be part of it, but if my hunch is right you'd better start knitting little booties."

Lucy's hand caressed her stomach. She looked shyly at Bessie. "You think that could be it?"

"I've seen that look in many an eye. Knew every time that Luther's missus was in the family way. You just stay right there and rest. I'll get on out and help Dovey clean up, and then I've got to get on home."

Lucy watched Bessie leave the room. Tenderly, she touched her stomach. A baby! Why hadn't she thought of that? Of course, that was what was wrong. She hadn't had her monthly sickness for three months. She thought of the doc's searching eyes. Wouldn't he be surprised? What about Holman—what would he think? He'd said he had him enough young-uns. She closed her eyes. She needed some sleep for now; she'd think about telling Holman later.

Voices echoed through the house. Lucy struggled to wake up. Why weren't the young-uns quieter? They knew she didn't feel well.

There was a banging on the door, and without waiting, John burst in. "Lucy, it's Pa. There's a man coming up the road leading a horse, and I think it's Pa laying across the saddle."

Lucy jumped up. Her head spun, and she stumbled backward. John reached out to steady her. "I'm all right. Just give me a second." She steadied herself for a moment by hanging onto his arm, then started for the door. "Let's hurry. Your pa could be hurt bad."

~ *21* ~

The clock on the mantle ticked away the time. It had been exactly sixteen hours since the sheriff had brought Holman home with a bullet in his chest. Now he lay on the bed, motionless, his face drained of color. Still, the clock ticked away. Lucy stood and rubbed the back of her neck. The doctor had said Holman didn't have much time left. Lucy had stayed by his bed all night, but there hadn't been any change. Her stomach felt weak. She'd forgotten all about her condition. What if Holman died? Her baby wouldn't have a pa.

Lucy lowered herself onto the chair. John came into the room as she buried her face in her hands. "What's wrong, Lucy? Is Pa worse?"

"No, John, there's no change." She squinted toward the window. "That morning sun is so bright. Would you get a quilt and hang it over the window to darken the room a bit?" A fly buzzed and lit on Holman's bandage. Lucy brushed it away, then checked the blood-soaked rags. She hoped Bessie would get here soon. This wound needed to be cleaned again.

John came back with the quilt. "Look's like Pa's bandage needs to be changed. You want me to help you?"

Lucy shooed away more flies. "No, John, we'll wait for Bessie. She said last night that she would be here to help. She's better at this than I am. You just hang the quilt."

John shook out a quilt top. "I brought this quilt top. Thought it wouldn't make the room so dark."

"Good idea, John. Bessie'll need light to work by."

"Lucy, who do you think shot Pa? He was a friend to everybody."

Lucy stood and stretched. "I know. He had a lot of friends. I've been sitting here all night trying to figure it all out. I wonder if it had somethin' to do with his public job."

"I don't know, but I aim to find out. Richard's pa was shot, and the lawman done nothing about it, and now my pa's been shot. I'm gonna go get the wood for the cookstove now, but I want you to be thinking. Did Pa ever say or do anything that would help me find the varmint who shot him?"

Lucy wiped Holman's face with a wet rag. She remembered the argument between Holman and Jake. Had they had another argument? No, Holman had told Jake to leave. What about Richard and that public job! That had to be it. Somehow Richard had found out about Holman and Luther. She knew whatever was going on, Holman was as honest as the day was long. She rubbed her forehead. Something bothered her but she couldn't quite figure it out.

The door opened and Bessie quietly entered the room. She whispered, "How's he doing?"

Lucy bent over him. "He's still alive. When the doc dug that bullet out of his chest yesterday, he didn't give him much of a chance. Said it just missed his heart."

Bessie took the rag from her. "I know. I've been worried sick all night. Would have been here sooner, but Richard got in this morning from his public job. Had to fix him somethin' to eat before I could come. I'll go fetch some warm water so we can wash Holman and change his bandages."

Lucy's head whirled with all sorts of thoughts. Richard and his public job was what was bothering her. Last fall when Holman and Richard were getting ready to make syrup, Richard had asked him to get him a job and Holman refused. Then when Richard rode away, Holman had been angry—so angry that he'd hit the barrels they'd just stacked. He'd sworn he'd quit if it weren't for his family starving.

Bessie came back with the water. She began to take off the blood-soaked bandages. Lucy's stomach felt queasy. "Lucy, in your condition you don't need to see this. You know that you could mark the baby. Besides, you've been up all night. You need somethin' to eat and some rest. I told Dovey to fix you some breakfast."

"Thanks, Bessie. When John comes in from cutting wood, I'll send him in to set awhile. You can come out and have a cup of coffee with me." Bessie nodded. Lucy pulled the door shut behind her.

Dovey set a plate of grits and sausage on the table, then sat down. "Lucy, Pa's not gonna die, is he?"

221

Lucy pushed the sausage around on her plate with her fork. She didn't know how to answer. She looked into Dovey's demanding eyes and sighed. "Well, honey, I'll be honest with you. The doc didn't think he'd make it through the night, but it's morning and he's still here."

Dovey filled Lucy's coffee cup. "Do you think it would help if we prayed for him?"

Lucy stirred a spoonful of sugar into her coffee. "It might, Dovey. Ever since I've been learning to read, I've been trying to find out more about this Jesus you talk about. I'm not sure . . ."

"Not sure of what, Lucy?"

"About this Jesus person. I don't know enough to believe."

"If I can teach you to read and write, I can show you how to believe. I'll be right back."

Soon Dovey returned with her ma's Bible. She opened it and pointed to a verse. "Read this, Lucy."

"For God so loved the . . . wo-r-ld, that he gave his only be-got-ten son . . . that who-so-ever be . . ."

Dovey looked over her shoulder. "Believeth. That means trusting in Him."

A soft smile curved the corners of Lucy's mouth as she continued to read. "Shall have ever-last-ing life. I ain't sure that I know what a be-got-ten son is."

Dovey read the verse again. "I suppose it means that it was the only son he got."

Lucy could feel her eyes grow moist. "And He gave Him up to die so I can live forever."

"Yes, Lucy. All you have to do is believe that's what He done."

"Well, if the Good Book says it, that's good enough for me."

"That's right, Lucy, and now that I've showed you how to believe, and I taught you to read and write, why can't I teach you to pray? All you have to do is pretend that God is setting here just like me. Bowing your head and closing your eyes helps. Then you just ask Him to make Pa better."

The room was quiet. A robin sang outside. Dovey waited.

"Do I have to say it out loud?"

Dovey thought a moment. "No, I reckon not. I pray lots of times just to myself."

Lucy bowed her head and thought a prayer.

≈　　≈　　≈

"It's a miracle!" Doc Rogers turned from Holman's bedside and snapped his black bag shut. "Yesterday at this time when I took that bullet out of him, I wouldn't give a plug nickel for his life." He handed Lucy a packet of powder. "However, looks like today he's going to live. He may still run a fever. If he does, just give him some of these powders. You know how to mix them, don't you?"

Lucy nodded. "You'll be back tomorrow, won't you?"

He picked up his bag and paused at the door. His eyes traveled down her body, then rested on her stomach. "I'll be back, and you, young lady, had better get some rest. A woman in your condition needs to take care of herself."

"What condition, Lucy?" asked John. "I thought it was Pa that the doc was worried about."

"John, your pa's gonna be all right! He's just took a turn for the better. The doc said that he still might run a fever, but he'll be all right."

John threw his arms around her. "Oh, Lucy! I've been so worried. I've been a-praying . . ."

"Lucy, I've got some fresh trout that Arthur caught today just coming out of the pan," called Bessie from the kitchen. "You ready to eat?"

Lucy patted John on the shoulder and went into the kitchen. "Bessie! He's gonna be all right! He's gonna be all right!"

Bessie hugged her. "Glory be! I was worried that you'd be left alone in your condition."

"What condition?" John asked from the doorway. Lucy blushed.

Bessie said, "John, why don't you go pick some poke salad? I'll sit with Holman while you're gone."

"That's funny you'd ask him to do that, Bessie. I've been craving poke salad."

John's eyes traveled over Lucy. "Uh-oh! I see." He picked up a pan

223

and went out. Lucy bowed her head and thanked God her baby was going to have a pa.

≈   ≈   ≈

Holman's fever began to creep up as the shadows moved across the mountain. Lucy remembered Annie May's struggle. The shadows had won that time. They wouldn't win this time. Doc Rogers had said only a few hours ago that Holman would live. Besides, she'd prayed that God's will be done, and she couldn't believe God wouldn't want her baby to have a pa. In Mary's Bible it had said the devil would make you doubt. It said when that happened to tell him to get behind you, and that was just what she was going to do.

"Holman, can you hear me? Come on, open your eyes." She emptied a packet of the powdery medicine into a glass of water and stirred it. Holman moaned. She tapped him on the cheek. He moaned again. "Please! Holman, wake up and try to take some of your medicine." He mumbled something she couldn't understand. Beads of sweat popped out on his forehead. She wiped at them with a wet cloth.

"You need any help?" Lucy glanced up. Dovey stood at the foot of the bed. Her long hair was pulled back and tied with a string. A deep furrow marred her forehead. Her lips were drawn in a thin, hard line.

Lucy pulled her chair close to the bed and sat down. A slight chill crept up her back. What if the shadows did win? Then she'd need all the help she could get. She was so thankful that she and Dovey were friends now. "Are the littl'-uns ready for bed?"

"Yeah. Hattie just took them out to the hayloft. I promised them that they could sleep out there tonight."

Lucy picked up the medicine and stirred it again. "That's a good idea. Holman don't need a lot of racket."

Dovey came over to where she sat. "I've been a-trying to keep them out of the house as much as I can."

Lucy smiled up at her. "And you've done a good job. Taking them up to the Joneses' house last night was a good idea. If your pa hadn't made it . . ." Her voice broke.

Dovey put her arms around her. "I know, Lucy. I know. I've been

224

a-thinking about this prayer business. You know it didn't help Annie May . . ." Her voice quivered. "And maybe it won't help Pa."

The room was quiet for a long time. The light from the oil lamp cast a dim glow across the bed. The quilt top had been drawn to one side, and a faint breeze blew through the half-open window. From the distance, frogs sang in unison. Lucy's mind wandered. It had been this time of year that she, Jake, and Annie May had found the dead fawn in the clearing. Then there was Tilman, dying alone in his shack. Typhoid fever had claimed so many lives. She remembered how the young-uns had prayed for Annie May.

Lucy lifted her face to look into Dovey's eyes. "If you remember, Dovey, Annie May did get over the fever, and she wanted to go to be with her ma."

Holman moaned again. Lucy wiped his forehead. "I've been a-thinking about God and prayer too, Dovey, and I *do* believe. Maybe things don't happen like we want them to sometimes, but we've got to believe that everything will be all right." She patted her stomach. "For you see, honey, life goes on. Your pa don't know it, but he's got another reason to live."

Dovey's eyes rested on Lucy's stomach. A smile relaxed the straight line of her lips. "You mean you're . . . ? I mean, are you . . . ?"

Lucy laughed. "Yes, Dovey. I'm in the family way."

≈   ≈   ≈

Holman's fever lingered and so did the shadows. It had been two days since he had begun to run a fever. It seemed to Lucy that every nook and cranny harbored some sort of shadow just waiting for a chance to reach out and snatch him. She wouldn't think that way. Holman was going to get well. She would stay by his side until he recovered.

John came into the room. "Lucy, it's getting on towards supper time. You go eat and rest a spell."

"Think I will. Your pa's been a-talking out of his head, but he's quieted down for now."

John pulled a chair next to the bed. "Could you make any sense out of what he said?"

"Naw, just mumbling most of the time. Once in awhile he'd say somethin' like, 'don't shoot,' or 'it's me, Holman.'"

John looked at his bandage. "Sounds like he knew the person who shot him. Did you remember anything?"

Lucy turned to leave the room.

"Well, did you?"

She glanced back at John. "Nothing that makes any sense, John."

"Pa, this is John. Can you hear me? Wake up!"

"I don't think that it's much use, John. We have to spoon his medicine down. We'll just have to wait it out."

Holman threw his good arm into the air. "Don't shoot! Please, don't shoot!"

"Pa, who shot you?"

"The boy! The boy!"

"What boy are you talking about, Pa?"

Lucy took him by the hand. "Holman, was it the Jones boy that shot you?"

Holman turned over, then called out, "Boy . . . No! Run . . . don't shoot!"

"Lucy! What are you saying? Why would Richard shoot Pa?" John looked down at Holman. "I know that Richard said he was gonna shoot the man who shot his pa, but you know Pa wouldn't shoot Luther."

"I didn't say he did, John, but you've got to admit that it looks a might funny."

"What do you mean, Lucy?"

"I've been a-thinking about Luther's death. Remember the day that Holman came home and told us that he was dead?"

John nodded. "I remember. Pa's horse was soaked with sweat."

"Well, he said Luther was involved in some illegal business."

John scratched his head as he stood up. "I don't remember him saying that."

Lucy pushed back the wispy hair from Holman's forehead. "You could've been taking care of the horse when he said it."

"I don't see what that has to do with Pa getting shot."

"How did he know what kind of business Luther was into?"

John paced the floor. "That's easy. He pro'bly just heard it at the general store."

Lucy shook her head. "I don't think so, John. Why was your pa's horse so sweaty? Ain't like your pa to ride a horse so hard. And how come there was no sheriff nosing around? You said yourself the law didn't do nothing about Luther's shooting. And remember when the peddler was robbed? Holman knew all about that, too."

John rubbed his neck and paced some more. "What you trying to say, Lucy?"

Lucy walked toward the door. "John, I've been giving this a lot of thought . . ."

"And?"

"The only sense it makes is that your pa is some kinda lawman."

"Lucy! You've been setting up too much. Pa, a lawman? We have a sheriff. You know, Mr. Thomas—Roy Thomas—he's our sheriff. Has been for as long as I can remember."

Lucy nodded. "I've heard about him, but last night was the first time that I've met him. Don't you think it's funny that he ain't been back out here nosing around? The only reason he hasn't is because he knows what happened."

John reached for a jacket. "You stay with Pa. I'm gonna pay our sheriff a visit."

Lucy caught him by the arm. "No, John, let's leave the sheriff out of this. I want to go up to the Joneses' house and see Richard."

John mopped his forehead. "You really think that Richard could've done it?"

"I hope not, but I want to handle it myself. I overheard Richard ask your pa to get him a job where he worked. Your pa turned him down. Said he couldn't."

John looked dazed. "And Pa was so willing to do anything he could to help the Joneses. Wonder why he turned him down?"

"Your pa was mighty upset after Richard left. He swore and knocked down some of the barrels they'd just stacked. Said if it weren't for his family starving, he'd quit his job."

John looked more puzzled. "But for Richard to shoot him just because he wouldn't help him get a job don't make sense."

Lucy took John by the shoulders and shook him. "You're not listening to me, John. If your pa was some sort of lawman, maybe Richard found it out and figured he was the one that shot his pa."

The expression on John's face changed as he sat down. "And that would explain why Pa couldn't help him get a job. He didn't want anybody to know that he was a lawman."

Lucy picked up Holman's hand again. "That's the way I see it, but we won't know till your pa wakes up. In the meantime, I want to talk to Richard."

"Ain't he gone? Bessie said he had a job."

Lucy shook her head. "That's why Bessie was late Saturday morning. Said she had to fix Richard's breakfast because he'd just got home."

"And he didn't go back?"

"Reckon not, John. Bessie said he was still home this morning."

John jumped up and grabbed his gun from over the fireplace. "I'm gonna go up to the Joneses' house and take care of Richard."

Lucy reached for the gun. "No you're not! Richard's mine. I'm just gonna go up and talk to him tonight. If I find out anything or your pa comes to, and he tells us it was Richard, then he's gonna wish he was dead."

John stepped back. He had never seen Lucy look this determined. He knew there was no use arguing with her. "All right, Lucy, but when you're through with him, I'm gonna have my turn."

Lucy took the gun and placed it back on the rack. "That's fine with me, John. Then we'll let that no-good sheriff have a turn." Lucy picked up her shawl. She bent and kissed Holman on the forehead and started for the door.

"Lucy?"

"Yes, John?"

"Do you think that maybe Richard didn't have a job at all? That he was just out to kill Pa?"

Lucy didn't answer. She hadn't thought about the fact that Richard had been gone all week, and he'd come home the morning after Holman had been brought home shot. She pulled her shawl tighter around her as she left the room. She was sure she smelled a polecat.

≈ 22 ≈

The shadows had deepened by the time Lucy entered the Joneses' yard. The half-starved hound got up from his place on the porch and greeted her with a slow wag of his tail. He eased himself down the steps. She watched him cross the yard and sniff at her feet, then lay down next to her. As she started toward the house, the dog watched her from droopy eyelids. She walked under a tall pine. A loud squawking came from the tree limbs. She looked up. The chickens were already roosting for the night. Droppings littered the tree trunk as well as the yard.

The front of the house looked dark. Lucy went around to the back. As she turned the corner, the black cat darted in front of her and perched himself on the kitchen step. She circled a spot of earth that had turned green. The foul smell of human urine, along with the chicken droppings, clogged her nostrils. A faint light showed from the kitchen window. A horse that looked just like Holman's was tied near the back door. What was it doing here? She could see a shadow moving around the room. The door stood part way open. She pushed on it without knocking and stepped inside.

Richard Jones turned to face her. "Well, if it ain't Miz Carpenter. If you're looking for Bessie, she ain't here."

Lucy never took her eyes off Richard. "It ain't Bessie I want to see."

He reached for a piece of cold cornbread. Lucy watched him crumble the bread into a bowl and pour buttermilk over it. "Guess you Carpenters eat good with Mr. Carpenter having a good public job."

Lucy could hear the bitterness in his voice. Was it because Holman hadn't helped him, or was it something else?

Richard cut off a large slice of onion and put it in his bowl. "If it ain't Bessie you want to see, what *do* you want?"

Lucy didn't answer. She eased her hand toward the knife he'd laid

229

on the table. Richard glanced up from his bowl of milk and bread. "Why are you looking at me like that?"

Lucy's fingers closed around the knife. "Why ain't you at your public job, Richard?"

He took a bite of the onion. "It's rained too much. I got myself a job over in Swain County helping a man make locust stakes. I can't work till it's dry enough to cut some more locusts. Why are you looking at me like that?"

Lucy slowly raised the hand that held the knife. Richard dropped his bowl of milk and bread. Glass shattered on the kitchen floor. He took a step backward. Lucy edged closer. Her eyes narrowed. She caught him by the front of his shirt and shoved him against the wall. Richard's mouth gaped open. He tried to speak, but only a gurgle came from his throat.

Lucy laid the back of the knife across Richard's jugular vein. "I think it's time you and me had us a little talk, Richard. You know Indians are knowed for scalping, and if you don't give me some answers, I'm gonna have yours!"

Richard nodded his head. He tried to speak a couple of times. By the third time he made a muffled sound. He looked down at the fire that sparked in Lucy's eyes and tried to speak again. This time he stammered, "I . . . I . . ."

Lucy pressed the knife harder. Richard cleared his throat. "I was upset with Mr. Carpenter for not helping me get a job, but . . ."

She tightened her grip on his shirt. "But what?"

By now Richard's face was deep red and his eyes bugged out. "All right! All right! Let me go. I'll tell you what I know."

She eased her grip on his shirt, but she kept the knife in place. "Start talking. I ain't got all night."

Richard took a deep breath and wiped at his forehead with his arm.

Lucy's eyes narrowed. "Talk or you're buzzard bait!"

"Well, you see, it's like this . . ."

Lucy tightened her grip again. "The only way I see it is that my Holman's been at death's door, and all because of a hot-headed boy."

"Now Miz Carpenter, you've got it all wrong. I said I'd tell you what I knowed. I didn't say I shot Mr. Carpenter."

Lucy could feel the sweat dripping from her face. "Then tell me what you know. I'll decide if you're telling me the truth."

Richard took another deep breath. "I didn't get no public job."

Lucy shoved him against the wall again. "Then John was right."

"I don't know what John thinks, Miz Carpenter. You wanted the truth. If you'll let go of me I'll tell you."

Lucy relaxed her grip on the shirt and moved the knife away from the vein, but she still kept it pointed at him.

"Can I set down?"

She shoved a chair toward him with her foot. "Set easy! Then talk!"

Richard slid onto the chair. "When Mr. Carpenter wouldn't help me get a job, I got suspicious 'cause he's been so good to us since Pa was killed. I just couldn't understand why he didn't want to help me."

Lucy rubbed her face with her arm. "I wondered about that myself."

"Well, last week I decided I'd find out just what Mr. Carpenter did for a living."

Lucy relaxed a little. "How do you plan on doing that?"

"I told Bessie I was gonna get myself a job, and when Mr. Carpenter left, I followed him."

"You did what!"

"I followed him. Nothing to it."

Lucy hooked her foot under the round of a cane-bottomed chair, pulled it toward her, and sat down. "Where'd he go?"

"He went mountain climbing. I followed him up on the backside of Big Chimney Knob. Looked to me like he was looking for somethin', but I couldn't get close enough to tell. He nosed around there and then camped for the night. Next morning he got up and started looking again. He found what he was looking for all right—a still, setting back in a cave. A big-un, it was. I watched Holman. He walked right in. I thinks to myself, 'Somethin's wrong.' Stills can be found all over, and I was purty sure Mr. Carpenter wasn't making moonshine. I think, 'There's more going on than moonshining.' Weren't but a few minutes till that mountainside was a-swarming with men. Holman was trapped inside."

Lucy scooted to the edge of her chair. If Richard was making up this story, he was doing a good job. "What were you doing all this time, Richard?"

"I was hid real good. I wedged myself in behind a bunch of rocks just inside the cave."

"Did you know any of the men, Richard?"

"One of them was that peddler man."

Lucy's felt her heart sink. Jake! Then what he'd said to Holman was true. Why would he want to do something that was illegal? He must have been involved all along. He'd lied to her. She'd never forgive him for that.

"Did you see who shot Holman?"

Richard turned and looked toward the door. "I could get in big trouble for talking about this, Miz Carpenter."

"Then you do know. Who was it?"

"It was that Herby Ledford. Ledford aimed his gun at Holman. Said, 'I should have finished you off a long time ago.' Fired before Holman had a chance to raise his gun."

Lucy cringed. That was why Ledford had tried to scare her. Him and the peddler were running some kind of illegal business. She remembered the day she'd seen Herby and the man she thought was Jake loading the wagon. No wonder he was so mean. And Jake getting beat up at Crying Rock. That probably had something to do with this illegal business, too. If what Richard said was right, it all made sense. "How did you get away, Richard?"

"The law rode in. You never seen so much shooting. You would have thought it was the Fourth of July. I scrambled out from my hiding place and ran to Holman. I could tell he was hurt bad, but he could still talk. Stuffed my handkerchief in his wound. Was all I could do. He told me to take his horse and get out of there. With so much fighting going on outside, no one seen me slip from the cave and crawl away. I found Holman's horse and hightailed it home."

Lucy stood. "I'd like to believe you, Richard. It would kill Bessie if you're the one that shot my Holman. I'll take your word for now, but when Holman comes around, and if I find out you done it, the sheriff won't be here for you. It'll be me, and you know what I'll do." She jammed the knife point into the wood tabletop.

Richard's face blanched as the air sang with the music of the quivering knife. He nodded and watched Lucy fade into the shadows.

≈   ≈   ≈

Lucy pushed open the door to Holman's room. John sat by the bed. Dovey spooned something into his mouth, and it dripped down his chin. She wondered what it could be. It wasn't time for the medicine Doc Rogers had given him.

John looked up. Lucy motioned for him. In the kitchen John took a plate of food and set it on the table. "Set down here and eat, then tell me what Richard had to say for himself."

Lucy sat down and picked up her fork. She pushed the food around on her plate. She didn't feel much like eating. "You was right about him not having a public job."

John started for the front room. "I knew it. I'm gonna shoot me a skunk."

Lucy grabbed him by the shirttail. "Wait till you hear all I have to say, then you and me will decide about Richard."

John sat down on the other side of the table. "Make it quick. I don't want that skunk sneaking off on me."

Lucy laid down her fork. "You know I said that I thought your pa was mixed up with the law somehow. Well, according to Richard, I was right."

John slammed the table with his fist. "My pa, a lawman? Ain't likely. Why does Richard think that?"

"He said he followed Holman last week when he went away." Lucy paused.

"And?"

"And he said your pa went snooping around up on the backside of Big Chimney Knob. He found a still. That's when he got shot. Thing is, why would the law be after moonshiners? Everybody back home makes moonshine. Wonder what they're doing that has got the law after them."

John tugged at his ear. After a few minutes, he spoke. "Lucy, my Uncle Sam's a lawman over in Swain County. Don't know. Maybe he'd know."

Lucy remembered her visit to Bessie's when she had first come here. Bessie had told her about Holman's brother. "Could be, John, but I think your pa's mixed up with the sheriff somehow."

John got up and took a dipper of water from the water bucket. He took a long, slow drink and threw the rest out the kitchen door. "What're we gonna do? While we're setting around here waiting for Pa to wake up, Richard could be gone—and the sheriff, too. That is, if he had anything to do with the shooting."

Lucy scraped her plate into the slop bucket. "We ain't gonna do nothing, John. Your pa'd want us to wait. I don't think Richard's gonna go nowhere, and as for the sheriff, he don't know we suspect that Holman's working for him."

John put the dipper back. "I'll wait till morning, but if Pa ain't come around by then, I'm gonna pay Richard and the sheriff a visit. If you need me, I'll be in the hayloft with the rest of the young-uns."

Lucy watched him go. She prayed that tomorrow Holman would be well enough to tell them the truth. The Bible said not to let the sun set on your wrath. She'd try not to be too mad at Richard. Maybe he was telling the truth.

≈   ≈   ≈

Lucy stood at the front room window holding back the quilt top. The sky turned crimson. She watched with a sense of anticipation. Holman had slept well all night, and his fever was gone. She turned to his bed and picked up the jar of light brown liquid that sat on a chair. Snakeroot! It had taken his fever away even though the doctor's medicine hadn't helped. While she was at the Joneses', Dovey had made snakeroot tea and began giving it to her Pa. After Dovey had gone to bed, Lucy had spooned it down him all night. Now he slept like a baby. She bent and kissed him on the forehead. She felt they would soon know if Richard's story was true.

Dovey stuck her head in the door. "Did the snakeroot help?" Lucy smiled and motioned for her to come in. Dovey walked over to the bed and touched her Pa's forehead. "He'll be fine now, won't he? I've been praying and believing, Lucy."

Lucy smiled and gave her a hug. Dovey turned to leave, then looked back at Lucy. "Please let me know when he wakes." She tiptoed from the room.

Lucy went to the window. The sun's rays streamed across the sky. "Ma," she whispered, "my baby's gonna have a pa." She touched the locket around her neck. ". . . And that's not all, Ma. I'm gonna have a husband. . ." Her finger slid over the engraving. ". . . and love."

A smile lit her face as she heard Holman softly speak her name. She turned to find Holman gazing at her. "Holman! Oh, Holman!" she whispered, crossing the room quickly.

A weak smile crept across his lips. She went to him and kissed him. He touched her face with his good hand. "My beautiful Lucy."

She blushed. "You're gonna be fine, Holman."

He drew her close. "With you as my nurse, how can I help but be?"

"Holman, I have to know what happened. Who shot you?"

Holman glanced toward the window. His lips drew in a tight line.

"Yesterday evening, when your fever was so high, you said somethin' about the boy. Was the boy Richard Jones?"

Holman looked back at her. "Why do you think it was Richard?"

"He's been threatening to shoot whoever shot his pa, and he had the chance. He was gone last week."

Holman tried to sit up. Lucy placed her hand on his shoulder. "You're too weak to set up."

"You know Luther was my best friend. I wouldn't shoot him."

Lucy pulled up a chair and sat down. She thought about what she had seen on the mountain. "I know you're weak, Holman, so just answer my questions. If I don't have some answers for John this morning, he's gonna go after Richard and maybe the sheriff."

Holman tried to sit up again. "Why would he go after the sheriff?"

"John thinks the sheriff might know more than he's saying."

"You've talked to Richard? What else did he say?"

"He said he followed you up on Big Chimney Knob. Said you found a still. He said it was Herby Ledford that shot you."

Holman rolled over to face her. Lucy took a pillow and placed it under his shoulder.

Holman reached for her hand. "Lucy, what I'm gonna tell you has to stay between us. Promise?"

Lucy sat down on the bed beside Holman. "I promise. But you'll have to help me give John some answers."

Holman took a deep breath. "Herby Ledford did shoot me. You see there's been this ring of moonshiners operating in these mountains. It's been my job to find them. All this ain't over yet. Tell John my shooting was an accident."

"There's nothing wrong with making a little moonshine, Holman."

Holman looked at her with a plea in his eyes. "No, Lucy, there ain't, but the law has a lot to say about who you sell it to." Holman caught his breath. His color paled. "Tell him my shooting was an accident. He'll believe you." He closed his eyes.

Lucy wiped his face. "Holman?"

He didn't answer. She looked toward the door. Somehow, she'd have to stall John. She didn't know if she believed Holman. She needed time.

≈   ≈   ≈

It had been a week since Holman had told Lucy who shot him. John had been satisfied with Lucy's explanation, or at least till he could talk to his pa. Today she planned on questioning Holman some more. She eased his legs over the edge of the bed and draped a quilt over them. "How's that? Feel all right?"

Holman touched her hand. "Lucy, how would we make it without you?"

Lucy pulled up her chair in front of him and laid her head on his lap. Holman smoothed back her hair with his good hand. She felt herself relax. She had won her battle with the shadows this time. Holman was going to recover. She looked up at Holman and smiled.

He patted her cheek. "What are you smiling about?"

She reached up and twisted his mustache. "Looks like I'm gonna have to trim that for you."

Holman caught her by the arm. "You didn't answer my question."

Her free arm slid down over the small bulge in her stomach. What would he say if he knew about the baby? He had said last spring that he had him enough young-uns. That was last year, before . . .

"Are you gonna tell me?"

She sat up and looked him in the eyes. "Yes, I'm gonna tell you, but first you're gonna clear up this shooting business. I was able to satisfy John with that accident story. I want to know if what Richard said was true."

Holman flung back the quilt and tried to stand. "I might have known you'd be asking more questions."

Lucy took him by his good arm. "You're too weak to stand up. Just sit back down and tell me all the truth, because you're strong enough to talk now."

Holman dropped back onto the bed. Lucy reached to cover him with the quilt. Her hand brushed his bare leg. Holman's good arm slipped around her waist, and he pulled her toward him. She pulled away. "First things first, Mr. Carpenter. Start talking."

He pulled at her apron strings. "I told you. It was Herby Ledford. What else is there to say?"

She retied the apron strings. "Herby Ledford might have shot you, but he didn't shoot Luther."

Holman reached for his pants that hung on the bedpost. He slipped his hand into the pocket, pulled out his chewing tobacco, and bit off a chew. As he put it back, his fingers curled around a piece of paper. The letter. He'd seen Lucy's sister, and she'd given him a letter to Lucy from her pa. What would she do when she learned the truth? Should he give it to her now? He bit off another wad of tobacco, chewed on it for a few minutes, and spit into a can Lucy held out to him. No, if she left, he wasn't well enough to manage without her. He'd wait a little longer. Wouldn't make any difference now. It was too late for her to do her pa any good.

"How do you know it wasn't Herby that shot Luther?" Holman asked finally.

Lucy's expression remained serious. "You're forgetting I was on the mountain the day Luther was shot. Now I know it was the sheriff with you." Lucy's forehead furrowed. "I've been half scared to death that it was you who shot Luther. Please, tell me it wasn't you."

"What did you see on the mountain?"

"You and the sheriff arguing with Luther. You went behind some big rocks and when you came out Luther had been shot." Lucy got up and opened the window partway. A cool morning breeze touched her face. She watched the young-uns for a few minutes playing hide and seek behind the barn. All the innocence in the world darted in and out of those bushes. How wonderful to be in a world free of lies and ugly truths, but the part of her that was a wife, and going to be a mother, had to know the truth, no matter how ugly. She turned back toward Holman. "Tell me, which one of you shot him?"

Holman spit and wiped the juice from his mouth with the back of his hand. "Luther was bull-headed. Wouldn't do what the sheriff wanted him to do. He pulled his gun on us. There was a struggle between him and the sheriff. The gun went off and Luther was shot."

Lucy sat down. "Just what did the sheriff want him to do, Holman?"

"Been a bunch of moonshiners bootlegging to the Indians over in Cherokee. It's illegal to sell to the Indians. The sheriff just wanted Luther to shut down till the bootleggers was caught. He didn't think Luther was selling to the Indians since his family was so poor. Just thought it would be safer for him that way."

"How did you get mixed up in this?"

Holman spit out his wad of tobacco. "My job was to find the stills that was selling to the bootleggers and let the sheriff know where they were."

Lucy looked up at him. "Was?"

"Yes, Lucy, I ain't going back."

There was a long silence, then Lucy asked, "What if Richard finds out the sheriff was the one that shot his pa?"

Holman swung his legs up on the bed. Lucy fluffed his pillows and helped him lean against them. When he was settled he said, "I'll have a talk with Richard. I think when he hears what happened, he'll understand."

Lucy spread a quilt over Holman's legs. "I sure hope so. It would kill Bessie if somethin' happened to Richard." She looked toward the window. She had to ask. She needed to know how Jake was mixed up in this. "What did Jake have to do with all this business, Holman?"

"He was helping Ledford haul it and sell it to the Indians. Being a peddler was a good cover. When some of the boys over in Swain County found out that he was cutting in on their territory, they beat him up."

"And that's why he quit the peddling business?"

Holman nodded. "He still worked for Ledford but not disguised as a peddler. Guess he was too scared." There was a long silence. Lucy and Holman were both thinking about what had been.

Lucy patted his leg. "You're mighty lucky to be here. Doc Rogers did a good job fixing you up, but it was the snakeroot tea me and Dovey spooned down you that got rid of your fever."

Holman reached for her. "See, I told you that she'd come around."

Lucy pulled the locket from under her apron bib. "See what she gave me for my birthday."

Holman sat straight up. "Your locket! Your birthday! Oh, Lucy, I was gonna . . ."

Lucy hushed him with a kiss. "You're here, and you're gonna be all right. That's all the present I need."

He pulled her close and let his hand slide down her leg. She glanced toward the window. "Holman, the young-uns!"

His lips brushed her hair. "It's a long time till supper, and they know the front room is off-limits to them while I'm sick."

Lucy let herself sink down on the bed beside Holman. He was right. They wouldn't see the young-uns till mealtime.

~ 23 ~

The old porch swing made a rusty squeak. It sounded harsh and grating against the whispering breeze of the tall pines. A full May moon bathed the porch in soft light.

"Holman," Lucy said as the swing cast shifting shadows.

He stroked her hair. "Yes, Lucy?"

She turned her face up to his as she cradled her stomach with her arms. "Remember last spring when you said that you had yourself enough young-uns?"

Holman twisted about in the swing and looked into the night. Why did she have to bring that up? So much had happened since then. Wouldn't it be better to let sleeping dogs lie? "I don't want to think about that." He touched the floor with his foot and pushed the swing harder. The squeaking grew louder. He looked up. "I'm gonna have to put some grease on this swing. That squeak would wake the dead."

Lucy took a deep breath. "Remember, Holman, the other morning when you told me how you got shot?"

Holman leaned back against the swing. How could he forget? He looked at her closer. Was there something else going on? "You do believe me, don't you?"

Lucy shivered and snuggled closer. "Yes, I believe you."

Holman wrapped his arms around her. "Are you cold?"

"Kinda."

They both were quiet for a few minutes; then Holman spoke. "Has John been asking any more questions?"

Lucy shook her head. "No, but I've been thinking about Richard. What'll happen? You think he'll try to find out who shot his pa?"

Holman stood and stretched. He'd planned on going up to the Joneses' and having a man-to-man talk with Richard. "He won't have to. I plan on telling him."

"That's good, Holman. He needs to know the truth."

Holman sat back down. He took Lucy's hands in his. He was so lucky to have a good woman to love him. Thoughts of Jake pushed in around the corners of his mind. Had she loved him? He pushed the thought away as soon as it came. Yes, he'd let sleeping dogs lie. She was here with him, and Jake was in big trouble with the law. "You're always worrying about somebody else. That's why I love you so much."

Lucy blushed and looked down at her hands. "I wonder if you'll still love me when I tell you what I have to tell you." Before Holman could answer, she said, "The other night, remember, I told you that I'd tell you why I was smiling."

Holman's eyes twinkled. He was sure he knew what she was going to say, but he didn't want to spoil it for her by saying he knew. "Sure do. I'd almost forgot. From the way you were smiling, I'd say you have a secret."

Lucy drew in her breath. "Well, you might not want any more young-uns, but you're gonna get another one."

A slow, lazy smile crossed his face. That was what he'd thought. Lord knew he didn't need any more young-uns, but Lucy did. A young-un would give her a reason to be, and somebody besides him to need her. "So that's your secret. I'm not surprised—that bloom in your cheeks, and there's a special sparkle in your eyes. And it looks like you're putting some meat on your bones."

Lucy felt the tension ease from her body. "You mean you're not upset? I wouldn't blame you. You've already got twelve young-uns and a wife to feed. And now you're saying you're not gonna go back to work for the sheriff."

He took her in his arms. "How could I not want our baby? Or babies?"

Lucy stiffened. "Babies! What do you mean, babies?"

Holman grinned. "Ain't you noticed there's two sets of twins a-running around here?"

Lucy gasped and felt her stomach. "Do you think . . . ? No, not me—ain't no twins in my family."

"Well, can't say as I remember none in me or Mary's family either." A frown edged its way across Lucy's face. Holman held her tighter. "Don't worry, honey. Whatever the Good Lord sees fit to give us, we'll take."

Holman felt her relax in the circle of his arms. The swing sang a lullaby. Maybe he'd not grease it after all.

≈　　≈　　≈

The next evening, as dusk crept over the mountains, the shadows grew deeper. The frogs began to croak. As if on cue, the crickets began to sing. The Carpenter young-uns gathered on the front porch. John eased himself down on the top porch step. He looked over at Holman and Lucy who sat in the swing. "Pa, tell us how your grandpa came to these mountains."

Dovey handed Martha to Holman. "Yeah, Pa. Tell us that story about how your grandpa settled here."

Holman twisted his mustache. Seemed like he'd told that so much they'd be sick and tired of it. "You young-uns have heard that story before, but I'd be glad to tell it again."

Arthur moved closer to the swing. "Every time you tell it, it gets better, Pa."

Holman chuckled. "Could be you just hear it different, son, but that don't matter. Where do you want me to start?"

Harley leaned back in his chair. "First tell us how great-grandpa got to this country."

Holman spit across the porch rail. "Haven't I told that part before?"

Dovey pushed her hair behind her ear. "I remember somethin' about a trip over on a boat."

Holman draped his arm over Lucy's shoulders. "That's right, Dovey. Your great-great-grandpa decided to bring his wife and four sons from England to America. Figured he'd get rich here."

Arthur glanced around. "He must have done good—we own the whole mountain!"

Holman chuckled again. It sure didn't take much for a young-un to think he was rich. "Truth is, son, he never made it to America. He and his missus both died on the boat trip over."

The little group was silent. After a few minutes, John asked, "How did great-grandpa and his brothers get to America then?"

"There was a family by the name of Carpenter on the boat. They took the boys in and raised them as their own."

Dovey sat down on the steps by John. "You mean we're really not Carpenters? If we're not Carpenters, who are we?"

"From what I've heard, Dovey, my grandpa's name was Woods."

Hattie wormed her way closer to the swing. "If that ain't somethin'—to find out you ain't who you think you are!"

Dovey said, "Hattie, a name change ain't gonna make you any different."

After the children's laughter died down, Holman said, "I think it's time for bed."

Hattie protested, "But Pa, you ain't finished the story yet."

Holman handed the sleeping Martha to Dovey. He looked at Lucy. No, he hadn't finished, but he needed some time with his wife. "We'll finish it tomorrow night."

After the young-uns had gone to bed, Lucy and Holman sat in the swing enjoying the quiet. She laid her head on his shoulder. He pulled her closer and kissed the top of her head. From the distance, an owl called. From the other side of the mountain, another answered. A cloud floated over the moon. In the distance a dog howled. Lucy looked up into her husband's face. "Holman, how did I get here?"

Absent-mindedly Holman answered, "I brought you here. Don't you remember?"

"Course I do, but that ain't what I mean."

Holman shifted in his seat and looked down at her. He'd been waiting for the right time to time to tell her about her pa. This was as good a time as any. She had to know. He touched the letter in his pocket. "Just what do you mean?"

She sat up. "Pa. Why did he send me away? I know you and him had some kinda deal."

Holman looked out into the night. "Why do you think that?"

"What you said to Pa the night you ate supper with us."

Holman twisted his mustache. "That was nearly two years ago."

Lucy pulled away from Holman and walked over to the edge of the porch. She leaned against the railing. "I ain't forgot. You said this

243

here trade'll work out fine for both of you. Why did Pa want to get rid of me?"

"Your pa . . . didn't really want to get rid of you."

"Then why did he do it?"

Holman ran his hand across his thinning hair. Should he tell her in her condition? Would it upset her too much? Maybe he should wait. No, waiting would only make it worse. He should have told her a long time ago.

"Your pa wasn't a well man, Lucy. He just wanted to make sure that you was taken care of . . ." His voice broke.

"What do you mean, not well? Why didn't you tell me, Holman? I want to go home! I want to make sure Pa's all right! When can you take me?"

Holman took the letter from his pocket. This was going to be harder than he'd thought. "Ain't no need to go home, Lucy. Your pa wrote you a letter. I'm sure he said his goodbyes in it."

"Goodbyes! What do you mean, goodbyes! I want to see my pa. Now! If you won't take me, then I'll find my own way." Lucy started toward the steps.

Holman reached for her. "You can't see him, Lucy. He's dead. Dead and buried."

Her eyes flashed. She bit her lower lip, then spoke in a even tone. "Why didn't you tell me sooner? I'd have gone. I'd have been with him." Sobs shook her body.

Holman reached for her again. "I just found out a few days before I was shot that he'd died. I went up to see how he was doing. That's when I found out. Your sister gave me this. Said he'd got the parson in Clayton to write it to you." He slipped the letter into her cold hand. "Your sister said he wasn't sick long. The letter's his way of saying goodbye to you."

Her hand shot out. The night air rang from the slap that caught Holman on his right jaw. "It's all your fault—your fault for making a deal with him! I should have stayed. I should have stayed and cared for him." She picked up the lantern and ran down the steps.

Holman started down after her. "Where do you think you're going?"

"Don't know, and anyway, it ain't none of your business. Just leave me alone! I need time to think." She vanished into the night.

≈   ≈   ≈

Lucy's back ached from lying on the hard church bench all night and her legs were stiff and chilled. She opened the church door. It creaked and groaned. She gently pulled it closed behind her. Another dense May fog hovered around her. She rubbed her aching back and stretched. The early morning fog pressed closer, but once again it wasn't the only thing closing in around her. The world she'd built with Holman and the young-uns had fallen apart. She felt that she had to escape. She was all alone except for the dead in the graveyard, and she may as well be dead with them. Everything she cared for was dead. Her ma, Annie May, and now Pa.

From deep within her came a faint flutter. No, she wasn't alone; there was the baby. The fog seemed to call to her into the graveyard. Her hand touched a tombstone. It was cold, hard marble, as cold as her heart. She'd promised to see that her ma had one. Now she'd have to get one for her pa, too. She pressed her hand harder against the stone, expecting it to give her some sort of comfort, but all she felt was its coldness. She pulled her shawl tighter around her and shivered. She needed to feel the warmth of her ma's love, the warmth of the sun. She needed to be above this fog. She needed to touch the edge of heaven again.

Her heart beat faster. Her pace quickened in anticipation of reaching another mountaintop. She followed a trail that left the graveyard. Soon the trees began to thin, and she stepped into a small clearing. A doe and two fawns grazed on the wealth of green grass that grew there. The mother raised her head and sniffed the air, then bounded off into the woods with the fawns following her.

Lucy remembered the deer Annie May and she had watched in another clearing and the dead fawn Annie May had found and Jake had buried. Now it was spring again, and another doe fed her young and protected them. Her hand touched her bulging stomach. She felt another quiver. She'd soon have a little one. It would need to be protected and loved. But she had her own needs.

245

She pushed on up the trail. The climbing was almost straight up now. She grabbed at a cluster of vines and missed, landing on her knees. Brushing the leaves and dirt from them, she pulled herself up by a limb. She couldn't give up. The decision she had to make was too important. Slowly, she worked her way to the top. With one last heave, she found herself up on top of the mountain.

Again she looked down into a sea of fog. The same tops of the Smoky Mountains welcomed her. A carpet of green moss covered the ground. She sat down and crossed her legs, Indian style, and waited. And as surely as day follows night, the sun streamed from behind the mountaintops.

She touched the locket that hung around her neck. "Ma, I've found myself in the family way. But that ain't all, Ma. I found out that Pa died! He'd made some sort of trade with Holman to take care of me. Wonder what it was?" She took the letter from her pocket and ripped it open. She was glad she'd learned to read.

Dear Lucy, I know this is hard for you to understand. I promised your ma before she died that I'd make sure you was took care of. She knowed I couldn't give you much from digging and selling ginseng and such other roots. This is the only thing I could do. Please forgive me. You know how your ma always wanted a tombstone with angels on it. Holman promised to get one for her. That was his end of the deal. He got it, and I was able to see it. Sure is nice. Two angels setting up on top. Maybe he'll bring you to see it sometime. Goodbye, my girl. I know that you'll do what's right. You're a good girl.

From the valley came "Loo-ou-cy!" The echo from the other side of the mountain answered "Loo-ou-cy."

"Ma, Holman's looking for me. He's probably got the boys looking, too."

"Loo-ou-cy, I love you!"

The valley echoed with "love you . . . love you . . . love you." The baby gave a real kick. Lucy looked out across the mountaintops. Thin wisps of smoke curled up in all directions. The fog had begun to rise. A few clouds floated overhead. "Ma, I've learned how to read and write some. I read in Mary's Bible all about forgiveness." The baby kicked again. "Ma, I guess that's what I'm gonna have to do. My

246

baby needs a pa, but more than that, I need a husband and a family."

She looked in the direction of Georgia. Smoke boiled from that way, also. She guessed somebody was making moonshine. A cloud slid over the sun. "And Ma, I ain't forgot Pa. I'll have Holman take me to see his grave and your tombstone. I'll find a way to get Pa a tombstone, too." She turned and looked toward Cherokee. "And I ain't forgot your people, Ma. I'll go see them, but I'll come back, for this is home."

Eva Carpenter McCall is the granddaughter of Lucy Davenport Carpenter. Eva lived with her grandmother in Franklin, North Carolina, for nineteen years. She has taken the many stories her grandmother told her and structured them into *Edge of Heaven* to provide a sense of what family life was like in the mountains of northeast Georgia and western North Carolina in the late 1800s.

Eva graduated from Franklin High School, attended Pfeiffer College in Misenheimer, North Carolina, and married George McCall, also of Franklin. They moved to Flint, Michigan, where George worked for General Motors and Eva became a beautician. Now retired, they live in Michigan but maintain a part-time home in Franklin. The McCalls have three grown children and several grandchildren.

In Michigan, Eva has attended writing workshops at Oakland University and Mott Community College, and she belongs to several professional writers groups. Although Eva has published short stories, inspirational material, and children's stories, this is her first full-length novel.